BEST
LESBIAN
EROTICA
2007

BEST LESBIAN EROTICA 2007

Series Editor

TRISTAN TAORMINO

Selected and Introduced by

EMMA DONOGHUE

CLEIS
PRESS

Published in the United States by Cleis Press Inc.,
P.O. Box 14697, San Francisco, California 94114.
Printed in the United States.
Cover design: Scott Idleman
Cover photograph: Celesta Danger
Text design: Frank Wiedemann
Cleis logo art: Juana Alicia
First Edition.
10 9 8 7 6 5 4 3

refreshingly original "Sweet Thing," the confident femme discovers something about the handsome baker she's just seduced on the breadboard beside the oven: despite having serviced most of the married women in town over the years, can it possibly be that "Petey the butch goddess is a virgin?" And unlike the straight do-me queens Petey is used to, this girl knows how to melt that stone.

"Your sense of your own power was what made me wet," writes the submissive narrator in Amy Babcock's "Last Ten Bucks." In a telling detail, the butch top bends her over a table she (the top) fixed herself: "It is an old wooden table—strong, stable, and firm—like you. You have been working on its repair for some time; skillfully crafting and successfully manipulating it to become what you want it to be—your very own." In the space between those two sentences, there is a moment of erotic blurring as the table flips from representing its owner to standing for the women she dominates.

A story like Sacchi Green's "Bright Angel" can be read as a smart commentary on the long literary tradition of wishy-washy nature writing about lesbian sex: all petals opening and fronds of seaweed. Green's butch protagonist rewrites all that on a Grand Canyon scale: " 'I suppose you think the water always flows gently, smoothly, taking forever to wear away resistance... But sometimes storms batter at the rocks, and spring floods from mountain snowmelt surge through the ravines.' I was really getting into it now. 'The water pounds, thrashes, filled with sharp silt and uprooted trees.' I raised my hand suddenly to the nape of her neck, still holding her hair roughly back. The scent of her juices on my fingers roused my own. With my fingernails, short but strong, I scraped a line down the valley of her spine..."

By its nature, erotica will always be somewhat conventional: we like surprises, yes, but we like compulsive repetition too. (Admit it, don't you often rely on a trusty old scenario to push you over the edge?) So most of the stories gathered here combine a quirky setup with a predictable conclusion of blissful orgasms for both parties. But there are some interesting exceptions. In the highly original "Sweet Desires," for instance, Tara Alton's character winds up having weird, uncomfortable, migraine-inducing nookie in her car with a really irritating coworker.

Since taboo is sexy, before I began selecting these stories I was expecting them to ring all the changes on the forbidden. What surprised me is how few of them are about situations in which a social law is being breached: no molestation of the underaged and only one official adultery, in Annette Beaumont's "Fruit of Another." Even when sex happens between client and employee, as in Kyle Walker's "Rosemary and Eucalyptus," the massage therapist is quite free to rip up the check and walk away. Consent is the rule.

Then it occurred to me that these writers are more interested in mental blocks than legal ones. It is at the private level, in the emotional intricacies of a scene of infatuation, compulsion or voyeurism that these characters knock down barriers. The protagonist in Rachel Kramer Bussel's "On Fire" makes herself learn fire-eating for a burlesque performance to fulfill the whim of the woman she wants. The nervous heroine in "Public Pet" by Cynthia Rayne has never yet been taken out in public on a leash.

Some of these stories are about sex in committed relationships, others about thrillingly unpredictable pickups (at parties, clubs, conferences), but either way, the excitement lies in achieving a contact so intimate, so naked, whether with partner or stranger, that you can really let go: angels and demons alike released into the shrieking sky.

Many of these tales are about the trembling pleasure of anticipation as much as the moment when sex actually happens; desire is as much about the past and the future as the now. The adult women in Anna Watson's witty "Homecoming Queen" get to resolve the angst of their adolescence by playing out the cheerleader-and-tomboy-loner scenario they never dared when they were in high school.

Unlikely pairings are a great tease, like that of the drop-dead gorgeous twenty-something Hollywood actress with the aging, crop-haired butch photographer in Sacchi Green's "Bright Angel." These stories range widely in settings: from the Grand Canyon to a dark wood where the babes in D. Alexandria's "Tag!" hunt each other down by—*mm!*—the scent of their juices. These authors reveal a fascination with the world of the richest lesbians as well as the poorest: homeless and crack-smoking in Jolie du Pré's oddly romantic "Kiki," bike messengers and strippers in Zoë Alexandra's gritty "French Handwriting," which concludes "...and then it hit me. I wasn't going anywhere."

The protagonist in Lynne Jamneck's "Voodoo and Tattoos" has both her dreams come true when she winds up in the hotel room of a corporate type and her pierced, tattooed bit of rough. In "Bingo, Baby," Radclyffe riffs cleverly on contemporary queer tourism when her butch character gets ordered into skirts by her femme for Drag Bingo in Provincetown.

Bathrooms come up a lot, either as places of privacy where you wash up or strap on, or as illicit places to have sex. The stories vary greatly in tone, and some of the S/M stories are the sweetest, oddly enough.

What's missing? I was surprised by how little anal sex came up this year. Lynne Jamneck's story is one of the only ones to feature even an uneasy moment of butch-butch desire. Bisexuality is oddly invisible, too: Suki Bishop's "Rupture" and Jean Roberta's "The World Turned Upside Down" are the only ones to include sex with a man (though the protagonist in "Public Pet" is ordered by her Mistress to give oral satisfaction to a strange man's wife while he watches). And I looked in vain for a story of two convent schoolgirls behind the bike sheds stuffing each other's every orifice with strawberries—but perhaps that's just me? Never mind, everyone's entitled to her own favorite flavor....

Several stories go well beyond the everyday of contemporary lesbian circles. As an aficionado of historical fiction, I was delighted by the aforementioned "The World Turned Upside Down," in which a Regency gentleman is appalled to realize that his rival for his promiscuous beloved's heart is her mannish maid! Girls who still ask "What's your sign?" will be highly amused by Andrea Miller's set of encounters with twelve contrasting "Heavenly Bodies."

One outstandingly atmospheric story, Skian McGuire's "Sweet Hunger," offers an unusual variant on the vampire: a mysterious maple syrup maker who seduces a different guest in the middle of the night every spring as a sort of erotic offering to the Goddess to bring the sap down. Our fantasies have infinite power: if the smorgasbord of stories in this collection add up to any message, that may be it.

Emma Donoghue
London, Ontario
August 2006

SWEET THING

Joy Parks

Watching Petey Ginoa knead bread dough is like watching a thing of beauty.

Watching her do it when she doesn't know anyone is watching her is even better.

First there are her hands, which are large but not too large; peachy pink hands that get washed soft over and over again every day, strong with short square nails and slightly knobby knuckles, the kind you get when you crack them too much. And flour. I don't think I've ever seen those hands when they weren't covered in flour. Strong hands, but not rough at all. Hands that can shape delicate flutes on a tartlet crust or fix a tiny broken motor on the mixer or, I believe, unfasten a button so slow and perfect, sliding a finger down the space between breasts, sliding past a slight mound of belly, sliding down. I take a gulp of Fair Trade fresh-ground something or other to keep me still and watch how she grabs a hunk of sunflower rye or cornbread with organic red pepper slices, or whatever delightful concoction is in her bowl today, and drops it onto the breadboard, her hands dancing it into a perfect round, her fingers disappearing inside, then out, inside again. Kneading. Needing. I watch those fingers turn and poke and stretch the dough. I feel heat welling up between my thighs, try not to squirm. I watch her with my lips parted like I'm waiting for a kiss.

And then she stops. I hold my breath. She pushes up the sleeves of the white shirt she's wearing beneath her apron and begins to knead some more, flexing her perfectly shaped muscles, girl muscles but firm and healthy and strong looking. The kind of arms that make you wonder what it would be like to be inside the circle of her body, to feel those muscles tighten and press against you, what that would be like. That close.

It's warm in here and the windows are sweating from the steam of the kitchen; it's still morning cold outside. I should go. I should get up and walk out of here as best I can and get to work on time for a change; the walk would do me good right now. If I could just stand up.

I could watch those hands for hours.

Yeah, I know I've got it bad. And I don't quite know what to do with it.

Everyone back home told me I was going to hate moving to a small town even if it was the only place I could get a job. In a small town everybody knows everybody's business and I'd have to watch my Ps and Qs, they said. Growing up in the city and having the natural luck to get away with a whole lot of stuff, I hadn't had to work very hard at being discreet. Who was going to know and who was going to care?

So I've been laying low, working at the library as the junior librarian in training, trying to make it look like I'm far more interested in learning how to organize the periodicals and start a community reading circle than I am in running back and forth to Petey's all day to buy coffee. I can't sleep most nights now. I don't know if it's all that caffeine or the fact that when I do sleep I keep dreaming about those hands on my skin and then I have to get up and drink a lot of cold water just to keep from melting in my own heat.

But bless the gossips in town for helping me learn all about Petey. I guess since some of them saw me spending so much time in the bakery, they wanted to warn me so I could be on guard and not fall prey to her seductions. You'd never know from looking at me that I've dealt with plenty of seductions by women like Petey and enjoyed every single one of them. From the very first day I walked into her shop, if she'd ever even looked at me with half a hint that she might be interested, I'd have fallen on my back so fast I might have ended up with whiplash. It's funny being femme. Sometimes you hate the fact that no one knows, and you have to go out of your way to make sure some butch realizes you're available, 'cause you look too straight. But the good ones know. The smart ones. They can look past the heels you wear to work and the lipstick and the girly clothes, and love all that about you, know what you are beneath your clothes, not just any woman, but special. One who would fall on your back for them, let them touch you all over, let them reach inside your body, fuck you hard and tender and whatever it takes to make you both feel so good about what it is that you are.

But since I'm not so obvious to normal people, I got the whole deal on Petey.

Petey Ginoa is a legend in town. Everybody knows she's a lesbian even though nobody's ever seen her with any woman at any time. She's too smart for that—to get caught. It's a small town and she's got a damn good business and she'd be crazy to take a chance on losing it all. Petey's not her real name; it's Pia, which is the name on the sign above the door. Her father named the shop that back when she was a baby. But everybody calls the place Petey's. They eat Petey's bread and take Petey's cake home for birthdays and baby christenings and stop by Petey's for coffee. Sometimes I think if not for her, the whole damn town would go hungry. Petey suits her more. That's just how it is with some lesbian children; they outgrow the names their mommas gave them, grow into something different, someone different from what anyone could have expected of them. Taking a new name is like being born all over again into who they should have been all along.

Not that Petey's the kind of woman who'd think about it that way. She probably just realized she was becoming someone for whom a delicate name like Pia didn't fit. It made her feel uneasy. So she gave herself a more comfortable handle. I get the feeling she's the kind of woman who would do whatever she needed to do to feel okay about herself and not give a damn about what anyone might think.

I wonder if any of her lovers—who no one's ever seen—call her Pia.

Wouldn't seem right somehow.

I want to be one of those women no one's ever caught her with.

I want those hands needing me.

On a belt under her apron Petey wears a measuring cup that looks like it was made by Black and Decker. She wears clean, crisp, white pants that cup her fine ass just right and a white button-down shirt with the sleeves rolled up to her elbows. She wears a full-length, white apron slung over her neck and tied real loose, and clean white sneakers that don't make a sound. Her dark hair is cut short and loose around her face, which seems a little tanned. Even in winter that hair curls up at the back of her collar when she's moving around the kitchen in the heat. That collar, those curls. I have to keep my hands in my coat pocket or flat, fanned on the counter, when I order my coffee. I look the other way when she slides the little waxed paper bag of cannoli my way; stop myself from reaching across the counter; stop myself from reaching out to touch her neck, smooth those curls. Touch her face real slow. I think her forehead would smell like butter, that her skin would be lightly glazed all over with a fine dusting of sugar, that if you put your mouth to her skin, you would come away tasting sweet.

I'm thinking Valentine's Day will be the time to make my move, 'cause that's when everybody's all crazed over romance and hearts and flowers and wanting to be loved. Petey can't be all that different from anyone else. Can she?

Today is Friday the thirteenth, and not a soul on the street fails to comment on it. I don't feel unlucky, just a little racy knowing I've got just today to figure out how I'm going to pull off the seduction of the town dyke. I wonder if she has a girlfriend now, but only for a minute, because something tells me I'd sense it if she did. At this point I don't think it would matter if she was dating my own best friend—if I'd been in town long enough to have one.

When I hit the doorway of the bakery, I almost swoon. It's the clouds of moist heat that gather inside, rain on the window, plus the scent of something sweet and deep, along with something fresh, like fruit juice, underneath it. And there's Petey. She's behind the counter, smiling at me. It must have been my reaction to the aroma that wrapped around me as I came inside. I wrinkle my nose like I'm sniffing for more and look at her grinning, as if to ask what's making such a delicious smell. Her eyes are actually lit, wide and open, more so than I remember ever seeing them. She motions me over. I've never been that close to her aside from her pouring my coffee or taking my money when I paid for bread or muffins or those slices of all-natural Queen Anne's cake with caramel-covered nut crust swirled with spidery feathers of toasted coconut. Or crème brûlée custard on a toasted almond crust. Or shiny pecan buns, moist and slippery as the flesh of my thigh right now. I'm weak. I don't think she's ever really talked to me. Specifically to me. And she still isn't—talking. I step up to the counter and she's still smiling and motioning me even closer. I move in like I'm in a trance, move in for a kiss, to touch my lips to her cheek, her lips. Desire bubbles up within my belly, there are tiny flutters inside my cunt. Like wings. I wonder if she can see down my blouse, see my breasts nestled in the pink, lacy, silk demi-cup I bought mail order from Victoria's Secret just in case something like this ever happened. I catch myself when my eyes start to close. She raises a fork to my lips like a present, speared with a tiny piece of something pink and fluffy, like cotton candy covered in chocolate. Oh baby. She directs the fork toward my lips as I open them on command, take the gift inside. Something sweet and deep breaks on my tongue; my mouth wells up with wetness. I think about the pink of it, pink like the tender underside of a breast set free, pink skin of a vulva, all shower fresh and warm; my tongue roaming my mouth to seek out and find every touch of sweetness, the citrusy aftertaste a surprise. I worry about drooling. I swirl it around my mouth, take it in, inhale it. Most of your taste buds come from scent. I taste an orange cream chocolate like from the Whitman's Sampler but warm. I want to tell her it's like sex on a fork, but that's too bold, too early in the dance. She's close still, watching me, silent. I open my eyes wide now, finally able to open my mouth.

Then she speaks real low, her voice deep but clear against the clang of coffee cups and beaters in the kitchen.

"So, you like? It's blood orange cheesecake iced with a bittersweet chocolate glaze. Did them special for Valentine's Day this year. It's the blood orange that makes it pink. They're in season right now."

She beams.

Oh the pride in her voice. Hands in her pockets, shoulders dropped back, slight smile drawing tiny lines around her lips like a frame. She makes me want to leap over the counter, pull her head down into the pink silk of my too-far-open shirt, whisper, "You are magical," wrap my legs around the clean white apron over her clean white pants, beg her to take me right there, right on the kneading board covered with flour and dabs of bittersweet chocolate glaze.

It takes three more trips to the bakery for me to get up the nerve to do what I have to do. All that coffee and anxiety is making me feel dry-mouthed, and it's now or never. So while she's ringing up the roasted red pepper and cilantro quiche with butter crust that's going to end up being my supper, I finally manage to find my femme courage and make my intentions known. At least to one of us.

"So, what are you doing for Valentine's Day?" I ask her.

She looks down at the floor like I've caught her in a lie.

"Nothing," she says. She kicks imaginary sand with the toe of her clean white shoe.

I'm tempted to look down too, but I keep my eyes right on her, make sure she can feel them.

"How come?"

It hurts almost to keep my voice this even.

More kicking at nothing. I've turned her into a twelve-year-old boy.

"I don't know. I don't go in for that sort of stuff. Romance and stuff. Phony."

Yeah, I think so too. If you do it their way. But I can't say that. Instead, I say, "Me neither. Maybe we ought to hang out and do nothing together."

She stops kicking. Goes still. I wait. There's a buzz rising in my ears. Bubbles flip upside my stomach, more tickle inside. I feel a coffee burp rising, wish it away.

She lifts her head, swings it up slow as if she's trying to get unstuck from something.

I don't think she knows. She doesn't see it. Too long stuck here in town. If she never saw my kind before, how would she know what I looked like?

Sweet thing, I think. *You ain't seen nothing like me yet.*

She finally speaks. "Sure. Why don't you come tomorrow night? I'll be here after we close."

frosting. Her want is hot enough to make me feel the steam rising from her body, her fingers kneading me inside, her mouth hungry on me, her tongue tracing sweet glazed circles, her head rising at times so I see her mouth wet and shiny with me, while I cry out, "Petey!" and tug at those mythical curls at her collar and wrap my legs around as much of her clean, sweet, white-cotton self as I can, try to take all of her inside. I can tell by her eyes and her moans and the way she keeps her lips on me; the way her fingers gather inside me, thrust higher and deeper without asking, simply taking, knowing it's freely mine to give; that Petey Ginoa has never had a woman want her wholly like this, has never had a real love to call her own. I arch my back, strain up against those strong knuckles slipping, twisting, filling me; those dear arm muscles straining to take me as I come screaming, shivering, crying out, grinding my ass hard against the smooth wood.

It's warm here lying beside the oven. Petey lies silently beside me while I come back inside myself, her fingers resting on my hip bone, her cheek against my hair. I snuggle closer; the board is wider than you'd think to see it in the daylight, but I'm not afraid of falling. I'm facing her now, her shirt is open, her T-shirt and plain white underpants still on. I cuddle against her, kiss her neck, then place my hands at the bottom edge of her shirt, slide up slowly, graze her breasts. She catches her breath. Stops my hand. Holds it tight against her heart.

"Aren't you tired?"

It sounds like she's afraid I'm not satisfied.

"Not tired, relaxed," I whisper, "and I want to touch you."

She stiffens slightly beneath my hand. Her heart is beating

hard enough for me to hear it; I expect to see it thumping up like a cartoon character's does when he falls in love. Or gets chased by something wild.

"I...usually...don't..."

It hits me. Petey's used to nice straight girls who like to get finger-fucked all night but don't offer to give anything back. No touch back, no tongue back. That might make them gay. And I sigh.

"Do you want this?" I whisper. "Do you want me to love you?"

She turns her face away from me. Mumbles into her arm, into the makeshift pillow the dish towel has become. I lean in to listen and there's only one word I hear.

Never?

Petey the butch goddess is a virgin?

Chaste despite sexually servicing what seems like a third of the married women in town, if you can trust the stories. Fortysomething and never been touched. *Jackpot,* I think, but then I panic; I want to get up and—presto change-o—my clothes would be on and I would be gone.

But that doesn't happen.

What happens is...

First I roll my eyes upward and curse and thank the Goddess for making me brave enough to bring Petey out. All the way out.

And I remember everything I know about butches and sex and surrender and what that means, and prepare myself for anything.

Then I slowly slip my hand inside the rib-knit tee she's wearing beneath her open shirt and caress her belly with my open palm. She gurgles something low and deep inside her throat. Her stomach contracts under my touch, new nerve endings coming to life for the first time. I feel terribly powerful and daring. She settles her shoulder closer into me, stretches out her legs; I try not to think of her feet in her white sports socks hanging over the breadboard, but I do and I giggle. She smiles at me as she strokes my hair with her hand. Slowly, oh so slowly, as if her stomach stretched for miles, I take my time and slide my hand further up her shirt, grazing her breasts with my knuckles. She sucks in air, twitches. I can hear my own breathing and hers, imagine it rising up into the moist steamy air that sits inside the bakery. Joined at the breath, I think. I kiss her neck, kiss her shoulders, raise her T-shirt further and bend to trace with my tongue the places my hands have been. Her skin is clean and sweet-tasting, and moist with heat. Glazed. All that sugar, all that goodness. She's moving down, rising up to meet my hand, still palm flat; my mouth, tiny sighs breaking from her mouth. My fingers find her breast; it's small and easy to cup within my hand and her nipple is firm as the dried currants I've watched her stir into dough and almost as dark. She gasps; I find my courage and rise up further on my side so I can move more easily. Gently, I gather her breasts under my hand. She likes a little more pressure than I would have expected, croons out soft little cries of want as I grasp her breasts and release them slowly, knead her gently as I have watched her do so many times. And eventually, when I'm not sure how much more she can take, I smile and kiss her lips and bend my face to her chest, sucking each hard curranty nipple; one, then the other, until her hips start to rise off the board. She's starting to get loud. With my mouth still on her, licking a trail over her breast, I retrace my path down her belly, further, further still, slipping my fingers beneath the waistband of her cotton underwear, moving slowly over a mound of damp curling hair, slowly, so slowly…. She widens her legs to greet me and she is wet and slippery and smooth as pearls underwater, she is open and gasping. In the dark, I imagine shiny deep pink like the filling of the cheesecake she fed me before. And I need the sweetness. She's rising and crashing into my fingers, so hard and so new that I rise up and turn, stretching out, never moving my hand, and use the other to push off what bit of her underwear still clings to her. Spread her open, slip a finger inside, gentle, so gentle, and she yells something I can't hear, as if part of her is far away now. And I move inside her slowly as she wriggles all over the cutting board, and all of a sudden, I need to taste her. I throw my head down between her moving legs, trade my finger for my tongue. She is sweet there too, sweet and fresh and slippery wet as cream. I lap her up, suck her sweetness into my mouth, my tongue fluttering hard and fast, then soft and slow inside her lips. I grasp her thighs on either side so I can hang on, stay with her, buckle in as if she's a wild ride in a small-town midway and she cries out loud, almost a scream, and comes shaking and gushing wetness into my mouth, the insides of her thighs stretching, ass grinding and bucking under my tongue.

And she is done.

For a few moments, she lies in my arms and we ride out her aftershocks with the heel of my hand nestled inside her lips and she sighs over and over, stretches arms out long and languid and pulls me close, and for a split second, I feel all Prince Charming come to curl up and sleep with the princess. Until she kisses me, tongue searching out all taste of her, until she rolls me onto my back, and I feel the wetness spreading out beneath me; I must have come too, when she did. She gathers up the wetness on my thighs and hair and slips her fingers inside me. Oh. One. Two. Yes. Three. More. Petey pushes my knees apart, spreads me wide open, lowers her still trembling body onto mine, grinds her wetness into mine with a fury I never expected, and I wrap my legs around her hips, shelter her as she rides me hard, her hands grasping my shoulders, my body rising up to meet every stroke. She is gasping now, breathing loud and calling out, sweet bits and pieces of words whispered, *fuck sweet wet baby, come, mine, mine, oh fuck, beautiful you, oh*. And I feel the climb and rise of us both as she comes hard and loud into me while I lock my legs around her, grasping, grinding, shivering, up, up and over, screaming and trembling against her as she falls into me, done, head full of dark sweet curls, fine strands of burnt sugar candy, warm and swirled over my breasts.

TAG!

D. Alexandria

"I hate getting older."

"Who doesn't?"

Keisha turned onto her side and propped herself on her elbow, looking at me. "We used to want to though, remember? I couldn't wait to get to eighteen, twenty-one, twenty-five."

"'Cause those ages mean somethin'. You ain't really legal until you can rent a car without the 'under twenty-five' surcharge." I remained lying on my back, staring up at the night sky. It was Keisha's twenty-ninth birthday and, understandably, she was upset. I had surprised her with a late-night picnic at one of our favorite camping spots, about an hour outside of the city. We were surrounded by dense forest and complete silence, save for crickets and numerous woodland animals going about their business. I'll be completely honest and say that camping really isn't my style. I'm a one hundred percent modern butch who likes my TV time, my PlayStation 2, and if I wasn't smoking a blunt right now I'd be seriously missing my tunes. But Keisha loves the quiet seclusion of camping and getting back to nature, so I deal 'cause I love her and making her happy is my contentment.

She sighed.

I looked over and took in the unbelievably cute pout on her cherubic face and instantly fell in love all over again. Keisha is one beautiful sista, and no one can tell me different. Standing at nearly five feet eleven, with a perfect brick-house body, she is the sexiest female to ever grace my bed. I could spend hours just looking at her whether she's curled up in a chair reading a book or languidly lying in bed after a break-your-back fuckfest. With her supple body, covered in the softest skin known to man, I can only hope I get to spend several blissful lifetimes enjoying this true model of what is Woman.

Out the corner of my eye, I saw her tremble. I immediately put out the blunt and headed for the stack of fallen twigs and branches we had collected to feed the fire.

"You don't care that you're turning thirty in a couple of months?"

I shrugged. "I dunno. I'm not crazy about it, nah, but I don't intend to lose sleep over it either. It's not like I can stop it, know what I mean?"

"I miss being a kid."

Oh, here we go. I rolled my eyes before looking at her. "Now, Keisha Everton, you know damn well you wouldn't want to be a kid again."

She looked at me with slight annoyance. "And what makes you so sure?"

I moved to where she sat, straddling her legs. My voice dipped low as I whispered in her ear, "'Cause if you weren't grown, you wouldn't be able to take my dick deep in that thick pussy of yours, that's why."

I swear I felt her body temperature rise as she took in a sharp breath.

"You're so bad," she whispered, giggling.

I gave her a soft kiss, barely touching her lips, just teasing her. She remained still, eyes closed and face turned upward, allowing me to touch her in any way I pleased. I love that about her. I prefer a woman who just gives in to whatever her lover wants. I'm not saying that Keisha doesn't get hers, 'cause believe me that body holds a very powerful sexual creature, and she can come at you like a pit bull to get what she wants. However, she has this perfect sense of when to just let me do my thing and that makes my head spin with countless ideas of how to make her sing those cums I feel to my core.

When I met Keisha, one of the first things she told me was that she wasn't a fan of kissing. I, for one, feel that kissing is one of the finer points of fucking. Kissing is an intimate act, I ain't about to front on that, but a single kiss, if done right, can make a female part those thighs for you. And right now, Keisha's breaths were becoming shallow as I gently sucked on her lips, letting the tip of my tongue quickly glide across them. I started to lightly nip them, careful not to bite down too hard, and I felt her thighs press together, my signal that she was getting wet and ready.

Despite wanting to just push her down and spread her open, I also wanted to draw this out as long as I could, and just as I was about to settle in for a little torture, she pulled back.

"You wanna play tag?"

"Excuse me?" I couldn't have heard right.

"Let's play tag."

I sat back on my heels, needing to look at her face to make sure she was serious. She was. "Keisha, baby, seriously…"

"Angel, c'mon, it'll be fun." She was already wiggling out from underneath me to get to her feet. "How often can we do silly things like this?"

"Uh, we don't, 'cause we grown," I said.

She made a face, but winked. "C'mon, baby, play with me."

Okay, now she really was losing it. "Keisha, it's almost midnight and we're in the middle of the woods. Who, in their right mind, would play tag right now?"

She reached for her K-Swiss, an old beat-up pair that she wouldn't be caught dead in back in the 'hood, and slipped them on. "Where's your sense of adventure?"

"I was about to show you before you moved."

She smiled. "Please, baby? Just indulge me."

I was already out here complaint free, wasn't I? That, right there, was some serious indulgence.

I hadn't answered her and she gave a dramatic sigh, hands on her hips. "Okay, what if I make it interesting for you?"

Hmm. "How?"

She thought for a moment, before a wicked glint came into her eyes. "I'll strip."

I chuckled. "Get the fuck outta here."

"I'm serious." She was now grinning. "I'll strip naked right here and then take off. All you gotta do is catch me. That ain't hard, is it? And if you want, we'll even play back and forth."

"*You* chasin' me?" I smirked.

"What? You afraid I'll be better than you?"

I rolled my eyes. "Whateva."

"Well, what then? Scared? Too dark for ya?"

"Oh, please!" I said sarcastically.

Keisha reached for the hem of her sweater and lifted it slightly, baring her soft stomach. "Don't tell me you're gonna punk out on me, Angel. What would your boys say if I told them you were too afraid to chase *me* in the dark? And naked, at that?"

I stared at her. Well, actually I was staring at the bottom curves of her bare breasts, which she teasingly revealed as she continued to slowly lift her top. I felt my clit twitch at the thought of touching them, getting my hands and mouth on them. Damn, I was aching for her in a serious way.

Her hips swayed provocatively as she pulled the sweater off, dropping it on the blanket. She stood before me, slowly writhing to a melody only she could hear, yet I could see her full hips bumping out the beat in the air. Her large breasts hung freely, moving with her, both nipples tight and hard. I caught myself biting my lip as I watched, and before I knew it I was wondering how long it would take before I could catch her—*if* I gave in, of course. When I said it was dark, I meant it. In fact, if the slightest bit of cloud cover had hit the moon, I wouldn't have been able to see my hand in front of my face. But thankfully, I could probably see about a good ten feet problem free, and even if I gave her a slight head start, I could catch her before we got in too far.

"C'mon, Angel baby." Keisha's hands found her dark nipples and she gently tugged on them. "You *can* catch me, right? I mean, your ass hasn't gotten *that* old yet."

And she knew that shit would work. My pride was too high. I grumbled as I got to my feet, pulling off my jersey. (I'd play along, but I wasn't about to ruin a perfectly good Patriots jersey while up in the mix.)

Keisha's face lit up at my acceptance and she began tugging down her jeans.

"Leave on your panties," I said suddenly, eyeing the pale pink cotton thong hugging her most intimate curves. I wasn't sure why, but I didn't want her completely naked...yet.

She gave me a sly look as she left them alone, pulling the jeans off her long legs and tossing them on top of the sweater. She stood before me in just her panties and sneakers, looking as fine as she wanted to be, and god help me if she didn't look as if she were in her element; her ebony skin glowing from the campfire, long limbs ready and taut; even how her hair, which was pulled in a tight ponytail earlier, now had strands that had fallen loose, kissing her cheeks. All she needed was some animal skin and a spear and I'd be at her feet in worship.

I silently appreciated my having had the foresight to wear my battered pair of Tims, before I crouched low, feeling my strap press against my left inner thigh, and shuddering in anticipation. "Ten! Nine! Eight!"

Keisha took off. I watched her slip into the darkness, the last sight of her the jiggling of her ass as she ran away. I took a deep breath to calm myself and finished counting, stretching out the last numbers to give her more time.

"Three! Two! One!" I called before I followed. It was dark as hell. I was rushing through the trees, my eyes darting from side to side to catch sight of her as I maneuvered around rocks and brush, batting branches out of the way. I had assumed I'd be able to find her right off the bat, but as I moved, I realized that my first instincts were right and it was going to be a helluva task to see anything. The night air was still, the darkness threatening to envelope me indefinitely. We might as well have been playing hide-and-seek. I was trying to think like Keisha, wondering how she'd try to move, when a branch snapped loudly under my boot. I silently cursed and slowed my pace.

As I moved, taking measured breaths, my heart was pounding and I could hear every pulsing thud in my ears. I was stepping gingerly, trying not to make a sound as I listened out for her, knowing that if she was smart, she would be trying to remain low 'cause of her height. I paused by a slim tree with low-hanging branches and squatted, my eyes now adjusting to the darkness. I was hoping to see the moonlight against her skin, but was having no such luck as I peered all around me. I figured I had been moving for almost ten minutes in one direction, and wondered if I should double back, just in case Keisha was purposely staying close to the campsite.

I was about to turn around when something in the air caught my attention. I stopped and inhaled deeply, my lips spreading in a wide grin as I recognized a scent almost as familiar as my own.

"You're wet, baby girl, I can smell it," I called out, my clit throbbing behind my dick as I surveyed the area. She was close, I knew it; unless she was *so* aroused her scent was just lingering in the air. I took a few steps toward the right and heard rustling to my left. I turned my head in time to see a quick blur of pink rush past a couple of trees.

I chuckled as I quickly followed, barely seeing her move ahead of me, but able to hear her quick, excited breaths. No doubt, she was completely worked up. I was right on her tail and able to smell her arousal even more, knowing at this very moment she wanted it just as much as I did. She suddenly made a right turn, and I did the same, knowing exactly where she was headed. I increased my pace, my breaths short as I pumped my arms, willing myself to pull ahead. In a few minutes I broke through the trees and stepped onto one of the hiking trails we often took, this one leading down to a small pond about a mile away. I stepped back into the trees, and quietly counted until I heard her footsteps.

Just as she was about to pass me, I lunged out, my arms looping around her waist, and pulled her close to me.

"Gotcha!" I roared as she struggled in my arms.

"Dammit!" She gasped heavily before accepting a deep kiss from me. I was feeling drunk on the adrenaline that was coursing through me. Keisha fell into me, her arms lacing around my neck as she hungrily returned my kisses while still trying to catch her breath. I relished in the feel of her naked body as my hands glided over her now slightly sweaty skin. I cupped her ass with some force and pulled her tighter against me so she could feel my dick through my jeans.

I pulled my lips away. "You want it?"

"Yes," she hissed, as her lips reached for mine.

I ducked my head, giving her earlobe a soft flick with my tongue. "How bad do you want it, baby girl?"

"Fuck, I want it bad."

"What do you want, Keisha?"

She gave a half groan, half whine. "Angel, I want your dick! Please! Now!"

I gave her ass a tight squeeze with both hands before pulling away. Just as she tried reaching for me again, my hand swung out, connecting with an asscheek, the smack echoing around us.

"You're it!" I smirked before I turned and ran.

"Asshole!" she screamed, but I heard her footsteps behind me.

I stayed on the trail, moving quickly until I was about a quarter of a mile away from camp, before turning left. This part of the woods had trees that grew closer together, and obviously, since there wasn't a defined path, I had to make my own, holding on to tree after tree for balance as I moved. I forced myself to move faster, as the sound of Keisha's footsteps started to fade. When I could still see a glimpse of camp far to the right, I darted to the left and crouched low behind a couple of bushes and waited.

After a few minutes of not seeing her, I began to worry, wondering if maybe the path I had taken wasn't as forgiving to Keisha in her sneakers. But before I could rise to investigate, I heard a branch break to my left. I had to grin. The girl had taken another route, hoping to cut me off as I had done to her earlier. But, of course, she hadn't anticipated my beating her and hiding out. I watched as she stood still, trying to listen out for me as she searched. She looked absolutely gorgeous. Her body glistened with sweat in the moonlight, her hair a complete and captivating mess, and every breath she took forced her breasts to slightly lift. Damn, I needed to have her pussy wrapped around my dick. She caught sight of camp and gave another hopeless look around before taking a step toward the glow of the campfire.

I jumped out and grabbed her, pulling her hard to me as I kissed the back of her neck.

"I guess we know who's best, huh?" I taunted as I held her arms to her side.

She couldn't help but giggle as she squirmed in my grip.

"You cheated," she gasped.

"You *wanted* to fuck up, so I could catch you again, don't front," I pointed out as I took a few steps forward, forcing her to move with me until she stood before a large tree. I placed a hand on her shoulder and forced her down to her knees, facing away from me.

Gasping for breath, Keisha planted both hands on the ground beneath her, her ass high in the air. My movements were quick, and before she knew it, I was behind her, jeans unzipped, dick in hand. I grabbed hold of her panties by the thin strip of fabric in the back, and was about to pull them to the side, when I thought better of it and gave a rough tug, tearing them away from her body. Keisha gave a loud gasp, bucking her hips in anticipation. There was no point in drawing this out, 'cause we were both primed. I pushed into her deeply, my entry the smoothest it's ever been 'cause of how wet she was. She groaned loudly, pushing back against me, her ass warm against my denim-covered thighs.

I sat back on my heels, getting a good grip on her wide hips as I pulled out to the head and then pushed back in, wanting to give her every inch of me. She was so wet that even in the dark I could see her juices glistening on the dick, and she was making guttural noises every time I entered her. My fingers dug into her flesh as I stepped up the pace, just enough to watch her asscheeks shake with every move we made.

"So, you got your ass caught up, huh?" I asked, giving a cheek a playful swat.

"Shiiit," she whispered.

"What was that?" I slapped her ass again, a bit harder.

"Dammit, Angel," she cried out, her ass starting to rotate on my dick.

"What, baby girl?" I asked as I gave her a quick thrust that made her body jump.

"It feels so goooood, fuck." She let her head fall forward as she quickened her hips.

I weighed my options and decided I wanted to enjoy a show. I stopped moving and removed my hands.

Keisha's head snapped up and she looked silently back at me.

"Who told you to stop? Keep going." I gave her ass a hard slap and she whimpered. "Come on, Keisha, move that ass."

Her eyes met mine for a moment, and I saw the lustful twinkle in them before she began moving her hips. I remained still, keeping my hands at my sides as I watched the woman I love fuck herself on my dick. She was working it like only a sista could, her pussy literally pulling my dick into it as she threw herself back and forth. I was mesmerized by every move she made; how her lower half seemed to have a life of its own and how my body was oh so willing to oblige its manipulations. She suddenly lifted her left leg, and I swear on everything that I am, my dick got sucked in deeper, and I quickly grabbed the leg to balance her as her ass started to ricochet off my body. In this position, I had a perfect view of her pussy greedily consuming my dick and her clit swollen and full, standing away from her body. I pulled her leg back, holding it against me, and reached for that clit, massaging it.

"Sweet Jesus..." Keisha wailed and I watched her fingers dig into the earth. I gently pulled on that slippery nub, feeling it pulsate and knowing she was gonna blow at any moment. I started tapping on one side of her clit, as I resumed moving, keeping her locked in her position.

"Yes, Angel, yes!" she cried as I fucked her. I was slamming into her harder and harder, hearing the slapping sounds of her ass connecting with my body, and I could feel the beginnings of my own cum. I was on a mission to fill and stretch that pussy to the hilt, jabbing her like a piston. She was back to whimpering, only louder this time, every lunge I made causing her entire body to convulse.

Just when I was sure she was 'bout to cum, I let go of her leg and quickly pushed a firm finger into her ass and she hollered, her body seizing and then freezing as she came, the song that I practically live for escaping her lips. I was still working her pussy as my finger dug in deeper, forcing every shudder out of her beautiful body. I bit my lip hard as I silently came, unable to take my eyes off her.

Keisha collapsed on the ground, and I knew that once morning came and she saw all the dirt and bits of leaves in her hair she'd freak, but I couldn't care less as I carefully pulled out of both her holes and lay beside her. We were both breathing heavily, and I found myself staring up at the night sky again.

"You were right," she said, still gasping.

"About what?" I turned to look at her and saw that familiar wicked glint in her eyes.

"About not really wanting to be a kid again," she replied. "'Cause only grown folks can play tag like that."

All I could do was laugh.

VOODOO AND TATTOOS

Lynne Jamneck

It started out so innocuously. Maybe that's why it turned out so fucking hot.

I've had enough of bartending in my life that when Annie asked me to pour drinks at a conference she was in charge of, my immediate instinct was to think—fast—of the first best lie I could offer in order to avoid the prospect.

"I—someone has to feed my cat."

Annie found that excuse pathetic, and gave me a look that said so. "Kyle, that cat died two years ago."

"Fuck, you remember."

"Of course I do. I was at the funeral."

"A little respect, please. Princess Leia was no ordinary feline."

"Sure she wasn't," she said sweetly. Sarcastically. Annie wasn't an animal lover. Curious, then, that she'd refer to her lover as a "tiger" in bed. Makes you think.

"So you'll do it?"

"Is this the fancy-schmancy do you've been planning for the last two months?" Annie was head of conference planning at the Sheraton Belgravia Hotel on Chesham Street in London.

"I'm thrilled. You remembered."

"How could I not—you've been yammering about it non-stop for weeks."

"Oh fuck off, Kyle." Then she went all sweet again. "So then you know how important this is to me, to my *career*." She sidled up next to me, running a long finger along my forearm. "I need the best bartender in London, and you're it."

Annie and I have never slept together. We've come close once or twice in moments when neither of us had been thinking. She was way too driven, and I liked Guns N' Roses. But she knew just how to play me.

"I take it the Sheraton pays well?"

"Oh, *yes*. And I'll get you a uniform... Just do us a favor?"

"I thought I already was."

There was the sweet smile again, laced with sarcasm. "I can see why you manage to fuck any girl you want. Your wit surpasses even my own. No dear, what I meant was the hair."

"The hair?"

"Yes. Yours in particular. Just...try not to look like Ringo Starr on a bad day, okay?"

I wouldn't argue with Annie. I'd just lose.

The night of the conference I showed up in my monkey suit at exactly 18:30 as Annie had instructed me. I'd never even asked her what kind of clientele I'd be serving overpriced cocktails and martinis to. It turned out to be some corporate thing. Loads of women in power suits. Blah blah.

When I went in through the service entrance somewhere in the bowels of the hotel, a group of waitresses eyeballed me. A couple of aviation blondes, their black roots starting to show. I smiled favorably and one of them brushed past me just a little too close. A spotty male looked at me like I'd stolen his wallet. Probably the usual bartender. I smirked. Annie could get away with anything. Probably because she was so fucking good at her job.

The conference started at 19:00 sharp. Between then and 21:00 I pretty much did stuff-all except verbally abuse Annie in her absence for making me show up so early. Control freak. Another reason why I would never have sex with her.

At some point, a woman sneaked out from behind the heavy conference room doors. She looked around furtively before making her way over to the bar. I was busy wiping down whisky tumblers, probably for the third time in an hour. When she saw the coast was clear she launched herself across the empty bar area, weaving through the unoccupied tables. and pulled out a bar stool.

She smiled disarmingly. "You'd be out of there too if you had to listen to that tosser."

"I take it the speeches aren't very entertaining."

She looked right at me and smiled widely. "Fucking understatement of the year, lassie."

"You have a great smile." *Stop flirting with the patronage.*

"Thanks." She looked as I dried off the glass. "God, you have really good forearms."

Oh. My.

I'd rolled my sleeves up before washing the few glasses my

perfectionist eye hadn't deemed clean enough. If Annie saw me like this she'd have a continental fit. But taking in the present company, I didn't really care.

She was a sort-of redhead. More like copper, flecked with golden brown. Her eyes were dirty emeralds and a crooked trail of freckles were scattered across the bridge of her nose. Her mouth appeared both demure and possibly foul at the same time.

"You got any Jameson back there?" she asked. "Make it quick, before the bastards notice I'm gone. Double, on the rocks."

"So you're Irish," I nodded, pouring the whisky with a steady hand.

"What on earth makes you think that?"

"Trace of the accent. Mild, but there. But in all my time as a bartender, an Irishman wants whisky, he wants Jameson."

"Then you know the Irish were the first to distil whisky."

"That's up for debate."

"Okay. You have something against the Irish?" She swallowed a mouthful of whisky and looked at me. Her eyes held mine for just a moment longer than need be.

"Hardly." An involuntary charge of arousal jolted up my thighs.

"One more. Quickly." She moved her glass closer and watched me pour the amber liquid. "If you don't mind me saying so, you look a little out of place here."

"Thank god for small mercies."

I could see the kinky smile around the edge of her glass. She swallowed the whisky in two, three quick successive tips of her wrist, then said, "Better prepare yourself. There's a lot of bored women about to come out of that conference room in serious need of booze. Hot little thing like yourself…" She slid off the bar stool. "You're going to have your hands full."

"Annie! Annie!"

She didn't see me at first, but how could she? The bar was packed. Women, everywhere. Then finally a gap as I served another Bacardi with a twist of lemon and everyone seemed to have a drink. For now.

Annie walked briskly over to the bar and tapped nonchalantly on the glass top. "Martini, doll."

I scanned the room whilst making her drink. I can prepare martinis in my sleep by now. Then I spotted her. Irish freckles.

I placed the glass on a serviette and slid it across the counter. "Who's that?"

"What? Where? Oh." Annie gave me a smarmy look. "Well, I can't say that I'm surprised; I did expect you to get your leg over. But I'm afraid you're out of luck on that one. That's Jamie Gallagher."

Annie looked at me expectantly. "I get the feeling I'm supposed to know who she is."

"Jesus Christ, Kyle; don't you ever watch the news, read the paper? Jamie Gallagher—as in Gallagher, Sabatini and Larue? The law firm?"

"Can't say I've heard of them. Besides, isn't she a bit young to be a partner in a law firm?"

"Jamie? She's thirty-two. I think. Anyway, like I said Kyle, forget about it. She's got a girlfriend with more piercings than you do. Tattoos up the woo-ha. Bad timing on your part." She took a lascivious sip of her drink. "She likes 'em young."

"Fuck. Double whammy. And to think, I just turned twenty-four last week."

Annie smiled. "Poor dear."

"Her girlfriend's here?"

"Yes. Probably waiting in their hotel room. She's not the type to go round in a business suit."

A woman came to the bar and ordered another vodka tonic. Annie watched, amused, as she blatantly tried to flirt her way into my pants. Sure, I'd be lying if I said I didn't feel flattered. Problem was I couldn't keep my eyes off Jamie. And I found it intriguing that she didn't drink after having come out of the banquet hall for the second time. What made the whole thing even more unbearable was that I noticed the stolen glances she directed my way, too. A quick look over the shoulder of someone she greeted with a hug, or an upward turn of the head when she bent down to say something to a friend or acquaintance sitting at a table...

Now look, I might be young, but I'm not fucking stupid, you know? Sure, I get teased all the time by superior femmes like Annie, and I become brainless at the thought of solving riddles or thinking logically. It's easy for me to let people think I'm a sweet butch who'd rather swing a wrench than fiddle with a pressure cooker. But if there's one thing I know, it's women. I've been learning my entire life.

So I'll tell you this much: every time Jamie looked up and we glanced at one another I could see there was a certain purpose to her. Not just in her eyes, but in the way she brushed the copper from her forehead; the two open buttons of her crisp, starched shirt; and the way her hands touched herself, slightly self-consciously.

She wanted me for something. And I was pretty sure I knew the extent of her motives.

Jamie made the flimsy excuse of ordering a drink from the bar for a friend to come and speak to me again. At the end of the night, when the bar was almost empty, she came up to pay the tab. I told her it wasn't a tab, it was one drink; she insisted.

She paid with a twenty pound note, which was completely over the limit of what she needed to cover. She was gone before I could give her any change. But she'd written her room number on a hotel serviette. It lay open on the counter, daring me.

Maybe Annie'd been wrong. Maybe Jamie was alone. And it's true—I can be morally inept if I choose to be.

So, soon enough, there I was, standing in front of room 27. I lifted my hand and knocked, short and sharp, twice. I waited. Tried to listen for any kind of distinctive sound, but there was none.

The door opened and Jamie stood inside, looking me over. "Hi," I said nonchalantly.

"Nice to see you…"

"Kyle."

"Come in." She closed the door. I was infinitely aware of her presence behind me. I'll admit, I expected her to touch me, but she didn't.

The room was a moderate temperature; comfortable and relaxed. I noticed the big king-size bed in the far corner had been turned down. With relief I realized there wasn't any music playing in the background.

"Would you like a drink?" Jamie's accent was more prevalent now. Her voice was laced with thick arousal. I heard her move behind me, then she stepped past and headed for the minibar.

"Actually—" I stopped when I saw the other woman step out of the bathroom. She was wearing jeans, heavy black boots and a wifebeater that accentuated her small breasts and flat stomach.

"Hi," she said in a gravelly voice, and smiled. "I'm Nicole."

As if by some form of sexual voodoo, the atmosphere suddenly crisped white-hot with eroticism. I looked over to where Jamie had started undressing by the edge of the bed. She was slowly undoing the buttons of her cotton shirt. I noticed with no small amount of satisfaction that the freckles repeated themselves between the cleft of her breasts. She was wearing a white bra and panties.

Jamie said, "Kiss her," and for a moment I wasn't sure who she'd said it to, or even if I'd heard her correctly. Then I felt Nicole step up behind me, her masculine presence heavy, and for a moment my body tensed.

I'd never fucked another butch. Maybe because of that, the coil of lust that started in my belly and slithered due south made me groan when I felt her hands, solid and firm from behind, on my hips.

I turned around and looked at her, knowing that Jamie, already naked, was looking at us. Nicole had a silver ring through the right of her bottom lip, and her left eyebrow had been pierced several times. Black, oily tattoos crept out from beneath her vest and veined down her muscular arms. Dangerous, distracting silver decorated all but the thumbs of her two hands.

I placed my hands on Nicole's forearms and felt the coiled tension there. I pulled her closer, just like that, and kissed her, tasting the tang of metallic as the silver ring slid against my tongue.

No matter how tough and rugged she might have looked, Nicole kissed like a woman. Don't get me wrong; she was as hungry as I was. Her tongue stroked mine slowly, probing keenly in a most exquisite way. The air in her mouth was hot. I felt her fingers waver near the waist of my black pants.

She pulled back, both of us breathing hard. All in all, the kiss had been a little demanding, but nothing too violent. As I looked into Nicole's gray-blue eyes I knew that it wouldn't be the two of us ending up in bed together. That wasn't the plan.

She stepped back from me then. We both looked at Jamie, who was lying on the bed, naked, looking back at us. No one said a word. I was ready to fuck her if they asked me.

Nicole tapped a cigarette from an open box on the table and lit it. She drew in deep and expelled a column of smoke. "Don't get undressed," she said to me and pointed at a chair next to the side of the bed. "That's your place. Don't forget it." She winked at me. Some sublime form of butch code passed between us.

As I sat down, one leg resting in a *T* across my knee, Nicole pulled her vest off and tossed it into a corner. Both Jamie and I watched as she unbuttoned the heavy buttons on her black cargos, the cigarette dangling from the corner of her mouth. The sound of the metallic buttons popping was followed by someone exhaling loudly—me, I realized. For an instant I felt as if it was me standing there. I realized my hands were grasping the chair. It took everything I had not to stand up and walk over to the bed.

Nicole stepped closer and held her half-smoked cigarette out to me. I took it, grateful for something to put in my mouth, and watched her strut over to the bed. I glimpsed a broad, black studded belt above the waistline of her pants. *That's a good-looking piece of leather.* Her crotch bulged fetchingly as she climbed onto the bed and crawled over Jamie like a snake. The bed creaked prettily.

Nicole and Jamie kissed, hard, and when I saw Nicole's tongue—which had moments before been in my own mouth—slip past her lover's lips a small sound of satisfaction escaped from Jamie's throat.

My senses began their slow but certain dip into overload. My groin was on fire. I heard the smooth *shhhk* as one of Jamie's legs moved against Nicole's clothed thigh and her heel hooked around the inside of Nicole's knee.

They were making the stimulated sounds of lovers flushed with arousal, and there I was, not four feet away, watching them. Nicole moved her mouth down. When her tongue flicked lewdly before taking Jamie's erect nipple into her mouth, I heard a moan. Involuntarily, I followed with one of my own, short and tight.

Nicole's hand moved down between her legs, and disappeared inside her cargos. When she brought it back out she held at least eight inches of dyke cock in her hand. I grunted at the sight of it; not because I wanted it in me, but because I wished I was Nicole.

Nicole turned her head and looked at me, smiling as Jamie reached down to take the cock in her hand. I was having a hard time taking my eyes off Jamie's hips as they rose eagerly from the mattress. Nicole put one of her big, decorated hands on Jamie's hip and held her down, making the muscles beneath the skin of her taut belly move.

"Fuck her," I snarled, quite unrepentantly, only then realizing how my jaw muscles were clenching. Nicole leaned forward and in one admirably executed move thrust herself into Jamie with a harsh grunt.

I sat and watched, rapt.

At first Nicole was nice and easy. She allowed Jamie to move up to meet her as she kept a fixed tempo. Every so often Jamie would make encouraging sounds, or those of pleasure when Nicole's cock hit the right spot. I watched the tattoos on the butch girl's back as they moved and undulated to the syncopated rhythm of that one weak spot in the mattress. At one point they both looked over to where I was sitting, their movements never faltering, their attention fixed on me. I felt my hand move down to my crotch.

Nicole began to fuck Jamie harder then, no doubt partly due to the fact that I seemed to have found my tongue and was egging her on. She was strong and held Jamie down, fucking her into the mattress while I implored her with rude remarks; ones I realized I'd wanted to say ever since Jamie had the balls to call me "lassie." I wanted to screw Jamie myself...but I knew the magic would end, the spell would be broken if I dared move from that chair an inch. All I could do was grind my teeth and cross my legs while watching the two of them on the bed.

When they were done, Jamie and Nicole fell against one another, kissing like longtime lovers. I wondered at that. Nicole couldn't have been older than myself. Maybe even younger. The idea that they had been in a relationship for some time was perversely thrilling.

I got up weakly to leave when Nicole went into the bathroom. The sound of a tap being opened brought reality back in full swing. Jamie, naked, stopped me when I was halfway to the door. "Thanks for coming," she said and laughed, realizing her pun. She patted and squeezed my ass before disappearing inside the bathroom just as Nicole came out. She walked me to the door.

I reached out to turn the knob but Nicole stopped me. Grabbing my wrist, she shoved my hand inside her cargos. Her clit was hard. I knew what she wanted.

I stroked her, stiff and rough. It was strange but thrilling to hear the low obscenities of another butch in my ear. My coccyx tingled with newfound lust.

It didn't take long for her to come. I didn't know whether Jamie was aware of what we were doing. Nicole pushed me against the door, grinding her hips against mine, and came with a cry of release still stuck inside her throat. I fumbled for the doorknob and fell out into the hallway. The door banged shut loudly behind me. For a moment I just stood there, flushed and getting my bearings back. When I checked my watch I saw that it was almost two in the morning. Too late to catch the Tube. Too late for a bus. Dammit. I should have asked for cab money.

BRIGHT ANGEL

Sacchi Green

Maura lounged against the railing, gazing out over the vast, bright gulf of stone dropping away at her feet. Dark sunglasses masked her green eyes, and those famous waves of long chestnut hair were tied down by an Hermès scarf rippling in the breeze.

"Are you trying to tell me all this was carved by that little trickle of a river?" In spite of her studied nonchalance, I could tell she was as awestruck as any other tourist.

"The Colorado's wider than it looks from this distance. And it was carrying billions of grains of rasping sand over millions of years." I didn't look toward the river at all, gazing only at Maura's slim, vivid form. The view of the Grand Canyon from Mather Point had gripped me often enough over the years, and

I had photographed it for many a magazine and guidebook, but long ago I'd come to terms with the inability of the human mind to fully comprehend its grandeur.

Comprehending Maura, however, might still be within my grasp. A year ago I had discovered how to penetrate her dark and bright complexities, to push her mind and body to the edges where she needed so desperately to balance. A year ago—and then came her first starring movie role, with filming on location in various exotic areas around the world. We'd only been able to meet sporadically, except when she'd insisted they hire me to do the still photos for publicity.

Did I even know who she was anymore? When I'd picked her up at the Flagstaff airport she'd greeted me with a Hollywood air kiss, nothing to raise eyebrows even when directed by a drop-dead gorgeous twentysomething toward an aging, crop-haired butch like me. Then she'd dozed for most of the three-hour drive across the high desert. But at least she was here, as promised, keeping the date we'd made all those months ago.

I moved up close behind her at the railing, not quite touching. The April wind tugged several strands of hair free from her scarf and lashed them across my face and chest, rousing a tingle in my nipples just as though they were naked to those flailing whips of silk.

"Hey Roby," Maura said, without turning her head. "Too bad you don't have the balls to fuck me right here."

Oh yeah. I still knew exactly who she was. "If you'd had the foresight to wear a skirt," I told her, "you'd be bent over that railing right now praying you could hold on long enough to ride my fist to glory." I pressed closer and reached around to unzip the fly of her elegantly cut jeans. "You could still drop your trousers and make all these amateur photographers rich on sales to the tabloids. Or you can let it simmer awhile, and I'll fuck you somewhere even better."

I could see out of the corner of my eye that we'd begun to distract a few tourists, most, of course, armed with cameras. Maura, even in scarf and sunglasses and denim, has the charisma of someone whose face could stare out at you with seductive arrogance from the pages of a fashion magazine. Whose face has, in fact, done exactly that, usually with the divinely sensuous participation of her body. More often than not the eye behind the camera had been mine, back before she moved on from the pinnacle of the modeling scene to her virgin attempt at acting.

"Don't they say that no publicity is bad publicity?" Maura turned toward me. I reached out to untie her scarf and remove her sunglasses, tucking them away in the pocket of my leather jacket. The old challenge was in her eyes. *Push me*, it said. *Force me to the edge. Make me feel.*

"So you don't think your acting can stand on its own," I asked, wrapping strands of her windblown hair tightly around my fingers, "without the scandal of getting thrown out of a national park before the movie even opens?"

She caught at my hands. I released her hair. "Maybe I'll give you a chance to show me somewhere you think is even better," she said, and headed back toward the car. I waited just long enough to appreciate the elegant undulation of her hips in tight jeans before I caught up.

Maura wasn't primarily an exhibitionist, in spite of her place in the public eye. Or possibly because of it. Her craving for danger was more complex than that. There had been times, once I had come to understand what my weathered skin and scarred body said to her, when she had begged me to mark the face the world saw so that it would become her own again. What she thought she wanted from me had nothing to do with tenderness. Still, whether she was aware of it or not, she needed something else from me, as well. *Push me right up to the edge*, her fierce eyes demanded, while a tiny tremor at the corner of her soft lips added, *but don't let me fall*.

While I checked in at Bright Angel Lodge, Maura watched the tourists signing up to ride down the nearby Bright Angel Trail the next morning. Even in April, well before the high season, there was heavy traffic along the route. This late in the afternoon we wouldn't have had long to wait to see the mule train returning from the river at the bottom of the canyon, four-fifths of a mile straight down and eight miles of switch-backing trail below, but I had no intention of waiting.

Our cabin out behind the lodge perched close to the edge, with just room for a narrow path and a wind-gnarled pinyon pine between its wall and the canyon's rim. Even a year ahead of time it had taken luck and the pulling of a few strings to get the reservation.

While I brought in the luggage, two-thirds of it hers, Maura stood looking outward, one hand tightly gripping a pinyon branch. The drop here was really not that abrupt at first. One could conceivably survive a slide down over a series of shallow shelves to Bright Angel Trail below.

"Are we going down there?" she asked.

"Not on that trail," I told her, "and definitely not on mules. Not all the way to the river, either."

"Oh, right, I'd forgotten about your poor knees." Her subtly mocking tone was just another variation on the game of challenge we played. I knew my old climbing injuries held a certain fascination for her, and she knew that my body still had more strength and stamina than hers would ever achieve from gyms and personal trainers.

"You'll get all you can handle," I told her. "Trust me."

"I'm more worried about how much you can still handle." Maura sauntered back to the cabin and stepped inside. I followed her eloquent butt, then stood in the doorway for a moment to watch her explore the interior.

The furnishings were of comfortably updated 1930s craft design, highlighting natural wood tones and artistically simple lines. The stone fireplace incorporated specimens of all the different rock strata revealed by the river's carving of the canyon, from Precambrian black Vishnu Schist to the Kaibab Limestone of recent millennia.

The platform bed was modern, wide, and inviting. Maura prodded the mattress with a manicured finger, sat on the edge, then lay back. She eyed me speculatively, but without enough challenge to make it worthwhile.

"You must need to rest awhile after your trip," I said with exaggerated solicitude. "Go ahead, take it easy. I understand." I began to unpack, hanging things in the closet, watching for her next move. She got up and started to unbutton her shirt. Not a bad idea. The day was getting hot. So was I, but I wasn't ready to take her deceptive bait. Maura is never that easy.

My own bait was more subtle. I moved into the living room, pulled open the curtains of the window beside the fireplace, and crossed to the far side to set my cameras and equipment out on a table. Maura followed.

I didn't let her catch me watching, but she knew I could see her in the mirror as she shed her jacket and peeled off a tank top damp with sweat. She hadn't bothered with a bra. Then, to enhance the temptation, she turned around to present a rear view while wriggling out of her jeans. Her lovely ass-cheeks paused in mid-wriggle as she saw the view presented by the wide window.

The vista, tinted gold and copper by the late afternoon sun, was breathtaking. Maura gripped her loosened jeans tightly and edged past chairs and coffee table to gaze out, spellbound. It was the same scene she had surveyed from the rim outside, but somehow intensified; made more personal, more decep-tively comprehensible, by the framing effect of the window. From inside it looked as though the cabin extended right out over the shining void.

I waited five seconds for the mesmerizing effect of space and light and color to take hold, and then I was on her, pushing her hard against the log wall and windowsill. I had her own silk scarf tight across her mouth and her pants and foolish thong undies down around her ankles before she could do more than gasp.

She could easily have escaped, even hobbled like that, although she despised looking ridiculous. While my weight kept her pressed into the wall, her hands were free, gripping the wooden windowsill. Now and then people strolled by just outside on the pathway; if she rapped on the window, they'd turn to look. She knew how to make me let her go. But gag-ging was a special treat she wouldn't risk losing, a promise that she was going to be driven to extremities, permission to let it all out without reserve. I wouldn't always humor her that far. More than once she had cursed at me and demanded a gag. More often than not I had refused.

I gathered her thick chestnut hair in my fist and yanked her head back. "Surprise, my knees aren't all that decrepit yet," I hissed into her ear, and brought my right one hard up against her ass. She jerked, but spread her legs to let me thrust between her thighs and nudge into her crotch.

"You wonder how the river carves a canyon through rock?" I asked. "You think you're stone? Haven't I cut my petroglyphs into you?" My other hand worked its way around to her belly and slid down to her shaved pubic mound. The scars I'd given her, where even bikini photo spreads wouldn't reveal them, were too shallow for my fingertips to find like this, but I knew they were there; four tiny, curving lines forming a delicate circle like a secret mandala, cut by the business end of an ice-climbing screw.

"I suppose you think the water always flows gently, smoothly, taking forever to wear away resistance." My fingers moved lower, stroking gently, too gently, over her clit and lush outer lips. "Working down through layer after layer," I went on, going deeper, sliding back and forth in her growing slickness, keeping it up slowly, slowly, as her accelerating whimpers of demand were muffled by the silk gag. She arched into my touch, desperate for more, harder, faster. I drew my fingers away and approached from the other side, starting with long strokes down between her buttocks and into the tender strata of her soaking crotch.

"But sometimes storms batter at the rocks, and spring floods from mountain snowmelt surge through the ravines." I was really getting into it now. "The water pounds, thrashes, filled with sharp silt and uprooted trees." I raised my hand suddenly to the nape of her neck, still holding her hair roughly back. The scent of her juices on my fingers roused my own. With my fingernails, short but strong, I scraped a line down the valley of her spine to its base. A shiver passed over her skin. Then I veered first to one side and then the other, tracing the delectable swell of her ass, leaving curving pink grooves just shallow enough to fall short of drawing blood. Her gluteal muscles flexed, and her muted voice rose in pitch.

A pair of college-boy jocks passed by outside; even through the gag she could have made enough noise to attract their attention. I felt a shudder wrack her body. She wanted so intensely for them to see...but would I pull back, drop her, rather than risk a scandal that might, at the least, distort her career?

I don't know, myself, what I would have done, but they moved on past. My teeth fastened on to Maura's right shoulder, and her taste filled my mouth. I had no more words. Moans and incoherent curses vibrated from her body through mine as she writhed toward my touch. I spread my fingers then and slapped hard, again and again, overlaying the scrapes on her buttocks with red handprints like the marks on the walls of ancient Anasazi cliff dwellings far below in the canyon.

Suddenly Maura lurched backward, pushing off from the windowsill, nearly toppling me. I lifted her just enough to swing her around and then dropped her hard onto the Navajo rug in front of the fireplace. In the seconds it took for me to get a latex glove from my pocket onto my hand she had torn off her gag and kicked her pants free of her ankles, and now she crouched, long hair falling forward to veil her face, her butt lifted toward me and her swollen labia exposed.

"Do it!" she snarled, so ready that there was no need for lube. I thrust into her, slid out, thrust again, and then she was pumping herself onto me, heaving, panting, her cries rising higher as my other hand pinched her nipples. When the spasms struck, tightening her cunt around my hand and wrist like a trap, I supported her until her grip finally loosened and I could withdraw, gently, holding her wide open for a few seconds and admiring her glistening folds.

"Dusky rose," I said softly. "Like the sandstone layers of the canyon wall at dawn."

Maura whispered something I could barely hear. I leaned closer.

"Was this the 'better place' you had in mind?" she said.

"No," I said honestly, not sure whether she was working up to another challenge. "This was just an opportunity seized. You'll know when you get there."

And she did.

It wasn't along the rim trail or at any of the famous points where cameras clustered, not even Pima Point at sunset when the river winding far below to the west turned briefly into a ribbon of gold. It wasn't the moonlit vista of the canyon as we leaned together against a spreading branch of the pinyon pine outside our own cabin. It wasn't anyplace that easy.

We were up at dawn the next morning, breakfasting on the Bright Angel Lodge terrace. "Why 'Bright Angel?'" Maura asked.

I told her about Major John Wesley Powell's exploration of the Colorado River, and the story that after his men named one muddy incoming stream the Dirty Devil, the Major had compensated by dubbing the first clear creek they came to Bright Angel, flowing down from the north to join the river across from what later became Bright Angel Trail. I thought, watching Maura's beautiful face, as luminescent in its own way as the morning light suffusing the mist rising from far below, that he must also have been thinking of Lucifer before the Fall, Milton's "angel bright" of *Paradise*

Lost. Or, just possibly, he had known someone like Maura.

Three hours later we were far below the rim, three miles along the Hermit and Dripping Springs trails. Maura's cheeks and forehead were smudged with rock dust, and sweat trickled down between her breasts. Her hair was tangled and tied back with a bandanna. Her eyes had never been brighter.

"Just a little farther," I said, urging her past the spring, its fringe of greenery lively with small birds. "We'll fill our water bottles on the way back." A hundred feet off the trail, through a crevice between boulders, we were on a narrow shelf out of sight of passing climbers at our own level. Our view of sky and rock seemed as wide as infinity, and hikers and rafters deep in the canyon could see us easily if they looked up; see us, but not clearly enough even with binoculars to recognize Maura's features from past magazine spreads or future appearances on the big screen.

Maura stood with her arms outstretched like wings and her back to the cliff. Just above her head a twisted juniper grew out from a cleft in the rock, casting a tracery of shadows across her face.

"This is the place," she said with certainty. "Right here. Right now."

I drew a wet trail with my tongue along her dusty cheek and kissed her, for once, gently. For once, she allowed the tenderness, kissing back with more sensuality than challenge. Maybe wearing her out was the secret. Or did the vastness of the world spread out before us make petty conflict seem too insignificant?

More likely, it was just that she had grander things on her mind than private games.

"Roby...do you think anyone is watching?" Her fingers

scrabbled in haste at the buttons of her shirt, and when she'd cast it aside and yanked off the tank top beneath, she went to work on the silver Navajo belt buckle purchased just yesterday. Sunlight glinted from its highly polished surface like spears of fire.

"I'd bet there are at least a dozen pairs of binoculars and as many cameras aimed right up there," I told her, pointing out the peregrine falcon riding the breeze above us, undoubtedly watching for one of the small birds by the spring to stray from the sheltering shrubbery. "And now that you've been wriggling hard enough to flash signals from that silver mirror sliding down along with your pants, most of them must be checking you out, and calling their buddies to look, too."

Maura kicked aside her jeans and raised her arms. Her fingers could just grasp the gnarled trunk of the juniper. "Tie me," she said.

I pulled the bandanna loose from her hair. A twist around slender wrists and up over the juniper, and she was bound just far enough out from the cliff for me to slide behind her and press my thigh hard up against her butt, bending my knee slightly, taking some of her weight. That juniper must have been clinging to life here for a hundred years or more; I hoped to spare its roots for another hard-won century, in spite of her thrashing. And she *would* thrash.

"So show them what you've got, girl," I muttered in her ear as I pulled on a latex glove. I'm not sure she even heard me. Her focus was far out over the bright canyon, past labyrinthine ravines and spurs and phallic turrets carved by water, wind, and time. The sharp pinch of my fingers on her breasts grabbed her attention, though, and over her shoulder I watched pink nipples swell and darken into nubbly peaks as wildly beautiful as any rock formation. To my tongue, they would feel tender as well as rigid, straining, begging to be sucked, hard....

No. In this tableau, this ritual of exposure, I belonged behind the scenes, only my hands coming between Maura's offering of her body and the sun-struck gulf of space and stone.

I reached around her and my hands went to work, one alternately flicking and squeezing her breasts, one stroking between dampening thighs. When she tried to press toward my touch, I moved the top hand down to knead her belly and hold her steady while the fingers of the lower one approached the growing slickness of her cunt. Approached, but refused quite to enter, slipping forward and back in the wet folds just short of where she needed me most.

Maura began to twist and strain. I nudged her clit erratically, lightly, too lightly; she rocked and bucked, muttering curses interspersed with gasps, making the juniper's trunk creak. Bruised bark added its scent to dried sweat and the intense musk of sex rising from both of us. The friction of her firm ass against my crotch was driving me toward the edge along with her.

"Now!" I thrust up inside her, fingers twisting, pressing forward, my upper hand sliding down to give her seeking clit the hard, fierce strokes it demanded. Short, sharp gasps punctuated my movements, intensified, accelerated...until, abruptly, she tensed, the arc of her slim body between tethered wrists and denim-bound boots so beautiful that I ached to capture the vision on film, but could only try to fix it in my mind. "Now! Let it out!"

And out it came; her long, triumphant cry, echoing from

rocky outcroppings, vibrating through her body and into mine as I crushed my mouth against the nape of her neck to muffle my own cries. Through the soft dark tangle of her hair, out of the sun-dazzled corner of my eye, I thought I saw, for the briefest moment, bright angel wings soaring off into the golden distance.

Then Maura slumped back against me. I cut her down from the juniper and crouched with her in my arms. Another beating of wings caught my eye, but it was only the falcon veering off toward her hidden aerie. Maura would fly again, to far-off places where I couldn't or wouldn't follow; but for this rare moment of surrender I knew exactly who she was.

PUBLIC PET

Cynthia Rayne

"Come on, pretty. It's time to go out," Lisa purred. "You've been such a good pet by putting all of our things away. Your reward is a walk." She unfurled the leather leash she used to lead me. It snapped open easily. "Come here."

I felt a rush of illicit pleasure at her words. She was actually going to take me outside the comfortable confines of our hotel room and show me off. Lisa and I had played bondage games in the privacy of our own apartment plenty of times, but this was the first time we'd be doing so in public. I kept my head bowed, my mouth shut, and my legs apart as instructed. When doing a scene, Mistress Lisa was very strict. Deliciously so.

I still couldn't believe I was doing this. I'd

had fevered fantasies about being put on display for ages, which I'd confessed to Lisa when we first got together; now I was really going to do it. I trusted Lisa completely. We both worked at a law firm in Chicago and she was my boss. We'd fallen into a relationship quite by accident. She told me she could see my desire to submit to her in my eyes. When I was late for a meeting once, she'd taken me in my office and berated me for my negligence. I was rushing to explain myself when she smacked my ass with a file folder. The anger had quickly elevated to sexual arousal. Lisa had watched with a knowing expression as my nipples peaked under my silk shirt and my breathing grew a bit shallow. We've been together ever since.

Now she fisted a hand in the short dark curls that framed my face. "Where is your head tonight, pet? Take off your shirt. I want to see my property."

I immediately complied. I stripped off the black tank top and neatly folded it before I placed it on the bed. I was left in my black bra and the leather miniskirt that my Mistress favored. She slowly walked a circle around me. It was a game we played often. She liked to make me nervous, but tonight I was in awe of her.

She was dressed in a pair of black leather pants and a red silk shirt. Mistress Lisa was over six feet tall and very thin, with long golden blonde hair that she kept in a ponytail. Her breasts were barely a mouthful and I loved to suck them. The hair between her legs was bushy; she smelled musky and sweet at the same time. Mistress reached over and undid the catch on my bra. I knew better than to try to stop her. It fell to the floor.

She pinched my left nipple, which was already stiff and upright. "Did you know that it's legal for women to go topless in public in Canada?" She grabbed a breast in each hand, roughly squeezing them.

I shivered. "No, Mistress Lisa." I only spoke when asked a direct question.

"It is. And tonight, I'm going to take you out, just like this. I want everyone to see these ripe breasts. But first," she said, slapping my right breast just slightly, "I need to get them ready." She grinned as she shoved a hand in her pocket and pulled out a long silver nipple chain. It had two alligator clips on the end so that it could be affixed to the nipples. Mistress Lisa had gotten me accustomed to nipple clamps. She always liked my nipples clamped and she'd stretched them daily. She pulled the right nipple out and clamped it, then did the same with the left.

I let out a small yelp. There was some pain involved but not enough to really hurt. It was exciting, more than anything else. I liked how sensitive they made my breasts.

"There you go, pet." She smacked both breasts slightly, enjoying the pretty shade of crimson they turned as they bounced. She slid her hand down my sides and over my hips. "And we can't let your pretty pussy go outside all covered up." She pulled my panties down my legs and reached up between them to smack my pussy lips. "Pets should always be accessible. Don't you agree?"

"Yes, Mistress."

"Good girl. What are pets for?"

"Fucking, Mistress." The instant I said it, I knew it was true. It's what I had always dreamed of and Mistress Lisa was the best there was.

"That's right. You are such a good girl." She pulled me close to her and claimed my mouth with hers. She kissed voraciously, as if she were trying to fuck me with her tongue and lips. When I was breathless, she pulled away. "Now, let's put your collar on." She took it out of her back pocket and fixed it tightly around my neck. It had a large O-ring in the front that she snapped the leash on. "Remember the rules, pet. Others may look but no one touches you without my permission. You may only speak when I ask you a question. Pets are for fucking. Not talking. Understand?"

"Yes, Mistress."

"Bend over and show me that sweet ass of yours."

I obeyed, bracing my hands on my legs and thrusting my behind in the air. She lovingly caressed the smooth white flesh before she brought her hand down sharply. "How does that feel?"

"Good," I moaned.

She smiled with satisfaction as she tugged the leash and I followed behind her. I was nervous and so excited about being seen by others like this. She pulled me down the hallway and into the elevator, which was empty. I wasn't sure if I was relieved or disappointed. Then, she dragged me past the front desk of the hotel. The night manager was on duty and his eyes nearly bugged out of his head.

Mistress Lisa decided to have a little fun at his expense. She pulled me along with her to the desk. "My pet and I need more towels in our room." Lisa played with my right breast, making it jiggle in her palm. "We shower after I fuck her," she explained. "So we shower a lot." Her smile was wolfish.

"Yes, Miss," the manager, said, eyes straying to Lisa's talented hand as it manipulated my breast, enhancing my pleasure. Between her mauling and the tightly clamped nipple, I was having trouble not making a sound.

"Thank you," Mistress Lisa said, turning and pulling me along behind her. "Come on, pet." She'd found a club near where we were staying called the Velvet Dog. It wasn't quite a fetish club, but it was fetish friendly. It catered to those people who'd had vanilla sex all of their lives but were too afraid to try something really different yet themselves. Those who were in the lifestyle were welcome to play in the club, as long as they let people watch.

Mistress Lisa had to give a password to the doorman but we were let in without a hassle. Inside, the lights were lowered; the windows were draped with long black velvet curtains. There were candelabra on every table. The music was low and throbbing with the chords of sex. There were several people doing scenes throughout the room. It smelled of sex. Middle-aged couples sat on long comfortable benches, waiting for someone exciting to join them. Mistress Lisa thrived in an environment like this. She was a sleek, predatory cat in a room filled with dozy mice.

She picked a couple in their late thirties to sit with. The man had been avidly watching us as we entered the room. What is it with men and lesbians? The woman looked nervous but her eyes kept darting toward us with a hint of excitement.

"Mind if we join you?" Mistress asked.

They both nodded and made room for us. "You needn't scoot over so far. My pet won't be sitting with us." She turned her attention to me. "Why is that?"

"Because I should be on the floor at Mistress's feet."

"And why is that?"

"Because pets don't have furniture privileges, Mistress."

Lisa sat down and pushed the table away from everyone, so they could view me between her legs. "My name is Mistress

Lisa and this is my little pet. What are your names?"

"Jane and Scott," the man answered. It was so obvious that they were fake names. "How long...how long has she been your pet?" He had a big boner in his pants. Disgusting.

She pulled at the chain on my breasts and I cried out. "A few weeks now. She's a good little pet pussy that knows her place. In fact," Mistress said, eyeing the prim and proper wife's white skirt and matching sweater set, "why don't you ask this nice lady if she'd like a little head from you, pet?"

Jane's eyes widened. "Oh, uh, thank you but that won't be necessary."

I was turned on by the idea of servicing a stranger. It was another first. I was already dripping wet, just feeling the couple's eyes on me was so terribly exciting. I hoped I could get through my performance without embarrassing myself. I crawled to Jane on all fours and rested my head in her lap. "May I please pleasure you?"

"You should let her, Jane. My little pet licks pussy three times a day, sometimes more. She'll give you the best head you've ever gotten." There were other folks in the club licking and sucking each other. Nudity wasn't something that was prohibited. "Come on, Jane. What do you say?"

Her husband nudged her. "It's okay, honey."

Jane blushed. "Well, I guess it would be all right."

I smiled and very deliberately licked my lips. I heard Mistress snort with laughter behind me. If I'd done it to her, she would have smacked my ass. I pulled up Jane's virginal white skirt and parted her thighs. She wore plain cotton underwear.

"Let me see," Scott said, pushing the skirt back, exposing his wife further.

I pulled the panties down and put my hands on her thighs

to push them apart. Then I gently pulled her ass forward, so that she was wide open to me. She was beautiful, with angelic blonde hair and white cream-cheese thighs. With a sigh, I bent my mouth to her. I lapped at her like it was my job. The small little berry of a clit, I took in my mouth and suckled. She tasted so sweet, almost innocent. She shouted and writhed against me like a wild thing. I bet her husband usually did a few obligatory tongue strokes and then shoved his dick in her. Not me. I was all tongue, all the time. I couldn't get enough. I licked her to completion, savoring the sweetness of her juices on my mouth and cheeks. I made a big show of wiping her juices from my face and licking my hands clean, like a cat.

Jane was undone. Her thighs were open, her face was flushed and she looked a little dazed. "So good," she whispered quietly. She patted my head.

"Make her do me," the husband ordered, going for the zipper on his pants. "Tell her to suck my cock."

"Sorry, my pet doesn't do pricks. She's strictly for pussy."

Scott looked like he was about to get angry but Mistress Lisa glared at him. "Can I watch you fuck her, then?" he said.

"Now, that I'll happily do." Mistress Lisa snapped her fingers. "Take off your skirt and get on the table, pet. Spread yourself like a good girl."

I stood up, feeling the couple's eyes on me as well as some onlookers at the bar. This was my moment. I made a big show of stripping off my skirt and running my hands over the exposed skin. Then I scrambled up on the table, eager for her attention. I lay down on the table with my legs spread. Mistress Lisa took the candelabra from the tabletop and blew out the candles. The whisps of smoke blew over me. She tipped her hand and the heated wax streaked against my tits and my belly. "Oh, how careless of me."

I let out a little scream. The wax burned at first, but then it soothed me, forming a warm wall around my flesh. Mistress Lisa began to peel the wax away from my belly, taking the fine little hairs with it. "Do you want one of those candles inside that hungry little pussy of yours?"

"Yes, Mistress."

"What did you say?"

"Yes, Mistress!" She shoved a long white candle up inside of me. It was warm and thick, but what I really wanted was Mistress Lisa's fingers inside of me. I knew that it wouldn't happen until I begged for it at home. "Oh! Yes!"

She found my clit with her expert finger. "Tell me who you worship, pet."

"Mistress Lisa!"

"Whose pussy do you crave?"

"Yours, Mistress!"

"Come now!"

Later, when we were walking home, Mistress Lisa yanked my chain. "Did you enjoy yourself?"

"Yes, Mistress." I was sleepy and sated. I never dreamt my fantasy would be so satisfying.

"Such a good pet." She slapped my ass. "I like this exhibitionist side of you. We may have to move to Canada. I like the idea that others can see you, but can't touch."

"Me too."

"We'd have to lobby for complete nudity, though. Your pussy is the best part."

"Thank you, Mistress."

"You will. As soon as we get home. I'm going to make you lick me until you beg me to let you stop."

"I never will, Mistress. I never will."

HOMECOMING QUEEN

Anna Watson

In the park after supper, Jenna leaned against a jungle gym and watched Pierre, her mother's middle-aged Pekinese, totter to and fro, lifting his curly leg. She was home for Thanksgiving, incognito, relaxed. She didn't know anyone in town anymore.

"Mind putting him back on his leash?" The voice was low and raspy, coming from somewhere behind her. Jenna startled, and snapped out of the postbrisket reverie she'd been enjoying. Her mom made killer brisket.

"Sure, yeah, of course. Sorry!" She whistled for Pierre, who obligingly trotted over and let himself be leashed.

"Thanks—it's just that Geordie can get a little too frisky." Jenna looked at the dog, a skinny, cheerful basset hound, then up at the woman, who was wearing a suit and tie, her salt and pepper hair buzzed, her biceps bulging. Jenna came to attention immediately, breasts up and out as if she were modeling the most delectable lingerie instead of her slouch-around-mom's-house tatty sweats.

"Hey—we were in high school together! You're Maude, right?" It came back to her all at once: the shy, nerdy girl who transferred to Christ the King junior year and became the star of the soccer team. The one who always wore loafers and white button-down shirts; the one Jenna's crowd avoided like the plague; the one, Jenna realized with a feeling like winning the lottery, who was, and always had been, butch, butch, butch.

"That's right." Maude looked her over, grinning and raising an eyebrow. Jenna blushed and put a hand on her arm, about to introduce herself, just as Pierre and Geordie got into a snuffling, yipping scuffle, and had to be separated.

Later that evening, Jenna emerged triumphant from her mother's walk-in closet, a pair of strappy, four-inch heels in one hand, and in the other, a little wisp of a dress, black, low in front and lower in back. Her mother puffed out her cheeks in embarrassment and made a grab, but Jenna held it out of reach.

"Secret life, Mom?" she asked, examining the dress more closely. There was a bust variation between the two of them, but she expected she could squeeze in there, which was good, because the fanciest thing she'd packed was jeans. Who knew she was going to need date wear this vacation?

"Oh, you know." Her mother smoothed the bedspread and straightened a few perfume bottles on the dresser. "Your father likes me to wear that. Not to go out, of course, just, you know, around the house. Now for heaven's sake, I have to go get started on that turkey or we won't have any dinner tomorrow!"

"Huh," Jenna said to her mother's retreating back, adding to herself, "then I bet you have something else I can use in here." Sure enough, after digging through the lingerie drawer, Jenna scored a pair of black fishnets and a lacy, red thong, but the matching bra just wasn't big enough. The dress, though, when she tried it on, was so tight around the chest and provided so much cleavage all on its own, that Jenna didn't need anything more.

After her parents had gone into their bedroom and Jenna could hear her dad snoring over the drone of the ten o'clock news, she got her mother's long down coat—actually, it had been hers for a brief and stylistically unfortunate period in the '80s during high school—and snuck out of the house. She walked to Maude's parents' and settled in to wait in the driveway where Maude had told her to. There was a motion light that came on whenever she shifted position, and she kept expecting Geordie to sense her out there and start barking. It was one of the tract houses near the electrical plant, and over the beating of her heart and the in/out of her breath, Jenna could hear the generator's low hum. She shivered, her feet swelling in the too-tight pumps, her pussy wet and growing wetter as she thought about the quick-but-thorough hug Maude had given her that afternoon.

At last, the lights in what must have been Maude's parents' bedroom clicked off. Almost immediately, the garage door opened, and Maude was beckoning to her. As soon as she got in, Maude wrapped her in another hug, holding her up as Jenna had a bit of a rag doll moment, succumbing to the sensations of Maude's biceps pressing against her ear; Maude's cologne, something with a hint of cedar; Maude's lips in her hair; the feel of Maude's dick pressing against her thigh.

"Come on, now," Maude whispered. "And don't make any noise—they're light sleepers. If my brother finds out you're here, it will be all over school tomorrow, and little Miss Popular won't be so popular anymore."

Jenna muffled a gasp against Maude's shoulder and let herself be led through the dark kitchen and up carpeted stairs to a room at the end of the hall. Maude shut the door quietly.

"It doesn't lock," she said in a low voice. "And my mother will come check on me if she hears anything—she's been worried about me because my grades are dropping. And you know why? You know why my grades are dropping? Because of you. All I can think about is you." She pushed Jenna against the door and ran her hands up under the coat, her breath deepening and catching in her throat as she felt the dress, the fishnets.

"I've seen you," whispered Jenna, arching her back so her breasts came into Maude's hands. "You sit in the bleachers and watch when we're practicing cheers. The other girls think you're so creepy. I can feel your eyes on me. It makes me nervous, but I like it. I don't know why. You're so strange—everyone says you're a dyke."

Maude pulled Jenna's coat off and let it slide to the floor. The room was dark except for light from a streetlamp shining through the window onto the single bed. "Your boyfriend sits in the bleachers watching you too, doesn't he? He doesn't know you're showing off for me when you do the splits and jump real high, your titties bouncing. He thinks you're doing it for him."

"But I'm showing off for you," sighed Jenna, as Maude's thumbs found her nipples. "When he kisses me, I'm thinking about you, and if he ever found out, he would kill you."

She was pinned to the door, Maude's body heavy against her, Maude's hands on either side of her head. "Don't make any noise, little Cheerleader," Maude hissed, and shoved the side of her hand into Jenna's mouth just in time. Jenna grabbed it with her teeth and moaned. "That's right," breathed Maude, her eyes gleaming. She pulled back her hand and gathered Jenna up, leaving the ridiculous coat crumpled on the floor. Maude laid her down on the bed, propping her head up on a pillow, straightening the dress over her thighs. "Let me look at you, baby. Let me look at Miss Popular, Miss Cheerleader. Let me see you now. Who's got you now, Miss President of the French Club?"

Jenna was panting, her whole body moving with her breath. No one had ever treated her like this, not even her last lover, who had claimed to be such a big bad top, and certainly dressed the part, but had only ever talked about spanking her and never did it.

"You have me!" she said too loudly, and Maude's forearm came down across her mouth, hurting her lips, making it so she could hardly breathe.

"That's right, I do. And you have to be quiet. If you make noise, I stop and you go home."

Jenna nodded, then shook her head, *No, I won't make noise, I promise, no noise.* She put out her tongue to lick the rough material of Maude's suit, then nibbled it. Maude took her arm away and put her lips to the wet spot, looking down at her.

"This is a slutty dress," she whispered, starting to move

her hands possessively over Jenna's body. "This is a slutty outfit—look at you, red lipstick, fishnets—you look like a whore in this stuff. I thought you were a wholesome girl, a good girl."

"No," whispered Jenna. "No, I'm not."

"Not a good girl?" Maude came close to her and brushed her lips in a brief kiss. Jenna moaned and arched, and there was the arm over her mouth again. "You aren't a good girl at all," Maude whispered, breath hot in Jenna's ear. "All the time you're walking around school with your pack of popular friends, and inside your Calvin Kleins your pussy is throbbing for this, isn't it?"

She grabbed Jenna's hands and pinioned them over her head, then straddled her face. She pressed her dick against Jenna's mouth, filling her world with its shape and feel. Jenna rubbed her cheek against it, her lips, trying to catch it with her mouth, struggling to get her hands on it.

"You can't wait to get a feel of my cock, can you, Homecoming Queen?" Maude held her hands tighter and all she could do was moan quietly into Maude's zipper.

"No noise," whispered Maude. "No noise, or I stop." She swung her leg over and stood beside Jenna, who closed her eyes in anticipation. She could feel Maude wrapping something around her wrists, tying her to the headboard. She whimpered, opening her eyes, and saw Maude standing over her, inspecting her breasts, her legs. "What a slut," she murmured. "Show me how much you want it, slut," and then she was on top of her, elbows and forearms trapping her head, kissing her hard. Jenna breathed and melted under her weight, letting it push her fully into the bed, opening to the tongue calmly fucking her mouth. She couldn't help herself, a loud moan escaped her, and instantly the delicious weight was gone, Maude had untied her hands and was on the other side of the room picking up her coat and holding it out to her.

"I won't do it again!" Jenna managed in a ragged whisper. "I promise!"

Maude stared at her, eyes narrowed, then nodded and dropped the coat, coming back to stand beside the bed. She placed Jenna's hands on the headboard, but didn't tie them. "Don't let go," she ordered. "Don't make any noise. Wait here."

Jenna closed her eyes, grabbing on to the posts, her body heaving and trembling. Maude left the room and didn't come back for a long time. Jenna could hear the heat in the house going on and off, the dog patrolling the hall, cars on the distant highway, and underneath it all, the steady hum of the power plant, a bass note that went on and on.

At last the door opened and there was Maude, pristine in her suit. Jenna felt rumpled and whorish in her mother's dress, sticky and wanting. Maude gave her a drink of water from a glass with a straw in it, holding up her head, smoothing her hair. Jenna blinked tears out of her eyes and hoped Maude wouldn't see, but she did.

"Been a long time since you were with someone who knew how to take care of you, baby?" she asked, and Jenna nodded. "Well, I'm going to take care of you, don't you worry. All that time you spend hanging out with those straight rich kids, and they just have no idea, do they, baby? No idea what a slut you are, how much you need to get fucked by the dyke, the one they make fun of, the one you don't say hi to in the hall, but the one you're thinking about when you lie in your bed at night and lift up your nightgown and touch yourself—because you do that, don't you? You're not such a good girl late at night when you're alone in your little Laura Ashley bed, touching yourself, are you?"

Jenna panted, shaking her head. "No, I'm not."

"Not what?"

"Not a good girl. I'm a bad girl."

Maude cocked her head. "What's that?" she whispered. "I can't hear you."

Jenna took a breath, about to say it louder, then stopped herself. It was a trick. Maude was looking at her expectantly and there was that sadistic gleam again.

"I'm a bad girl," breathed Jenna, so quietly that Maude had to lean over to hear her. "Your bad girl." She gripped the bedposts tighter as Maude dropped onto her mouth, kissing her softly, sweetly.

"Hey! What are you doing, slut?" Maude had Jenna's earlobe between her teeth, her hand pressing on Jenna's bucking cunt.

"Please." Jenna pressed her pussy into Maude's hand.

"You want me to do something with this?" Maude asked coolly. "Hmm." She left Jenna's side and knelt on the bed between her legs. She ran her hands up and down Jenna's thighs and calves, the sensation exquisite through the fishnets. Jenna pumped her pussy up and down, past caring about anything but her own pleasure.

"Hmm," said Maude again, slipping her fingers under the waistband of the fishnets and beginning to peel them off. "Let's see." She took the stockings down to ankle level and Jenna hoped she would take off her heels, but she didn't, leaving her hobbled. Maude smiled at the lacy red thong, then slid it down to rest above the stockings.

"Well, well. Do your preppy friends know you shave your pussy, Miss Cheerleader? Does your boyfriend know? Or did you do it just for me? I think you did it just for me, didn't you? And look how wet you are! Just like an animal in rut." She settled into a more comfortable position, her face right above Jenna's pussy, but not too close. "You want to give it to me so bad, then go ahead, baby. Feed it to me."

Jenna grabbed hard on to the bedposts and lifted her ass as high as she could, but she couldn't go quite far enough. She moaned in frustration and Maude smirked. "What are you waiting for? I can smell it, but there's nothing in my mouth. God, you're wet, you whore. All right, I'm going to help you out a little. Stay like that."

She lowered her mouth. Maude hovered there, breathing, then slowly dipped her tongue along the slit, just the slightest pressure, and the warmth of her breath. Jenna trembled, her thighs and belly spasming as Maude brought her hands up under her ass, cupping the cheeks, allowing Jenna to rest there. Maude lifted Jenna's pussy to her mouth and rubbed and licked, sloppy and wet, no pattern, no rhythm, just random pressure, slobbery tongue, spit trickling down the crack of Jenna's ass. If Maude hadn't been holding her up, there was no way Jenna could have kept the position; as it was, her calves and feet were starting to cramp and her hands were falling asleep, although there was no way in hell she was going to let go of the bedposts. Just when she thought she wouldn't be able to stand the rush of conflicting, crazy-making sensations any longer, Maude pulled her face out of Jenna's cunt and growled, "A nasty girl like you can probably come more than once, am I right?" Jenna made a groan of agreement. "So show me," Maude ordered. "Ride me." She lowered her face again, this time her tongue flat and businesslike against Jenna's clit. She pulled Jenna close with one arm and gave her a hand to bite, just in the nick of time, as Jenna was already coming, pistoning herself against Maude's face, screaming as quietly as she could.

"Shh, shh," cautioned Maude, lowering Jenna to the bed and rolling on top of her. "You can let go now. I'll hold you."

Jenna gratefully abandoned her grip on the bedposts and grabbed hard on to Maude who had started rocking against her.

"You liked that, didn't you, baby, you liked feeding me your hungry little pussy, didn't you, Homecoming Queen; you pretender, what would your boyfriend say if he saw you here with me, letting the big dyke eat you out, begging for her dick? Let me hear you, baby. Beg me for it."

Jenna could think of nothing clever to say, only, "Yes, please, I want your dick, fuck me, put it in me, fuck me!"

Maude's eyes were half-closed and her forehead was shiny with sweat. Her breathing quickened as she moved against Jenna, then she rolled off and turned her over, pulling off the pumps and fishnets and thong, and shoving her knees apart. Jenna could hear her unbuckling her belt, unzipping her trousers; then she was covering her, easing her dick in, slowly filling her pussy. Jenna made noise into the pillow, pushing back. Just rocking gently at first, then gaining momentum, hitting her stride, Maude fucked her, reaching underneath to find her tits, squeezing them with both hands, using them for purchase, pinching the nipples hard.

"Such a slut, such a slut," she whispered.

Jenna lifted up onto her hands and knees and pushed back,

panting and groaning. Her throat hurt from all the screams she was keeping inside. Maude reached down with one hand and found her clit, and Jenna bucked against the hard fingers, coming with a roar of pleasure that stopped them both cold.

They heard a door open and footsteps in the hall.

"Maudie?" an older woman's voice called. "Maudie, do you have the dog in there with you? Are you all right?"

Maude drew in a breath, trying to stop laughing. The two of them were giggling like fiends, clutching each other, practically falling off the narrow bed.

"Fine, Mom! I'm fine! Nightmare or something!"

"Well, all right." Slowly the footsteps went back down the hall.

"You almost got me busted," Maude hissed, no longer laughing. She had pulled out and was holding Jenna tightly. "I won't forget that. I told you to be quiet, and you weren't quiet. You can't follow the simplest rule. I won't forget that, either, and next time you're going to take your punishment, aren't you, Cheerleader?" She reached for Jenna's ass, roughly shoving aside the dress Jenna had yanked down, squeezing her cheeks, painfully raking them with blunt fingernails. Jenna shuddered.

"Yes," she said so softly she could barely hear herself. "Yes."

Maude pressed her lips together and shook her head, frowning. "Such a slut, such a bad girl. Someone obviously needs to take you in hand. Your boyfriend certainly can't keep you in line, that's clear, and he sure isn't giving you what you need. So next time, we'll go somewhere you can make all the noise you want, little Cheerleader. All the noise your nasty little heart desires. I'll get you alone and you can just go ahead and scream and scream, but your friends won't hear you, no one will hear you, no one will come rescue you. Now come sit on my lap and be good to me until we're sure my mom's gotten back to sleep and I can sneak you out of here. We have school tomorrow. Come here, Homecoming Queen. And remember. Be very, very quiet."

And Jenna was.

SWEET DESIRES

Tara Alton

My coworker Sarah was really going too far. I had begun to dread going to my desk in the morning, afraid of what she might have left for me as a little present—to say hello. She was making me feel as if I was back on the playground in grade school with a girl/girl crush that had gone too far. It's not that I'm opposed to the girl/girl stuff. To be honest, I was rather partial, but I couldn't see myself with Sarah, and I don't think it's professional to bring your love life to work.

You couldn't say she was a bad-looking girl; a little nerdy or geeky maybe, with her pigtails and thick glasses. Someone once said she looked a little Asian, but I couldn't really tell with her bangs in her face all the time. The worst thing about her was the way she dressed. Mostly, she wore little stiff cotton blouses over khakis and tennis shoes. That was her idea of business casual. I couldn't believe our boss hadn't said anything to her about it yet. You would never catch me wearing anything less than a pencil skirt, a silk blouse and kitten-heeled shoes to work.

Oddly enough, I think her infatuation with me started when she learned about my migraines. I had to admit my headaches were the bane of my existence. Two or three times a month, they plagued me. It had become so bad that I couldn't even eat chocolate or have an orgasm because it triggered another headache.

Regrettably, I had let this piece of information slip to another coworker in the break room one day and Sarah overheard it.

That was when I began to find candy left on my desk. Sarah was searching high and low to find things for me to snack on that didn't include chocolate. Jelly beans, licorice and vanilla fudge all showed up next to my keyboard.

At first, I thought it was a sweet gesture and I thanked her, but it only seemed to encourage her. I caught her giving me puppydog eyes all the time, her gaze constantly following me around the office. When a five-pound bag of candy corn showed up on my desk before Halloween, I couldn't take it anymore. My desk drawers were starting to look more like a candy store than a place to hold office supplies. I lugged the bag of candy to her desk and told her that I couldn't accept it.

"But why?" she asked.

"I'm going on a diet," I said firmly.

She looked as if I had slapped her, but to my relief, she put the candy corn in a dish for everyone.

I thought I was in the clear with Sarah until the little stuffed animals started showing up on my desk. The first one was a little teddy bear wearing a bunny outfit. She left a note with it that said, *Just something to brighten your day.*

Then one day she left a little rubber duck. It was a small one that fit into the palm of my hand, and it had blue eyes. Her note said that I should take it home and use it for my bath, which I thought was a little personal.

I didn't know what to do with all her unwanted attention, but I wanted it to stop. I asked my supervisor to have my desk moved to the other side of the room. I figured she might find someone new to latch on to if I wasn't around her so much. When my supervisor asked me why I wanted my desk moved, I told her that my personality wasn't meshing with Sarah's and the conflict was distracting me from my work.

Once my desk was moved, I felt things were going much better—until I felt another headache coming on one afternoon. I was having a very stressful day, and I could feel the tension beginning to radiate from my neck and shoulders. I went into the bathroom to run a paper towel under the cold water for the back of my neck when Sarah came in after me.

"Did you like your rubber ducky?" she asked me. "Did you take it home?"

I frowned at her.

"It's still in my desk," I said.

I started to put the damp paper towel on the back of my neck.

"Oh, you've got another headache," she said.

She tried to grab my hand, but I pulled it away. What was she doing now?

"I've been reading up on headaches and reflexes," she said.

"Please let me massage your hands. It's supposed to help."

She gave me a beseeching look. I didn't know what to do. Letting her have my hand seemed like a bad thing to do, but what if she actually helped my headache? I didn't want to spend the rest of the day in pain at my desk.

"What if someone comes in?" I asked.

"I'll just say I'm doing reflexology on you," she said.

Putting down my damp paper towel, I surrendered my hand to her. To my surprise, her massage felt even better than when my manicurist did it. Sarah had the most amazingly warm, nimble fingers. She opened my palm and started gently stretching the muscles of my hand. Then she massaged each finger and joint. I could feel the tension draining from my body. I was actually relaxing.

Another coworker came into the bathroom. She gave us an odd look before she entered a stall. I looked at Sarah, waiting for her to explain about the reflexology, but she stood there mute, hanging on to my hand.

Giving her a stern look, I whisked my hand away.

"Please take the duck home," she begged. "You'll love him."

In the parking lot after work, I spotted Sarah. I was still a little peeved at her after the bathroom incident, and yet I had to admit the hand massage had helped my impending headache. Therefore, despite my better judgment, I had put the rubber duck in my tote bag so that if she started pestering me about it, I could at least say I had taken it home.

"Night Sarah," I said firmly.

"I really need to talk to you," she said.

"Can't we talk about it in the morning in the office?" I asked.

"I can't discuss it at work. Will you please get into my car for a moment?"

Beckoning me over to her, she bit her lower lip. Cautiously, I approached her car. On her rear bumper, I spotted a sticker that read, *I brake for Gumby.*

She motioned for me to get inside with her, but I hesitated. Though I wasn't so sure about doing this, it might give me a chance to set her straight about ceasing with all these little gifts.

The moment I shut the passenger door, my thoughts escaped me as I took in the interior of her car. It was like a mobile kitsch store with bobble-head dogs, Betty Boop stickers and Hello Kitty accessories everywhere, not to mention more little stuffed animals and bags of candy necklaces and ring pops lying all over her backseat.

I clutched my tote bag to my chest for protection as she stared at me with those puppydog eyes again.

"I wanted to give you these," she said, ripping open the cellophane packaging on a candy necklace. "Here, put it on."

"Sarah, I don't need any more candy," I said. "I've eaten so much sugar lately my teeth are going to rot out of my head."

Her expression fell.

"Fine," I said. "Give it to me."

I hadn't put on a candy necklace in years. The fit was a little snug, but I managed to get it around my neck. I was sure I looked ridiculous.

"And a ring," she said.

Undressing a ring pop from its wrapper, I slipped the strawberry-flavored jewelry on my pinkie.

"Is this why you asked me into your car?" I asked. "So you could dress me up in candy?"

For a moment, I actually thought she was going to say yes, but she slowly shook her head.

"I wanted to know, did the hand massage help?" she asked.

"A little," I admitted.

She seized my hand again.

"I bought a book on reflexology," she said, motioning to a book on the floor.

Once more, she began massaging my hand. I wanted to whisk it away again, but it felt so damn good, the way she worked my palm and made little circles around my knuckles. She had certainly learned a lot from that book. I was glancing at the book on the floor to see what the title was when a thought occurred to me.

"Isn't reflexology about feet?" I asked.

"It's both," she confessed. "But I need to tell you something else. I really wanted to touch you, and I thought this might be a good way."

"Look Sarah," I said.

She was really holding my hand now, her fingers locked between mine.

"I have the biggest crush on you," she said.

Before I could stop her, she kissed my hand, between the knuckles, featherlight kisses from very soft lips. This tingling feeling went up my arm. Turning my hand over to expose my wrist, she kissed up my arm, giving me gooseflesh the entire way.

When she reached my shoulder, she turned my face to meet hers. Slowly, she took off her glasses and brushed back her bangs. She had the prettiest blue eyes I had ever seen.

"I'm thinking if you were really to relax," she said, "you

might not get too worked up and get a headache when you orgasm."

"I don't know," I said.

She pulled the rubber ducky out of my tote bag and squeezed his back. To my surprise, it started vibrating. Did rubber ducks do this?

"Think about it," she said. "You're relaxing in a warm bath and you put your rubber ducky in your special place."

"What do you mean?" I asked.

She looked down at my skirt, between my legs.

I swallowed, getting her meaning.

"Shall I show you?" she asked.

Words escaped me. Balancing the duck on my knee, she slowly moved it up my thigh, then flipped up my skirt when it got in the way. My breath caught in my throat. The duck was under my skirt.

"Mr. Ducky wants to visit your happy place," she whispered.

Suddenly, I had a vision of Sarah using this duck at home in her own bath.

"Is this your duck?" I asked.

"No, silly," she said. "I've got the full-sized one at home. I bought you the travel size."

This was feeling rather good on my thigh. It felt like an intense purring. She was backing him up tail first. His little yellow body completely disappeared under my skirt.

I couldn't help but shift myself in my seat as she angled him toward my inner thigh. The vibrations were more intense as she hit the softer skin there. His upturned tail was almost on top of my pubic bone. I opened up my legs a little. I hadn't worn nylons today so he was touching my cotton panties.

Wiggling him in deeper so the width of his body fit between my thighs, she used his flat base against me.

I wasn't sure how the vibrations managed to be soothing and yet stimulating at the same time, but they were. I could feel my clit beginning to beg for some individual ducky attention all on its own.

The base of the duck suddenly just wasn't enough.

"Turn it around," I said, thinking the point on the tail or the bill might just be the ticket.

"No. It's too soon."

"I'm ready. Do it," I said.

Turning the duck upside down so its bill was directly on my happy place, she nuzzled up to me and began sucking on the candy necklace around my neck.

"Sarah, you're tickling me," I said, squirming.

Picking up my hand, she stuck the ring pop in my mouth.

"Suck it," she whispered in my ear.

I got a chill as the sweetness filled my mouth and she watched me lick the edges. There was so much desire in her eyes, as if I was a piece of candy myself and she wanted to eat me completely.

Brushing away my hand that wore the ring pop, she kissed me again, licking and nibbling the sugary strawberry flavor off my lips.

The vibrations from the rubber ducky were almost becoming too intense. My head was starting to throb. I started to push him back a little, but Sarah must have thought I wanted something else. Turning him off, she pulled him out from under my skirt, propped him on the dashboard and slid her hand back under my skirt, where she pushed aside the crotch of my panties.

With her eyes nearly closed, she petted me as if I was one of her little stuffed animals. For a moment it felt strange, as if she was taking this to some weird place in her head, but then she found my clit under its hood. Pressing her fingertip just inside my lips, she got it a little wet and brought it back up to my clit. I gasped as she made little circular motions on top of it, massaging it much the same way she had paid attention to each one of my knuckles during her hand massages.

Every time she made several rotations, she dipped down further inside me to remoisten her fingertip. She was getting so close to actually entering me that I was beginning to squirm with anticipation.

The moment she entered me, she stayed there, sliding in one finger and then two. Keeping her thumb on my clit, she slowly finger-fucked me. My breath caught short. It was hard not to clamp my thighs down around her hand.

"Suck the ring," she said. "I want to hear it."

With the ring pop back in my mouth, I sucked loudly. She moaned and pressed her lips back to my neck. I could feel her teeth against my skin and the candy. She cracked the little sugar disks with her teeth, the thread getting moist as she reached over with her free hand and gave my breast a hard squeeze.

Suddenly, I felt the sensation of my clit exploding like a firecracker. It was unlike anything I had felt before. *Pow!* My entire body shuddered as the sharp feeling washed over my skin, and then just as quickly as it had come, it was gone.

Sarah was so caught up in what she was doing she hadn't even noticed that I had an orgasm. Her fingers were trying to go even deeper inside me. It was too much. I was becoming too overstimulated. I could feel my blood pressure beginning to pound in my ears. I was going to get a migraine any second if she kept it up.

"Stop," I cried.

She didn't stop.

Pushing my hands against her, I tried to break her grip on me.

"Let go of me," I cried.

Suddenly, there was a rap on the window. We stopped and looked up. To my horror, our supervisor stood at the passenger door, a concerned look on her face. She must have heard my cries.

"Are you all right?" she asked me through the glass.

Quickly, Sarah jerked her hand away from under my skirt. Smoothing down my clothes, I rolled down the window, wondering what I looked like—out of breath, face flushed and clothes disheveled. Not to mention the half-eaten candy necklace around my neck and a soaking wet ring pop on my hand.

Words failed me as my gaze met hers.

"We're playing with her rubber duck," Sarah volunteered.

Our supervisor gave me a quizzical look. I knew what she was thinking. I had asked to have my desk moved because I wasn't getting along with Sarah, and now here I was in her car, candy everywhere, doing who knew what with her.

Still, I could salvage this. I could tell her that Sarah was still bothering me, but glancing over at Sarah as she pushed her glasses back onto her face, I felt a surprising affection for her.

Picking up the rubber duck, I wiggled it in the air at our supervisor.

"Quack," I said.

FRENCH HANDWRITING

Zoë Alexandra

It is pouring buckets in front of Beatrice's
steps where I sit beneath the overhang, pants
already soaked at their bottoms. I am used to
this. Bike messengers must learn to bear the
elements. Bea is not home but her telephone
number is smudged on the paper so I can't
quite make it out now. I want to call her. The
pay phone is a block away. I could walk there
and get even wetter, breathe into the receiver,
say her name as if it is a blessing, a mantra.

When I was little my mother used to tell
me to cross my legs. The skirt was made of
wool and scratched the insides of my thighs.
Catholic school is the best place to meet
whores or become a lesbian. I did both. In the
bathroom I used to bum cigarettes from this
blonde girl named Molly. I used to smell the

tips of her hair as she walked away. They smelled like fresh mangoes and blackberry sherbet. She would always play hard to get. I would tell her I had to show her something important. It was in the bathroom stall. She would come in there with me, rub against the front of my skirt, kiss the insides of my wrists and bite my neck like a vampire. That bitch was crazy but I loved her. But this isn't about Molly, it's about Beatrice.

I met Beatrice on the R train. My hands were locked around the pole I was holding on to. When the train stopped short, my bike would jostle around and so would I. She appeared like some fucking angel. Black hair, straight as a pin and the skinniest thighs I've ever seen. Her voice was paper thin and she carried a large backpack that wasn't much bigger than she was.

"Can I hold on here?" she asked.

I nodded. I was thinking about Molly. Molly's lips were bubble gum pink and her tongue tasted like oil pastels. I never tasted oil pastels but I'm sure that's what they'd taste like. Beatrice held on next to me. Her hand brushed against mine. It was rough like sandpaper. My stop came. Astor Place. Beatrice spit and followed me out the door. I was halfway down the block before I noticed her there. She lit a half-smoked cigarette and looked up at me with those huge blue doe eyes.

"You have a buck?" she asked.

I did have a buck, but I didn't want to just give it away.

"What do I get if I give you a buck?" I asked. She shrugged before she spoke.

"I work on Forty-second Street, you could give me a ride there on your bike and I could show you something."

I thought about it. I had errands to run. I had to stop on
Waverly Place and then 42nd Street.

"If you want to run my errands with me you could tag
along," I said.

I amazed myself with how agreeable I was being. I was a
stone-cold butch dyke and I made no apologies for it. I didn't
need some cute femme to come along and fuck up my shit.

"Get on," I said and she did. I gave her my helmet which
was too big for her tiny head and we rode on into the night.
Well, actually it wasn't the night. It was midday, but riding
off into the night sounds better so for this purpose we'll say
it was the night.

I did my drop-offs and pickups and then we flew down
Sixth Avenue and onto 42nd Street until we reached the Kitten
Inn.

Beatrice walked in and I followed her, past a mean-looking
bouncer with enormous snake tattoos across his arms, and
into the dressing room. She put on these shiny red platform
heels and a big blonde wig that made her look like Dolly
Parton without the huge breasts.

"What's your name?" she asked.

"Ian," I said.

"That's a boy's name," she answered.

"No," I said. "It's my name." I think she understood.

"I'm Beatrice," she said. "But here, I'm Venus."

I looked up at her as she slipped into a rhinestone thong
and bra. Her arm had a giant heart tattoo on it. I grabbed
a sharpie out of my pocket and wrote my name inside of
it. "Now, you're mine." I said. She smiled and nodded. Her
two front teeth were crooked like swans' necks. It made her
look even prettier. She smacked her lips together and applied

vampire-red lipstick to them. She walked over to me, reached down my pants and sighed. She had found it, the softee. Okay, so it's not mine and maybe I do have a Napoleon complex but it was necessary to maintain a sense of power which only the softee could provide.

"Sorry, it's not hard," I said. "I wish it was but I left that one at home. I didn't plan on meeting you today."

"It's okay."

An older woman came over and nudged Beatrice's shoulders. "Venus, you're on in four," she said. The woman was thick and fat like a cheeseburger. Her eyes were lined in kohl and she was wearing very unflattering giant fake eyelashes.

When Beatrice went out into the box, I decided to leave. The box was impersonal, clear with a bubble machine inside that blew tiny bubbles into the girls' hair as they danced around. The windows in the box were two-way so they could see out, could watch who was watching them.

Sadie always waited for me, on the bench smack-dab in the middle of Washington Square Park. Her blonde wig sometimes sat crookedly on her head but she was beautiful. There was no way around that. Her ample thighs and voluptuous breasts made her more woman than most actual women. She opened up her red patent leather purse and pulled out a heart-shaped flask, took a long swig and held it out to me.

"It'll do you good," she said as she lit a Gauloise. Sadie would only smoke French cigarettes. "Live like the French, die like the French," she'd say. They were hard to get. There was a tiny tobacco shop on Madison Avenue that had them, but whenever Sadie walked the blocks between Park Avenue and Madison Avenue it was always like a scene from *Pretty*

Woman. "I'm just waiting for them to tell me I can't shop here," she'd say.

Sadie sighed; her dress was made out of that bizarre holo-gram material and had tiny comic book characters saying racy things like, *Fighting for peace is like fucking for virginity.* It glimmered under the streetlight.

"You know what I want more than anything?" Sadie began. I shrugged.

"I want a sugar daddy to take me shopping. I saw this show on television. It tells you how to be a gold digger. See, you have a guy take you out to eat near a store you like. Then you walk by the shop and say, 'God I love that dress, but I could never afford it.' When he offers to buy it for you, which he inevitably will as this is a test to see how much of a man—a provider—he is, you have to say, 'You can't buy that for me, it's way too expensive.' Then of course he buys the dress. It's all a big game," she said before laughing so hard it caused her to make this terribly guttural cough.

It was getting late. I decided I should probably try to pick Beatrice up from work, so I kissed Sadie's cold cheek and got back on my bicycle.

The door guy took my three dollar entrance fee, and I walked down the dark corridor. The place was made to make its patrons feel smarmy and perverted. The passageway led to the booths. There was a plump Italian-looking girl bending over in her box, thrusting and shaking like a robotic doll. I tossed a dollar through the crack in the window. She smiled and came toward me, blew me a kiss and proceeded to spread her legs. I asked her if Beatrice was here but she shrugged as if she couldn't hear me. I grabbed a receipt from my bag and wrote *Is Venus here?* on it. She pointed to the dressing room.

I knocked on the door and a high-pitched voice said, "Just a minute." The door swung open and a young-looking girl in cutoff shorts stared blankly at me.

"Is Venus here?" I asked.

"I don't know," she replied. "Come in and look around if you want."

The vanity mirror with the big fluorescent lights stung my eyes. There was a tiny blue piece of paper tucked into its corner. I picked it up. The letters were written in perfect cursive. The kind of handwriting you thought only French girls had. It said: *Ian. Come meet me in Union Square on the steps facing 14th Street.*

I got back on my bike and pedaled hard and fast. I was going to be late. I sped through intersections and some taxicab driver screamed, "Watch out you fucking dyke!" but I didn't care. For once I wasn't thinking about Molly. I was thinking about Beatrice. The park was quiet and dead. There was a homeless guy asleep on the bench but other than that it was completely silent. I walked to the steps and saw her. Her back was turned to me but her black bob made her look like a 1920s film star. She was drinking a 40 from a crumpled paper bag. I held in that moment for a second before approaching her. When she saw me she looked up and held out the 40 to me. I took a sip. It was slightly warm and tasted like piss but I was nervous and it helped.

"So how come you wanted me to meet you here?" I asked.

"Well..." she said, pulling out a wad of dollar bills. "Do you think this is enough to take a plane?"

I took another sip of beer.

"A plane to where?" I asked.

"To France?" she asked.

"Probably not," I answered. I felt bad disappointing her like that.

She closed her eyes then opened them looking me dead-on. She had such cartoonish blue eyes like Betty Boop or something and her lips were so small and pouty, like if she asked she could have whatever she wanted. No one could say no to her.

"Je suis morte parce que je ne ressens pas de désir. Le désir me manque parce que je pense posséder. Je pense posséder parce que je n'essaie meme pas de donner. Lorsqu'on essaie de donner, on se rend compte que l'on a rien. Comme on a rien, on essaie de donner de soi, et alors on se rend compte que l'on n'est rien. Quand on est rien, on désire devenir. C'est à ce moment là que l'on commence à vivre" she said. "It's broken French, but I will tell you what it means. 'I am dead because I lack desire. I lack desire because I think I possess. I think I possess because I do not try to give. In trying to give, you see that you have nothing. Seeing that you have nothing, you try to give of yourself. Trying to give of yourself, you see that you are nothing. Seeing that you are nothing, you desire to become. In desiring to become, you begin to live.'"

I smiled.

"I'm waiting for my boyfriend—I mean my ex-boyfriend— here. He owes me money."

The thought of Beatrice's ex-boyfriend made me nervous. I chugged her beer as if it were mine.

"I'll pay you back for this," I said.

"Don't worry about it."

"So where did you learn all that French?" I asked.

"I used to live in Paris. I was a maid for this wealthy family."

First I saw the lights, then I saw the shiny wheels. He pulled up on his motorcycle like some evil spirit from the crypt. He was a heavily tattooed white boy. The kind of person I hated most. They reeked of privilege and they were always the first to throw down. They'd say they'd never hit a girl but I wasn't a girl to them. I was some kind of genetic mutation, a fucked-up Y chromosome. He walked right up to Beatrice without a trace of hesitation. He put his thumb on her chin and moved in, kissed her like a snake. I could smell the disgusting mix of beer and his saliva. He hadn't noticed me yet. It was a good sign or so I thought.

"So where's my money?" she demanded. Her voice had changed. It wasn't the sweet paper-thin voice I remembered. This voice was loud, sharp and bossy.

"I got it, baby. It's right here." He moved her hand toward his package. I cringed. She slapped him across the face, hard. I knew shit was going down and I wanted to get the fuck out of there but I was frozen. It was as if someone had hit the PAUSE button.

"Oh," he said. "So it's like that, huh?"

Beatrice spit hard on the ground and stamped out her cigarette. He grabbed her by her perfect black hair and held her down.

"So you think you can talk to me like that, huh?" He was very close to her face. I was terrified for her.

"If you want your money, you'll have to get it yourself you stupid cunt."

He looked over at me. "And who's this?"

Beatrice let out a tiny shriek. "Don't touch Ian," she screamed. He hadn't let go of Beatrice yet but he was staring me down.

"What are you going to do about it?" he asked me.

I had a blade in my pocket and if I wasn't stuck on PAUSE I'd grab it and rip this motherfucker to shreds. I somehow found the strength to reach into my pocket and grab the blade. I lifted it up so he could see it.

"Oh, you think you're a tough guy, huh?" he said.

"Ian, don't...just don't, okay...?" Beatrice screamed. I didn't care. I wasn't going to listen. I wasn't going to die over this. He turned to look at Beatrice, stroked her shiny hair and breathed in her face.

"You really are a little money-grubbing bitch," he said. I was ready. I came at him full force, held the knife up to his big thick neck. He laughed.

"You wouldn't hurt me," he said. "Uh-oh Bea, your little dyke boyfriend's sticking up for you. How sweet."

I was ready to fuck this guy up but it was too late. He'd knocked me onto the ground and I took some pretty mean punches. My lip was bleeding and my eye was definitely black.

I don't remember what happened next except that when I came to Beatrice was there and my head was on her lap. We were still in Union Square and the sun was just barely peeking through the trees.

"Are you okay, Ian?" she asked.

I nodded but my neck felt like it had been struck by a hammer and my eyes stung.

"You took a fucking beating," Beatrice said.

"Yeah, well I'm not going to run with your crowd anymore," I said.

I biked home hard and fast. My legs felt twisted and my bones ached. My face felt like it'd been smashed to pieces.

I carried my bike up the five stories to the apartment. I unlocked the door to find Sadie sitting in her favorite spot. She calls it "the parlor." She says it sounds very Southern and sophisticated. She was polishing her toenails, her leg hiked up onto the table, wearing pink spandex leggings and a Siouxsie and the Banshees T-shirt that she had cut and tailored into a halter top.

"Damn, Ian, you look like a fucking car wreck. What the fuck happened to you?"

I mumbled about some fucking asshole trying to kill me but my face hurt too much for me to raise my voice.

Sadie walked over to the freezer and pulled out a bag of frozen peas and placed it on my left eye.

"Thanks."

Sadie laughed. "I used to get to black eyes all the time when I lived in Harlem. Guys used to think I was a girl. I guess I passed and when they reached down my skirt, they realized I wasn't. Once they know you're a guy, all bets are off. So, they'd never hit a girl, but I guess I'm not a girl to them."

"Yeah, me neither," I said.

"So what are you doing today? You can't work like that can you?"

I sighed, slipping out of my jeans and down to my boxer briefs.

"God, even your legs are tore up."

I nodded. The sunlight was seeping through the drapes, making shadows across Sadie's heavily painted face. When Sadie and I went out together people sometimes thought we were a couple, boyfriend and girlfriend. We liked that, because it meant we were passing. The man at the deli would say, "Sir, you're lucky to have such a beautiful woman in your life. Treat her right." I'd smile and say, "Of course, man. Of course."

There was a knock at the door. I walked over to my bed and hoped Sadie would get it.

"Hello," I heard Sadie shout through the peephole.

It was J.T. J.T. lived on the floor below us with his butch dyke girlfriend. We called him J.T. because he was young-looking and he reminded us of Jonathan Taylor Thomas from that show "Home Improvement."

"What do you want now, mister?" Sadie asked. I could smell J.T. from my bed. He smelled of beer and dirt and some-times urine. He was always scratching like the sick junkie he was. Not a heroin user but a T addict. T is pure poison if you don't get it from someplace reputable. J.T. bought his on the street. There was a man called Doc who'd come around and you could buy a vial of what he said was testosterone for twenty bucks a pop. It was T all right but that wasn't all it was. It was street T, probably cut with Drano or some other sick shit, and the needles were never clean. You could count on that.

"You got a couple of bucks?" J.T. asked Sadie.

"I thought you'd come to ask for a cup of sugar. I don't have a couple of bucks," she said.

J.T. stormed through the apartment to my room where I was lying in the dim light. "Got a couple of bucks, Ian?" he asked. "Rent's due this week."

I sighed. "You don't want rent money. Fucking be honest with me. Say 'I want to buy some fucking junk for my arm,'" I answered.

J.T. scoured the room, found my jeans that had been tossed on the floor and dug through the pockets.

"What the fuck are you doing? I didn't say you could go through my shit."

He had found my wallet and was skimming through its contents. There was exactly two bucks in there.

"You got two bucks," he said. "I'm gonna borrow it. 'Kay?"

It was a rhetorical question. He already had taken the money. "Hey, dude, what happened to your face?"

"I'm trying to get some sleep, J.T. You got the money so just get out of here, okay?"

He stormed out the door and was gone. I thought about Molly, how she was probably married with one and a half kids by now. She never thought about that dyke from high school who was still so fucking stuck on her. She thought about white picket fences and playdates and PTA meetings. It was all pretty sad really. I thought about my five-year high school reunion. Was I going to go? I had wanted to but now the possibility of ever having anything with Molly was gone. What was the point? I could go and stare at her, shake her husband's hand, maybe even have a man-to-man talk with him about cars or the price of oil but what would be the point?

I woke up at five thirty. It was raining outside. Sadie was watching "Soul Train" on the television and dancing around. She was wearing her Roller Derby outfit with the white roller skates that had pink and gold hearts on the sides. I was thinking about Beatrice. I was thinking about trying to find her.

"Wanna take a walk?" I asked Sadie.

"I can't," she squealed. "It's raining. I'll melt like the Wicked Witch of the West."

I got dressed and grabbed my bicycle. I walked downstairs and headed down to 42nd Street.

The club was packed. Men were getting out of their Wall Street jobs feeling lonely and horny. I walked straight to the dressing room and banged on the door. The young-looking girl appeared again.

"Looking for Venus?"

"Yeah."

"She's not working. She's got fines now. She'll have to pay Dottie a hundred bucks if she wants to work again."

"Do you know where to find her?" I asked.

"We got information sheets with addresses and phone numbers but most of the girls lie on them. I know I did." The older woman from the other night put her fat hand on my shoulder. It felt heavy. I was still sore.

"She lives on Bleeker Street, number eleven-sixty-six," said the lady. "If you see her, tell her to come in to work." I nodded.

I rode off into the rain. My hair was soaking and my shoes squeaked at each turn of the pedal. When I arrived I walked up the front steps and hit her buzzer. No one answered. I buzzed again. Still no one. I walked out the door, sat on the stairs underneath the overhang. I reached into my pocket. Her number was there but it was smudged by the rain so I couldn't make it out. I knew the first three numbers were 4-1-7. That's all I knew.

I waited about an hour, and just as I was standing up, about to mount my bicycle, she appeared. She sort of floated like above the water. Her eyes were so clear, her hair was so wet. Her red bra strap peaked out from underneath her white T-shirt. She kinda just stood there for a minute, looking me over, making sure it was really me.

"Ian. You're here." I nodded. My body felt heavy and

exhausted. I wanted to go inside. She walked up the stairs.

"Are you coming with…?" she began.

"Yeah, okay," I said.

Of course I had every intention of following her. I'd been waiting out in the rain for nearly an hour now. I wasn't about to just up and leave. We walked through the door. The building smelled musty and sort of like linoleum. If you live in the city you know that smell. It also smells like food, an undiscernable smell like foreign food but you don't know where it's from. We walked up the creaking steps to the seventh floor. It felt like it took forever. It was probably only a minute.

She paused by the door. She was breathing heavily. She pulled a cigarette from the pack with her teeth, which I always find to be extremely hot. She lit it and slid the key into the lock like she knew what was up. She turned the lock and the door flew open.

The apartment was dark. The floors were made of wood. There was a dim light on in the kitchenette. She bit her lip and exhaled. There were maps on the walls, maps of other places. Places I'd never been. Paris, Barcelona, Egypt. The walls were a deep yellow, the tarnished color of a room that had been smoked in for years, centuries. There was peeling wallpaper in the kitchenette.

"I'm trying to pull back this awful wallpaper. There's a fucking vault of information underneath. Newspapers. They had put newspapers under the wallpaper. They are old. Like very old. From the early immigrant days when people came over from Ellis Island. The days when people still liked a good story…." Her voice trailed off.

I didn't care about wallpaper or maps anymore. I wanted her. I wanted her legs spread on the bed like a quilt. I wanted to take her in my mouth like a juicy orange, a warm vowel. I wanted to push her tiny body against the wall and grind into her cunt.

"Want a towel?" she asked.

"Okay."

She went into the bathroom and came out with a small blue towel. First I dried off my hair, then I took off my jacket. I dried my shoulders and then I felt her in back of me. She had grabbed the towel. She was pulling at the pockets of my jeans. She was taking them off. I stood there in boxer briefs and a wifebeater. She leaned over and pulled off her jeans. She was soaking wet. She grabbed the towel and dried her skinny legs, then her hair; then she pulled off her T-shirt. She stood there wearing a bra and panties, shivering. Her body was covered in goose bumps. I thought I saw her smile. I could have been wrong. I was nervous. I was still sore but I wasn't thinking about that anymore.

I'm in control. I'm in control, I kept telling myself.

She slid onto the bed. She was lying on her back. She was waiting for me. I hesitated before walking over to her. I slid on top of her. We fit like puzzle pieces. She smelled like graham crackers. I bit her bottom lip. It tasted like a mandarin orange. She took my tongue in her mouth. I was ready for her. I tugged at the sides of her panties. They slid off. I fiddled with the back of her bra. I couldn't get it off. I felt like an amateur. She laughed. She grabbed hold of my hands and helped me take it off. She threw it on the floor. She was shivering and naked and pale. Her lips glistened red like Dorothy's shoes. I pushed down hard on her pelvis. I felt my body shake. I slid my hand down, rubbed her clit slowly. It felt warm. I licked my first two fingers and slid them into her. I felt the little hills and canyons on her insides. I felt her melt into me, grind onto my hand. I kept fucking her. She was getting wet.

When I moved down to taste her, her pussy glistened like a waterfall. I slid my tongue against her clit and continued to fuck her with my fingers. She slid her hand down, tried to touch my breasts. I had bound them earlier. I moved her hand away. She tried to slide her hand down my boxers but I had forgotten the penis. I moved her hand away. I fucked her furiously with my fingers and tongue; she moaned and purred like a small cat.

"Ian," she said. "You feel so good." I smiled.

I rubbed my fingers along her small breasts, moved toward them, licked her nipples, felt my weight shift onto her again. I ground against her. She made a tiny sigh. I felt her wet pussy engulf my fingers like a hungry mouth. She thrusted and ground against them in a frenzy, until, in one smooth shift of energy, she let out a loud moan and her pussy lips quivered. I slid my fingers out of her and rubbed my entire palm against her moving cunt.

She leaned into me. Kissed me like it was the last kiss she'd ever have. There was a certain end-of-the-world feeling about the whole thing. I sat up. I surveyed the room. Where had I put my pants, my bag, my bike? I remembered that I had left my bike out in the pouring rain. I hadn't even locked it up. Someone had probably stolen it by now which was pretty sad as it was the only true material possession I had and my means of earning a living.

Beatrice's eyes closed. I got up, found my jeans and slid into them, threw my jacket over my shoulders and headed toward the door.

"Where are you going, Ian?" I heard her ask.

"Nowhere," I said, and then it hit me. I wasn't going any-where. I sat back down on the side of the bed, stroked the ends of her damp hair, kissed her lips and looked into her pale face. I wasn't thinking about Molly, although I didn't even realize I wasn't thinking about Molly at the time. I was there and it was where I wanted to be.

ROSEMARY AND EUCALYPTUS

Kyle Walker

My lover gave me an inordinately expensive Christmas present, then broke up with me on January second.

"I knew this was coming..." she told me. "But I didn't want to ruin the holidays."

I didn't know it was coming, but kept the present.

I made the first appointment (of twelve) for a one-hour massage at our local wellness center the second week of January. My lover, I mean my ex, gave good presents. Somewhat numb; well, more like a block of ice, I still felt the cutting wind and curled into myself as I made my way through the icy streets.

It was already dark as I sat in the warm, spice-scented reception area at the second-floor suite. The traffic outside seemed muffled and far away. A dark-haired woman in loose cotton garments offered me a cup of herbal tea. I accepted and inhaled its steam as I filled out the form: *Check yes or no: Back problems? Allergies? Heart problems?* No, no, and no, unless you counted broken hearts. The woman took the clipboard from me.

"This looks fine," she said. "Do you have any problem areas I should know about? Or anything special you want me to work on? I'm Marlena, I'll be working with you today." I wanted to explain that I needed to be taken apart and put back together as a better-functioning, more desirable person. Preferably one with a better income and a smaller ass.

"My shoulder is sore sometimes from too much computer work," I told her instead. "And my lower back."

"Modern life, huh?" she said with a wry smile, as she opened the door to the treatment room. "Too complicated, right?" I nodded in agreement.

I turned away as I disrobed, folding my clothes, tucking my watch and ring into my shoes. I instinctively reached for the other ring, the one I got for Christmas two years ago, but remembered I wasn't wearing it anymore.

I draped myself over the massage table, and noted gratefully that Marlena had a heated pad under the sheet. This winter, the cold had been getting in my bones in a fierce, awful way. I fit my face into the cradle and she gently laid the sheet over me.

"I like to start with a little aromatherapy," she said. "Is there a scent you prefer?"

"Do you have eucalyptus?" Years ago, I went to Australia, and the Blue Mountains were the coolest place I ever saw. They smelled so good, and there was that blue haze created by millions of eucalyptus trees and the koalas eating them all day and getting high. Yes, I love the smell of eucalyptus. And I suck on Halls lozenges all winter, as much for the memory as the head-clearing.

I heard her rub her hands together and then she held them under my face and the scent of mountains on a faraway continent started relaxing my muscles before she even touched me. Which she then did, letting one hand rest on the middle of my back. My breath got slower and deeper, and the ice in my bones started to melt.

I'm not much of a talker during massages; I like to dissolve and let my mind go where it wants. But a first massage is like a first date; you have to get to know each other, tell the masseuse where to go and what you like. Hmm. That's not quite what I meant. Maybe a first massage is like the first time you make love with someone. Except you have to pay for it... Oh wait. This metaphor is really headed in an awkward direction. Sorry. The thing is, you have to tell the person how deep and how hard and how soft and where it hurts and where it feels good... Oh well. That's not even a metaphor.

At any rate, we exchanged the usual information; what I do (a nonprofit thing), where she trained (Swedish Institute, got out about ten years ago); I hold my tension in the lower left calf; yes to caffeine and meat; I don't get enough sleep, take vitamins, don't exercise nearly enough. Spend a lot of time lately wrapped up in a blanket, rocking back and forth. And I don't even own a rocking chair.

"The holidays can be very stressful," she told me.

"You don't know the half of it," I replied as she dug at the knots in my right shoulder. As she worked at them with strong, probing fingers, and even applied her elbow, I could feel myself letting go, and at that moment, that wasn't a good thing. I started crying, shaking with heavy sobs.

"That happens," she said soothingly. "Better to let it go than hold it in." The digging in my shoulder changed to light, soothing pats. No doubt I drooled and snotted on the floor, but she didn't say anything as I eventually cried myself out. She asked me to turn over, then worked up my legs and my arms, enveloping my hands in hers and pulling on the fingers, popping the joints.

She rubbed my scalp and I could both feel and hear my hair rubbing against her hands. I'd had most of it (my hair) cut off the week before, and the ends slipped through her fingers easily. She rubbed my forehead, working her thumb in the "third eye," then pressing under my cheekbones, as I worked my jaw and breathed deeper and deeper.

"Do you need a little something to clear your head before we finish?" Marlena asked. "A different scent? Something refreshing?"

"What do you recommend?" I was sad the massage was almost over.

"I could put a little rosemary on. That's very invigorating," she told me. So I said she could, and she stroked the oil on my temples, and I inexplicably craved chicken.

She said "Thank you," and left me alone to dress. I put my clothes back on, slowly, feeling their texture as they moved across my skin, feeling my muscles slide over bone, feeling a dull ache inside, emerging from the ice as it dripped, dripped, dripped. I looked at my watch and realized she'd worked on me for well over an hour.

"Thanks for that," I told her when I emerged from the room. "If you'd like, I can pay for your additional time."

"No thanks, on the house today," she told me. She had a kindness to her that almost brought me to tears again. "You want to schedule another appointment?"

"Oh yes!" I agreed. I wouldn't have minded a massage a day until I used up the certificate, but I had to ration them. Had to get used to living on a reduced budget. When these ran out, it would be hard to pay for more. I scheduled another session for two weeks later. Two a month would take me til June, which seemed like a magical, imaginary place from here in the second week of January. She gave me one of her cards. "Marlena O'Reilly? You don't look Irish," I feebly joked. She had long black hair and light brown skin; not tall, but well-upholstered with large breasts and rounded hips.

"I'm Dominican," she said. "O'Reilly was my husband. My daughter's Irish, though. Consuela O'Reilly."

"Only in New York," I clichéd back at her. "See you in two weeks."

O'Reilly hadn't been on the scene in a number of years, I found out at our next session. "Oh, really?" I remarked, and to her credit, she didn't pinch or poke me. He'd split when Consuela was young, and Marlena, who'd been working as a secretary, decided to get her massage certificate, so she could have more flexible hours to take care of her child.

"Turned out to be a great decision," she told me as she ground the heel of her hand into that right shoulder. I whimpered and shed a few tears. "I found out this is something I really like, and care about. Being a secretary, working in an office, wearing those clothes, stuffing into the subway with a zillion other people. So boring. So terrible. Oh. I don't mean to insult you...."

"No, I understand," I grunted. "You have to do what fulfills you. Not just what brings in the money. Believe it or not, I actually have a law degree. I could be one of those downtown assholes making a ton of dough, but I like my nonprofit thing. Makes me feel like I'm doing more than taking up space."

"Exactly!" she said.

"I wouldn't mind a ton of dough, though," I said wistfully.

"Eh...you have enough for what you need, I guess," she told me. "I don't know you, but you seem all right. Except for being so sad right now."

The goddamn groundhog saw his shadow. Winter would never end. I went out for dinner with some friends and it turned out to be a fix-up, which I wasn't remotely ready for, and I got quite drunk and had a terrible time.

"You are very dehydrated today," Marlena scolded me as I dragged in the next day, still wondering whether it would ever be light out when I showed up for my six o'clock appointments. She made me drink a large mug of herbal tea before she got me on the table, and later pressed a couple of teabags into my hands as I left feeling revived, if not quite alive.

Her daughter was waiting for her when we finished the next time. I recognized her as Marlena's child, though she was tall and had red hair. She had Marlena's eyes and carriage. I knew she was in the ninth grade at one of the more competitive high schools in the city, and that she was very good at science. Marlena greeted her with a hug and kiss, and proudly introduced her to me. Consuela wasn't embarrassed, the way a lot of kids might have been (if *my* mother had kissed me in public? Forget it...). We walked out together, and they headed off to dinner, arm in arm.

March came in with another snowstorm, but it melted very quickly, and I leapt from the street to the curb past the over-flowing storm drains. The air smelled wet, not cold, and theoretically, spring was coming.

Marlena had to cancel our first appointment that month because she got a flu that was going around. When she called to reschedule, I teased her that her healthy diet and lifestyle hadn't kept her from getting sick as a dog.

"It's you..." she said through a stopped-up nose. "You are the sick ones. And then I put my hands on you and the next thing you know, I am sick as one of you office people with the windows that don't open and the artificial light!" I begged her pardon, and asked if there was anything I could do. She told me her friends were helping her out and Consuela was a good girl who took care of her mama. *Of course she has friends*, I thought. We rescheduled for the following week.

I brought her a jar of chicken soup when I saw her.

"Not from the store," I told her. "My mother's recipe."

"In that case, I'll take it home and have it," she said. "Mother medicine is very powerful." I shrugged.

"She's not really *that* much of a cook," I said. "But it's good when it's hot."

I saw Marlena again the next week, and it was a treat to have two massages in just over a week. I fantasized about being rich enough to afford one...or more! a week. I think that's the first thing I'd do if I hit the lottery: hire a full-time massage therapist. I'd do good works the very *next* thing.

Maybe it was because the temperature was creeping up and the leaves were unfolding and I was starting to get spring allergies, but I started having sex dreams again. They were rather comforting, not just because they were sex dreams, but because I was feeling less like a tossed-out shoe or paper bag, and the prospect of touching someone, having her touch me, was something I'd not dreamed of in a long time. I'd stopped having erotic dreams a few months before the breakup, I realized. Maybe I *had* known something.

That April was one of those months when New York makes you fall in love with it all over again: daffodils down the middle of Park Avenue; little kids driving their Big Wheels around and around in my neighborhood (What? You think I can afford to live in Manhattan?); the first of ten million repetitions of the tinkling song of the ice-cream trucks as they start to prowl the neighborhoods; big guys in muscle T-shirts walking their pit bulls. I wouldn't live anywhere else.

I opened my eyes during our next session. I usually kept them shut during a massage, but I chanced to look up and saw Marlena's breasts as she stroked my forehead. They were really large and beautiful, and they swayed as she worked, and I became hypnotized by them. My mouth began to water.

I dreamed about her. She was massaging me, and we were both naked. She rubbed her breasts against mine, then held them up to my face. I suckled first one, then the other. In my dream, I tasted eucalyptus.

"Did you pay your taxes?" she asked me during our next session.

"Huh?" I astutely replied, jerked from a guilty memory of what was becoming a recurring dream. "What? Yeah...back in February. What about you? Have you filed?"

"My accountant retired," she told me. "I've been looking for a new one. I was so used to him, we were so comfortable with each other, that I've been putting it off. That's very bad for me. When it's over, it's over, you know? I need to move on." I recommended my accountant, who also works with a lot of freelancers.

"You have to file quarterly," I told her.

"I know," she said with a sigh. "I wouldn't care about it, let the government go to hell, but when Consuela goes to college, she's gonna need loans and stuff. They can't have me down as not paying my taxes."

"Yes... It is hard to move on..." I agreed with what she'd said earlier.

"You're doing better, though," she told me. "Your hair is getting longer."

"You like it better that way?" I asked, hopefully.

"Yes," she said firmly. "Much better."

I spent a lot of May feeling guilty. I dreamt of her, more and more often. There was one dream that was very short, but memorable. I saw her, and she kissed me, and I felt her mouth, all wet. I woke up, touching my lips. *It's transference*, I told myself. *She's a nice lady who gets paid to touch you. Easier to get a crush on her than go out in the real world. She's not there to be your fantasy.*

But I don't like the real world, I whined to myself. *I like Marlena.*

I apologized to the friends who had fixed me up in February, and asked if they knew anyone else. I even went on a date with a perfectly nice woman who seemed interested in more than just a good-night kiss, but I couldn't follow through.

As Marlena's hands touched every part of me, I scolded myself for objectifying her. Her hands. Her breasts. Her sweet voice. As I turned over, my nipples were hard.

"It's not too cold in here, is it?" she asked. "I can shut the window."

"No, no, I like the breeze," I managed. As she circled her thumb in the palm of my hand, it took everything I had not to grasp on to her. I let out a huge sigh.

"That's it, breathe," she told me.

I thought of canceling our next session, but knew I didn't have the willpower.

The days were longer, and I wore my sunglasses out on the street and up the stairs to my appointments. The room was dark, then I took off the glasses, and there she was, and my heart leapt.

It would be over soon anyway. June barreled down on us, and I had two sessions left. I went over my budget to see if I could manage at least one session a month, and told myself just to let it...let *her* go.

"Summer's here...you go to the beach? Coney Island?" she asked me. "It's fun down there." She wore a light, sleeveless top and was a little sweaty. She hated air-conditioning, and told me she wouldn't put it on unless the client asked. Client. I reminded myself that's what I was.

"I always mean to go...but summer gets away from me," I told her. "Like I always mean to go to baseball games and outdoor concerts; I like the idea of them, but I've lived here so many years and haven't done so many of the things you're supposed to in New York...."

"You need someone to make you have fun," she commented.

"Yes, I do," I agreed.

That night, I dreamed we were riding the Ferris wheel at

Coney Island. As we whirled around and around, my stomach rising and falling, the ocean coming into view as we reached the top, she kissed me and reached up my skirt and touched my thigh. The world rocked around us as she pulled me to her with one arm, and I spread my legs to welcome her other hand. We rocked and rolled and I came so hard.

It was full summer on the day of our last appointment. The solstice had come and gone and I knew, even if I couldn't tell by sight, that the days were getting shorter again. I like autumn better anyway.

"So Consuela's going to be in tenth grade soon?" I asked.

"She's so big...so grown up," Marlena sighed. "Talking about colleges and where she wants to go. I'm not ready for her to leave me."

"Well, she could end up going someplace around here," I said. "Lots of good schools in the city."

"I tell her that. But what if she wants to go to Stanford or someplace? She would hate me if I moved to California to be with her, right?"

"How embarrassing for her," I said without thinking.

"Yeah, she should be ashamed of me," Marlena said angrily. "Is that what you think? I shouldn't love her? I should let go of her?"

"No, no! That's not it at all!" I said.

Marlena stepped away from the table. Her hand, which was always touching me, suddenly wasn't there. I sat up, and the sheet fell away from me. I got off the table, and she moved to the other side.

"Hey!" I said. "Hey..." and I followed her, and she kept going and I kept following and it must have been a sight to see naked me chasing her around and around the table. Then

I caught up with her and what was I going to say? I couldn't think of anything, so I just hugged her.

"You have a beautiful daughter and she has a beautiful mother, and...and..."

"And what?" Marlena said, not angry. Challenging.

And then we were kissing. It was much better than I had dreamed it. She didn't seem surprised. She didn't push me away. She kissed back.

"It's not right..." she said, between kisses.

"I'm a client..."

"Ethics..."

"Not real..."

"Sometimes I get..."

"But it's okay..."

"If we both..."

"Yes...I think we both..."

"Yes..."

We broke for a moment, and she pulled off her top and her bra, and stepped out of her loose cotton pants.

"Get back on the table," she told me. "I'm not finished."

I did as she said, and stretched out on my back. She got on as well and straddled me. She poured the lotion in her hands and rubbed it on herself: breasts, arms, belly. Then she loosened the long hair she always kept pulled back. She leaned over me and it fell like a silken veil over my face. Her breasts brushed, then rubbed against mine, and she massaged me with them, letting them slide and roll all over my front. I moaned.

She shifted so that one of her legs was between mine and lay prone on top of me, using her whole body to stroke me, her leg to grind into me, her teeth and tongue to nuzzle my neck, chin, face. As in my dream, she clasped me to her with one arm, and reached down, and I opened my legs.

Her oiled fingers slipped easily into my cunt, and the hand that knew every inch of my outside began to massage me from the inside and I was beyond thought, beyond words, just capable of moans and grunts and sighs. She rubbed me expertly, but with more than simply a professional touch. She wanted me, she wanted to claim me, to be part of me.

"You're with *me* now, understand?" she whispered fiercely. "I don't care how we found each other, because we're here now, okay?"

"Yes...yes..." I managed.

She slipped out of me, and told me to turn over. She turned round on the table, and bent over my buttocks, squeezing and kneading them hard. She'd never touched me that low before, and along with her hands, I felt her mouth, her breath, blowing, licking, nibbling around my ass. No one had ever done that to me before, and I instantly understood what I'd been missing. I could feel her pouring more oil on me, then rubbing it in, circling my hole with her finger, touching, seeking; quite suddenly, easily, sliding in. Oh yes, oh yes. Her finger rode me and rode me and I grabbed the table and begged for more.

She climbed off the table, and pulled me toward her so my feet were on the floor. She kept working the finger in my ass, and put her other hand back in my pussy. I bucked and rocked and she kept rubbing and stroking, massaging me to greater heights.

"I'm going to come..." I stammered.

"So come, baby," she said. "Come with both my hands in you." So I did.

As I lay there, trembling and weeping, I felt Marlena lying

on top of me, resting her head on mine. Something dripped down my cheek, and I licked it and realized it was salty. I managed to get up and turn round, and she was weeping, too.

"Today's not the last time, right?" she asked, and I held her.

"Today's the first time," I told her. "We get to go outside. Out of this room."

She sighed happily.

"But not just yet," I told her, pushing her back on the table. My hands, all slippery and soft, worked their way up to her breasts.

RUPTURE

Suki Bishop

It begins like this: We are driving down the highway. I feel frisky, mischievous. I want to play a little, set something in motion that takes on its own life so that when it happens, it just happens. I want to throw something out and see how it returns to me.

Mark sits in the backseat. Dara drives. I am in the passenger seat with my legs spread, the AC funneling under my dress. Later, Dara will say I called her to me. It is true. I pictured her hand under my dress until it happened. *What does it matter?* I think. *Why not?* I marvel at how easy it is to cross over a line, to cross back.

I look at her, the driver, who must keep her eyes on the road, who does not keep her eyes on the road. I run my hand up her shorts, pull it away and laugh. I close my eyes and will Mark not to speak; his voice will pierce this fantasy. I want to imagine I am in a car heading nowhere, that I have nowhere to head, that it is raining out suddenly, that drops are hitting the windshield and their shadows fall over my skin—hydrating, penetrating drops.

She puts her hand on my leg. I watch it inch under my skirt. I don't know where to look, how to hold my head. Mark must be watching. Her hand inches up. I focus on my breath, the sound of rain against the windshield.

He rests his hand on my head at first. "I feel like a puppy," I say as he strokes my head awkwardly, brushes my hair aside. He moves his hand to my neck. I drop my head back. He grabs my throat as Dara's hand enters me. I feel myself bend and open. I am in it now; I am in this speeding car, this driving rain; I am in her hand fucking me, his hand grabbing my throat, this throat fuck. She is supposed to be driving, but she watches his hand. She knows about hands and me. So she fucks me harder. I'm opening and opening my legs; I slide down the seat. His finger is in my mouth. I suck it. I am in this thing now; this thing I began with mischief, from a distance; this thing I set in motion last night when I said to him, "What do you imagine it will be like to fuck us?"

She is the one who says yes or no. She has said no all along. Ever since the day the three of us met and she and Mark competed for my attention. She and I kissed then, on a staircase in front of a window. We knew he saw her push me onto the stairs and lift my skirt. *See how she lets me fuck her? See how she has chosen me?* But Dara is afraid of something.

Today she says yes with her fingers inside me. What happens for her while she tries to watch the highway; catches quick glimpses of his hand on my throat, my shoulder, my chest?

He grabs my hair, wraps it around his fingers. The pain calls me to myself, brings me back to my body—her fingers, his pull, calling me back to this thrusting and spreading and opening body. His hand fills my mouth. I bite him so hard I leave teeth marks.

How can I explain that thing at the center, the destination I never reach, this impossibility? Her hand cannot break me open and fill me. His hand cannot break my jaw and drown me. I cannot bite through his flesh and swallow his palm. I cannot spread my legs so far that I become an endless, open hole. Something releases, but where will it go? Aside from my breath, I do not make a sound. I have lost sound's language, as if all release is useless. I come, but I cannot break myself open into a thousand drops pouring down on glass, the drum of it, the endless patter of it, the flood outside our car.

Later, he enters our room without knocking. A bold move, yet we have not locked our door. I rise to greet him and he pushes me against the door, hard kisses me. Dara sits on the twin beds that have been pushed together as one and pretends not to care, but she can't hide her disgust. I am careful. I stiffen at his touch. I lead him to the bed and tell him to kiss her, while I watch her face for signs of pleasure or anger.

He leans over her. The kiss is too hard and too sloppy; I know what she likes. But she lets him continue. The way he just pulls down her shirt and sucks her. The way her nipples are hard, her mouth open. The way he arches over her, like he's going to devour her. I see their bodies arch and push against each other—there is something fierce there, some kind of war. I get angry when he kisses her too long, and yet the anger excites me.

A reaching hand pulls me in. We become a gross mathematical equation, a rotating lock with endless combinations, the search for a winning number to open a vault. What are we after? Not the skin (though Dara's skin is so soft); not the hand approaching the bull's-eye (the brain says, *Yes! Yes! Go there!*); not the gentle lick of a nipple, the release of air and sound from a mouth; not the kiss (Mark's is a penetrating kiss, Dara's a delicate probing); not the hand grabbing the hair of the head below him (such violence—her mouth could not hold him).

This feels different than the boy who obeyed us, who asked, "Can I touch her there?" That boy was nervous and new to this kind of thing. This one is tricky. Mark creates a tornado around him. He wants something; he is hunting us, and even as he slips—no, thrusts—his fingers inside me, I retreat somewhere deeper than his fingers can reach. Something familiar is happening, as if someone hums a haunting tune that I have been hearing and losing and hearing again all my life.

It takes me here: to a windowless room with a raised bed like an altar, to a time that now seems a lost precious gift. She is sixteen. She is on the bed, tied up, stripped down, and her boyfriend cuts her, tentative at first, until she writhes under the blade and he can see that she is coming. He is hard and confused at this pleasure he gets from cutting her, but he does not run from it. She begins to cry and says stop and he wants to, he really does, but it seems to him that something has already started; the knife now cuts him as it slices her. She is crying but she is also writhing and her crying sounds like a plea for something—something he cannot give her, he thinks, so at least maybe he can give her this.

I am on my back when Mark fucks me. When Dara watches

him fuck me. Perhaps she sees the way my body bends in grief from an invisible source—a hair pull, a petting, an echoing touch calling up a resonant past. It is grief fucking me when Mark does, a phantom grief, a seductive, sweeping grief that enters and opens and steals me.

But Dara hears no haunting tune. With the obedient one, she and I kept each other's gaze. This time, we do not. I do not retreat, in this moment, to the embrace of my lover, who is caught outside, feeling excluded, reaching tiny tendril hands onto my thigh, little cat paws pulling at me, calling me back.

When we lie together, I am in the middle, my head supported by an unfamiliar chest, pale white skin. She rests against me, a little lone bird on a log out at sea. The twin beds have begun to split: she and I on one side, Mark on the other. "The abyss of gender," Mark calls it.

I think: if only it were that simple.

FRUIT OF ANOTHER

Annette Beaumont

It was the same every time. She lay back in my bed, the features of her face now faded in my mind. Those details were diminished, but not the intensity of my desire. As I kissed her neck I heard her breathing quicken; her curves, soft and full beneath my hands, a reminder of this forbidden love. My mouth moved slowly down her body, exploring, hoping, coming alive with cravings. Her moans were soft, a whisper, trying to keep our secret. I lingered on her hips, feeling them rise to me, wanting me, wanting more. In my mind, the teasing was relentless, taunting her, torturing myself. I pulled the inside of her thigh to my lips, her leg bent at the knee. She moaned, louder this time. She wanted me, needed me, called for me. So many times I had heard her call my name and longed to answer. Though I would never be with her, the image of this woman dominated my fantasies, invaded my mind and left me helpless to forget. In the painful absence of her touch, I succumbed to my own, feeling the wetness that only thoughts of her could bring. Years passed and time and again I dreamed of this woman with a frenzy of desire, always the same woman, always the same dream, only to watch her float away before I could finally taste her passion.

More than a decade ago her face was still fresh in my mind. Her eyes were big and brown with smile lines that had come from years of happiness on the river. She was beautifully round, even slightly heavy, with womanly curves my tomboyish shape had never known. Her natural ways enhanced her beauty. She had absolutely nothing to hide. Free from makeup and jewelry and attention to fashion she nevertheless radiated femininity. Her honesty permeated her appearance. She was modest, but not insecure. Her gestures, her laugh, her love of the nature that surrounded us were all quite genuine. She was simply beautiful to me. She had no idea that she held such beauty, and certainly no idea that I, of all people, appreciated it.

It was on the river that she looked most at home, and on the banks in the evenings, the sun casting its last rays on the canyon wall behind her, that I realized I wanted her. She was a bona fide river guide, with calloused hands and a faded life vest, skillfully rowing guests through turbulent class IV rapids, giving them a wet and wild adventure they would never forget. It was my job, on the other hand, to organize the trip, to plan and pack five days of rations and supplies: Bisquick and bacon, cold cuts and steaks, tents, sleeping bags and Dutch ovens. I would meet and greet the twelve anxious guests, help orient them to camp life, and encourage them to pare down their new L.L. Bean wardrobes to stuff into their assigned dry bags. Both in our twenties, we embraced the freedom of life on the river, welcoming the constant sound of rushing water that drowned out the world and its expectations.

By the end of that summer on the Lower Salmon I was in the throes of my first lesbian infatuation, and I had the makings of a fantasy that would sustain me for more than a decade. We had spent months on the river and countless evenings around the campfire in the sand, no one ever suspecting my hidden lust. The end of each trip was marked by our small rafts floating peacefully into the larger flow of the Snake River, leaving behind the isolated, remote and hidden canyons of the Salmon. Just beyond the place where the two rivers meet, vehicles awaited to return our guests to the world they had only briefly escaped.

The confluence of two rivers, the legends say, is a magical place. I personally have known this to be true. That summer, however, every wish I made with each crossing of the confluence would need to stay forever secret. My longings would remain in the safeguard of the canyon walls we left behind, lost in the river's constant whispers. No one could know what I dreamed that summer. No one could know because it had been exactly one year earlier, on that same river, that I had met my fiancé.

Eleven years passed since my heart was first tempted. Countless crushes followed. Unsuspecting friends, colleagues at work, fellow students in graduate school each touched a part of me that I was not ready to concede. The attractions were real. So, too, was my commitment to my marriage, to the man who was my best friend, the father of my children.

He had known about my lustful attraction before we ever married. I loved him too much not to tell him. He dismissed it as natural and circumstantial. He asked me if I was in love with her. I replied, with clarity, that I was not. I simply wanted to sleep with her. The wedding had taken place as scheduled. Still, through the years, my very first love of a woman pervaded my fantasies, remaining the one place I sought refuge. I refused to abandon the one imagined encounter that made me feel whole.

Over the years, my longing for a woman was kept alive by my riverside fantasy and thrived just below the surface. As my marriage wavered, it didn't take much for that hunger to invade my every thought. Playfully, without guilt, I found myself searching the Internet for someone to talk to. The anonymity of the computer and the absolute certainty that I would never act on my desires kept my conscience clean. I found a sympathetic ear on several occasions, and almost laughed at the distance I was able to keep between myself and these acquaintances. The game went on for months, and it was surprisingly fulfilling. Then, one unremarkable evening online, I by chance met a woman named Beatrice.

Even her name set her apart from the others, timeless and wise, resonant of a distant era. Beatrice was playing a game of her own. Only a few years older than me, she had already given up on real relationships, and entertained herself by corresponding with a host of women scattered across the country. She had a strict policy of never dating or even corresponding with married women. I will never know what compelled her to break her own rules that evening, but the decision sent both our lives in a direction we couldn't have anticipated.

My first contact with her was less than appealing. *My name is Anne and I'm kind of new at this. I am thirty-three years old, and I am married. I have two amazing kids, a little boy who is four and a little girl who is three. I hope you write back.*

Stunningly, she did. *If you are married and have two fabulous kids, why are you writing to me?*

I've longed to know intimacy with a woman, I explained. *This is not a "bi-curious" phase, but a long-term, innate need to understand these desires. I don't want to do anything about it, I just need someone to talk to. I'm not looking to date you, just to correspond with you. Trust me, we may never meet.*

And so we exchanged emails. Over weeks that flowed into months, we shared an outpouring of thoughts that spanned pages and pages. Because neither of us was seeking a romantic relationship, we were free to be ourselves; free to think, divulge, explore anything, without the pressures or tensions that accompany a budding relationship. Unwittingly, we had discovered the lost art of letter writing.

Topics expanded from sexual orientation to personal histories, politics and literature, art and humor. Instead of getting to know one another through small talk and red wine, we used long letters to paint vivid portraits of ourselves, prompting each other to reveal ever finer brushstrokes. Her favorite color was black, her favorite food was chocolate. Her only brother was gay, her mother was ill. Her sarcasm was clever, biting. She adorned her apartment walls with Georgia O'Keefe and Ansel Adams, and her shelves were scattered with bones collected in the Southern Utah desert. Her bookshelves were bursting with worn copies of Carson, Leopold, Abbey, McPhee, Thoreau, and Tempest Williams; the greatest environmental minds standing shoulder to shoulder with Kant and Nietzsche. Her bedside table was overflowing with everything from Anne Rice to Ayn Rand. Her desk was stacked with legal textbooks. She dreamed of fighting for the civil rights of others, of the GLBT community, of the elderly, of those who had no voice. Without ever exchanging pictures, her beauty was most obvious to me. She was a songwriter. She was a poet. She was a student. She was a comedian. She was a cancer survivor. She was a musician. She was a philosopher. She was full of passion she didn't even realize. Some of those passions we shared, like our mutual love of the natural world. With others, like her music, I could only sit back and listen in awe.

The game soon changed to a battle of wit. Creative energy flowed from our fingertips as if our souls were newly awakened. She shared her history and her ambitions, her past and her future, woven into stories that evoked tears of both sympathy and laughter. With every free moment, I would run to the computer to see if a musing from Beatrice had graced my inbox. For the first time in years I felt intellectually stimulated. My brain came alive. I was excited and inspired and filled with anticipation. I was writing again. I was feeling again. I was falling in love.

Eventually our physical distance, our anonymity, shifted from something we relished to something excruciating. Twice we made plans to meet. Twice we canceled them. Neither of us wanted to cross that line, to change or risk losing what we had. Both of us knew we were destined to.

Finally, one evening after work, Beatrice drove to my small town thirty miles from her home and waited in a local bar. I arrived with impossible expectations. I inched down the steps into the darkness and as my eyes adjusted I saw her in the corner on a sofa. She was dressed atypically conservative, having come straight from work, her tweed suit and high collar catching me off guard. Her hair was unexpectedly coiffed and sprayed to hold it in place. Who was this buttoned-up woman? Where was my Beatrice? Where was the wild free spirit I had come to know so intimately online? Had I only imagined her? Had it all been an illusion?

I walked into the room and cautiously to her. Petrified, I sat a comfortable distance away from her on the sofa. I couldn't look at her face. I had urges to run, to fly up the stairs and back to the safety of my house, of my marriage. I do not even remember our first words. I went to the bar and got us drinks, but when I returned I could only sit quietly, staring down at my glass, avoiding her gaze. She was talking, but her words were muted by the thoughts of escape spinning in my head.

I'm not sure how much time had passed when by chance I looked into her eyes. They were the bluest eyes I'd ever seen, shocking against her otherwise dark mane and complexion; glacial blue, like those of a cat, but full of mystery and danger, like those of a wolf. It was at that moment that I recognized her. Every word she had written to me, the secrets of her heart that she had dared to expose in her letters, the strength of spirit that her words had reflected, her hopes and passions and dreams and desires all at once came flooding over me, through me; an entire sea breaking as a single wave.

Like old friends we walked arm in arm down the street to the small but crowded Italian restaurant that I had chosen. We spent the evening lost in each other's eyes; lost in conversation, laughing, learning, completely oblivious to the world around us. When we eventually looked up, the waiters were sitting at a table at the other end of the room with looks of amusement at our expense. The restaurant was otherwise empty. I glanced at my watch and realized that it was long past closing time. For hours we had floated in our bubble, sheltered from the real world. Table by table, the other patrons had paid their bills and left the place completely deserted. We had not even noticed.

I was parked right out front, and Beatrice's car was several blocks away, so I offered to drive her there. During those brief moments, I was panicked at the thought of her getting into her car and driving out of my life. I was tempted to turn the wheel and head for the highway with Beatrice as my captive. As I pulled up beside her SUV and shifted into PARK, my eyes could only follow her hand as she reached for the door handle. In a flash, the door opened and she slid out of the car. The car door was already swinging back toward me when I managed to whisper, "Beatrice?" The door opened again and she leaned inside. "No kiss?" I asked timidly, knowing that she wouldn't, knowing that the crowded parking lot in my small town was a dangerous location for my first lesbian kiss. She paused, smiled sheepishly, and climbed back in the car.

Beatrice stared at me in silence for a moment, an eternity. Throughout the evening her every thought, her every gesture, had been stimulating. Now, the eye contact was almost unbearable. I waited for her to explain that there would be no kiss; that she couldn't, that we must never talk again, that we would never meet again. I knew deep down that she would be right. I was lost in those thoughts, waiting for those words when suddenly her lips were on mine.

So soft, so tender was her kiss, yet so unexpected. My body responded instantly. For a split second I stiffened, breathless, and then I slowly relaxed into her. As her hand brushed my face and her lips explored mine I knew that I had never really kissed before. She playfully nibbled, and indulged me with the softness of her tongue...gentle, teasing circles. The taste of her mouth was intoxicating. Time passed and I was suspended. Again I felt the accidental brush of her hand, this time on my thigh, and I shuddered, drawing her closer, aware of her body, her curves, moving against my own.

With that kiss I was transformed. She awakened a part of me that had waited patiently for far too long, and the feeling was overpowering. The passion in her lips was genuine as she breathed warmth and renewal into my very soul. To simply describe the aching between my thighs would belittle the magnitude of my response, as every cell in my body simultaneously opened to let her in. Later, when I climbed in bed beside my sleeping husband, I knew I could never kiss him again.

It took several days for me to arrange my schedule so that I could get to Beatrice's apartment. I showed up unannounced in the middle of the afternoon. Without a word, she let me in, took me by the hand, and led me to the bedroom. We lay in each other's arms and kissed as time paused for our emotions. For the first time I really noticed her body, clad casually in torn, faded blue jeans and a black V-neck T-shirt that better suited her true self. She was curvy and feminine; voluptuous but not overweight, sexy beyond words. Her large, full breasts and hourglass hips accentuated her petite waistline and flat belly. Her dark untamed curls swung freely that afternoon, framing a face of unspeakable beauty from which those radiant blue eyes glowed with anticipation. I lay motionless, emotionally exposed, mesmerized.

Before I knew what had happened my blouse was unbuttoned and my jeans were around my knees. "Beautiful. For me?" she asked playfully. She was running her fingers along the outline of my black lace panties, soaked completely through, although I wasn't sure which detail she was referring to.

I tried to answer her, to hold my composure and think of some clever and sexy retort. Instead, my head was swimming with intrusive thoughts of my husband, of nearly twelve years of unwavering loyalty to the man who was home with my children. True, our marriage was not one of passion. He had not touched me in years. He had once told me that he thought of sex as a chore, but I knew he was fucking someone else. Our marriage had died a few short years after it had begun. Neither of us had the guts to leave it. We were living the common lie of separate lives under the same roof. I felt abandoned and emotionally battered by the man who was once my closest friend, but now would go for days without speaking to me. While I wasn't looking, he had chipped away at my self-esteem and stripped me of any knowledge of my own beauty. Still, infidelity was a line that I never, in my entire life, had dared to cross. While I had in fact chosen those panties just for Beatrice and drenched them at the mere thought of her touch, all I managed to say at that moment was, "I'm so sorry."

Overcome with guilt and fear, and without another word, I jumped up, pulled my jeans to my waist and ran, not even looking back, leaving her hurt and confused. I was still breathing heavy when I merged onto the highway that led back to my house, not sure if my gasps were those of desire or panic. This journey would not be easy.

The next several days were filled with a flurry of emails. I revealed all my fears and trepidations in heartfelt explanations and apologies. Our letters had become a refuge for unquestioned honesty and the only means by which I felt I could safely explain my behavior, declare my regrets, and plead for another chance. Beatrice was understanding and graciously agreed to an evening together.

She welcomed me back with a new sense of closeness and without hesitation. But this time she was more cautious. We sat comfortably on the floor of her dimly lit living room eating take-out Thai food and rediscovering our shared laughter and infatuation. She brought out one of her three guitars and gave me a glimpse of the passion behind her music, serenading me with "River Waits," a song of patience and seduction written and performed just for me. Later, we danced slowly in the candlelight, melting in each other's arms. When we finally kissed, I knew there would be no turning back.

"Do you want to go into the bedroom?" she asked, almost with forgiveness in her voice. Her words were invigorating, making my heart race, making my chest ache. Yes. Every inch of me screamed *yes*. Without pause, I took her hand and led her there.

Through all our writing I had let her words take me. She was already a part of me. She had already replaced the worn fantasy of my river beauty with images of what was to come. I had shed my guilt and fear like the skin of a snake, leaving it shriveled in the path behind me as if it never had been a part of me. She was in my heart, yes, and in my brain, entangled in my every desire, distracting me from anything but her.

Images still flash in my mind of those first moments when I felt her body against mine, luscious and warm, naked but for her own lace panties, and so very still, as she allowed me to explore the female form for the very first time. My mouth found her ears, her earlobes, the tender place behind them so erotic for me. My heart pounded and I wondered if I could handle any more than simply this. Her ears led so easily to her neck and my mouth began to know where to go. My thoughts relaxed, and I found myself caressing her breast with my hand, her dark nipple tightening as I dared to pass over it with my tongue. She was exquisite.

I was restrained at first, unsure of myself. My instincts, however, soon took over, my mouth finding that hardened nipple and taking it in as if it had a thousand times before. Her body began to move, ever so slightly, and I knew then that I wanted so much more. I found her arm, so delicate, and followed its length to the inside of her elbow, soft, so perfect for kissing, and then to the tender skin of her wrist, the open palm of her hand. I mindlessly took her finger, calloused from guitar strings, and caressed it with my tongue, sucking it in familiar ways. Even now I am swept away with desire at the mere thought of it.

I continued on in my explorations, a little embarrassed by my diversion, a little excited by the thought of her watching me. My tongue found its way slowly down and around the inviting curves of her waist, stopping briefly on her hip bone, moving anxiously, desperately across the top of her bikini line. As if from far away I heard her faint, stifled offer. "Baby, you don't have to."

Only then did it occur to me that she thought this was for her. No, I needed no excuse, no escape. I was selfish in my lust. I wanted her for me, and only me. For years the lesbian in me had lain dormant, waiting passively for her release, sustaining a lifetime of unquenched thirst. With the slow and meticulous survey of Beatrice's womanly form I was sipping, savoring that long-awaited drink, motivated not by her seduction but by my own wanting; a desperate wanting that throbbed and dripped between my thighs. Make no mistake. It couldn't have been just anyone. No, it was Beatrice who held my trust, held my heart, and made me feel safe and loved and beautiful as no one else ever had. But this was for me, not her, and I ignored her selfless words.

Her scent filled my head and I was drawn to her inner thighs by a craving I didn't yet understand. It was familiar yet new, erotic, exhilarating. I accidentally felt the trickle that had escaped to her inner thigh as it brushed against my cheek. Her bent leg fell to one side and I instinctively ran the tip of my tongue along the edge of her panties, just at the crease where her thigh gave way to the source of all that wetness. With a hint of her flavor swirling in my mouth, I began to lose my thoughts and drift in reverie along her body, swept away in a current of lust. Despite her efforts to lie still for me, her back arched in anticipation. The last of my inhibitions gave way.

First with my teeth and then in slow motion with my hands I pulled her panties away, feeling the weight of their saturation as I cast them aside. I hovered momentarily in front of her, my eyes closed, lost in a trance, drunk with the beautiful aromas, picturing her wetness but not really looking, not thinking, just needing.

My warm breath against her made her squirm impatiently and I realized how long I had lingered there. All my senses were heightened. I felt that I could not wait another second, that I must finally know. I immersed myself in her with a raw and untrained passion that was tempered by the delicate pace of a woman in awe. My mouth was alive with the feeling of her softness, her wetness, trying to take it all in at once, overwhelmed with new sensations yet comfortable in its new home. My tongue was searching, wondering, finding her clit and moving with a mind of its own, in motions reminiscent of her own teasing kisses. I heard soft moans, but couldn't bring myself out of my dreamworld enough to know if they were hers or my own. The music left playing in the other room mingled with those muffled sounds, a hypnotic combination. The room faded around me. Time seemed to flow strangely slowly. I found myself floating effortlessly, momentarily leaving my body, taking her taste with me and seeing from above the wonder that was us.

The moans grew louder. As her hips rocked beneath my mouth I rocked with her, rhythmically, as though we were one, as though I was not sure whose mouth was on whom. The more I drank the more I craved. I was drowning in her but it was still not enough. I was where I needed to be, oblivious to my own actions, oblivious to her cries of pleasure, to her convulsions as the orgasm ripped through her, to my own thrusting against the bed, to her ultimate whispers for me to stop.

She reached down and pulled me to her. I felt the shaking but it was several minutes until I realized that it was my own body. I honestly did not know why she had asked me to stop; why she had broken my trance.... I wanted more and more. After so many years of waiting, I was insatiable. I lay against the warmth of her body, still half-hypnotized by the experience, still shuddering and at the brink of orgasm. My stomach muscles contracted, intensifying the sensation; I was sure that the slightest touch of my hand would send me over the top, not knowing if I should, not knowing how to ask for it. I rolled into her and pressed my aching clit desperately against her hip. Suddenly remembering that she had cried "*Fuck!*" as she came, I pushed harder against her, the rawness of that word as it flashed in my mind sending me soaring, coming indescribably hard at the mere thought of her pleasure.

The cries that burst from my throat held more than a decade of yearning and frustration. Someone else's voice seemed to rise from deep within me, explode from my mouth and dissipate into thin air like steam escaping from a screaming kettle. With her arm wrapped around my shoulders, my head against her chest, I felt Beatrice's other hand push between my thighs, the heel of her palm against my clit, her fingers sliding rhythmically inside me, one then two then three, I wasn't sure, it didn't matter. Tears streaming down my face, I came again and again while she fucked me relentlessly and held me tightly in the safety of her embrace.

As the torrent of emotion waned and the world came slowly into focus, I was left awestruck by the force of our passion, amazed by my own potential. We stayed motionless in each other's arms well into the night, neither of us daring to separate, and without so much as a single word, until sleep inevitably inched in like the evening tide.

I know that my first time was so intense because my love for Beatrice was so very great; because only she could have released me so powerfully and with such permanence. I look into her eyes, even today, and I know this is so. I know I am free. I know I am whole. I know I am beautiful. When I look into Beatrice's crystal blue eyes, I always, always know that I am home.

ON FIRE

Rachel Kramer Bussel

"I would do anything for you—anything," I said boastfully, caught up in the throes of lust as I looked at Brenda, all luscious curves that extended from her beautiful breasts down over her slightly rounded stomach to her killer ass and along her thighs. Every part of her made me want to lie down and worship her—with my tongue. Yes, I wanted to make love to her, to push my fingers deep inside her until they unlocked her coils and made her hiss and moan, but I also wanted to take each of her carefully painted toes into my mouth, wanted to trail kisses up the seams on the backs of her stockings, wanted to dig my palms into her shoulders and caress her into oblivion. We were friends, and hung out almost every night. She maintained that she was straight, but that didn't stop her incessant flirting, and sometimes, about once a month or so, we'd come so close to kissing that I'd feel dizzy afterward. She knew I was hopelessly besotted, and she teased me, stringing me along, but I was so turned on I couldn't help it. I really would do anything—almost.

"Okay. If you do this one thing, you can have me—all of me," she said, spreading her arms wide, letting her luxurious red curls bounce along her shoulders. I couldn't believe it, and sat up straight, putting my drink down, my eyes wide with anticipation. I was ready, for sure.

"I want you to eat fire for me. There's this amateur burlesque competition, and I know you could win. I want to watch you shake your ass, showing off those tits you've got buried under there, and I want you to put a flaming torch inside those pretty little lips and make it disappear. I want to hear the crowd go wild for you, and then I want you to come home with me and breathe your fire onto me."

I stared at her like she was crazy. Certifiably nuts, like she was speaking her own language and belonged in a mental hospital. What kind of person wants someone to light her mouth literally on fire to prove her devotion? I knew that other people ate fire, but those were trained professionals. All sorts of images flashed through my head, and none of them involved me in a skimpy outfit trying to impress a crowd of jaded hipsters with an orange flame. I looked at her, my face drained of color, and said, "I'll have to think about it." Then I got up, put some money down on the table, kissed her weakly good-bye on the cheek, and went home.

The first thing I did was lie down on my bed, grateful I lived alone and wouldn't have to contend with any pesky roommates asking what my problem was. I just didn't have the energy to explain. If it were anyone else, I'd tell them where they could put their fire stick, but Brenda was different. She was a ray of light with her bubbly, infectious laugh; bright green eyes; freckles and red hair and anything-goes attitude. Sometimes I half expected us to wind up on a flight to who-knows-where before the night was out. One time she even got me in a taxi headed toward the airport, but I managed to talk some sense into her and we turned around halfway there. That was on a Monday night, mind you. I've found myself in areas of New York City I not only never would've ventured into without her, but also hadn't even known existed. She's an expert at unearthing the overlooked, at figuring out just what someone's limits are, then pushing them to the hilt. She thrives on it, and I knew she'd asked me to eat fire to see if I was really her kind of person, if I'd really go over the top for her, or if I was all talk and no action. I'd been saying I'd do anything for her, but by that I meant take her out to any restaurant, take the day off of work— pamper her, do something *for* her. Not necessarily just do something myself with no obvious payoff for her except to watch me be humiliated.

Yet even as I lay there dramatically on my back with my hand across my forehead, I knew I would do it. How could I not? I hadn't seen most of my other friends much in the last year, unless they came out with me and Brenda, and had let my online profiles languish into oblivion. I wanted Brenda, Brenda, Brenda, and no one else. If this was how I was going to get her, then I'd just have to do things her way. I fell asleep and had dreams of flames licking the walls of my bedroom while I had my face buried inside Brenda, but I didn't wake up scared so much as energized. I was really going to do this, and suddenly, I felt a little bit more powerful, a little cooler—I was going to eat fire.

The first thing I did was go online and read as much as I could about the topic. I'd seen someone do it once at a circus, and the flames had been extinguished almost immediately upon entering the performer's mouth. He'd opened wide like he was eating a s'more, not something that could obliterate his whole face. I wondered whether I could do it—both swallow the flame and make it look effortless. But I knew I'd try, because I'm never one to back down from a challenge, and I *had* said I'd do anything. This feat almost seemed even more exciting than the chance to sleep with Brenda—*almost*.

I asked my best friend, Courtney, who'd run away with the circus when she turned eighteen and done a yearlong stint as a clown, mime and general overall trickster, to help me practice. First, we went out shopping. I thought I had plenty of sexy bras and undies in my drawer, but our trip proved me wrong. Courtney took me to a few shops frequented by strippers where every single item was more flamboyant than even my most risqué outfit or undies. We settled on a plush maroon bra with tassels hanging down below, the kind that made you want to pet it as much as you did my pushed-together breasts—whoever you were. As soon as I saw my cleavage in it, my breasts seeming twice their normal size yet supported by the sturdy material, I knew I had to have it, along with the matching thong. I found some maroon fishnets and tall, shiny black heels to complete the look. I turned this way and that in the mirror, admiring my own ass, sure that I was halfway there.

Now for the hard part. Courtney patiently watched as I made many attempts, chickening out before the flames got anywhere near my lips. I'd always thought there were some things you couldn't simply learn by reading about, fire eating being one of them, so I was also going to learn in the tried and true way—trial and error. I envisioned my mouth moistening around the flame, putting it out in one smooth shot, as the instructions commanded. The torch looked scary once I'd lit it, but I thought of it like my old pet snake, Zilly, who everyone else in junior high had been petrified of, but I'd spent hours sitting around the house with him happily coiled around me. It had been a learning process, but one that made me a better person.

When I wasn't envisioning the flame roaring out from between my lips, I was picturing Brenda, with her tumbles of hair and searing gaze. My fantasies could only go so far because I didn't know what she looked like naked or even what she was really like in bed, so I just focused on her presence; on her stretched out next to me in my queen-size bed, her red hair splayed across my black sheets. Even though I had to focus immensely on what I was doing—holding the torch high above my head, then tilting it upside down, tipping my head back, arching my long tongue out and dipping the wick between my open lips before wrapping them around it to cut off the oxygen supply—somewhere, hovering over everything else, was Brenda. The flame became an extension of her fieriness, her red hair, her laugh—except those were things I didn't want to extinguish.

Keeping my new hobby a secret was pretty easy after I'd made the mistake of telling another friend, Deb. "You WHAT?" she shrieked, then demanded to know every detail, grilling and admonishing me until I felt myself start to doubt my mission.

"Can we change the subject?" I finally asked, my heart beating faster than it had holding that first torch. I was getting better, and under Courtney's steady guidance and patient waiting, I'd even attempted my whole routine, music, fringed bra, fire and all, once. I needed practice, and needed to move faster and steadier, not showing an ounce of the fear lurking below the surface. The fire should reflect my beautifully made-up eyes, my bravery, my tongue boldly going where few had gone before. I knew that Brenda wouldn't be able to resist me, even if she hadn't made this stupid challenge herself. I'd been working out, too, honing and sculpting my body until it looked exactly how I wanted, until I was strong enough that I could literally lift Brenda up and carry her around my apartment if I'd wanted to.

The big day finally arrived. Trying to calm my nerves, I made my way through the theatre to join the other burlesque contestants backstage. I'd attended many shows here, but never thought I'd be the one to take the stage. This time, my audience would be much bigger than simply Courtney in my living room. I peeked out from backstage through the mascara haze, hardly able to stand the jitters and energy coming from the other girls, and smiled to see Brenda shining up front in an elegant black wrap dress and mother of pearl necklace that made her simply sparkle. She outclassed everyone else in the theatre. I stepped back behind the curtain, running my hands over my bra, down the very small curve of my belly, along my ass. I knew I looked good, and I shut my eyes for a moment, picturing my moment of victory. No, not the flame sliding between my elegantly parted lips. The real one, when Brenda walked out with her arm linked in mine, the two of us the belles of this wacky, downtown ball.

I listened as the crowd hooted and hollered for the other performers, snuck glances as the contestants shook and shimmied to everything from classics to punk rock to R&B, from love songs to "fuck you" songs. And then it was my turn. At first, I'd wanted something slow and sensual, something I could dance and writhe around to, but the more I'd thought about it, the more I'd wanted a song that was in-your-face, the kind of song best illuminated by disco balls and dazzling flame. I wouldn't need to move fast as I'd have a stick of fire burning before me. I'd rummaged through my CD collection and found a classic from my early twenties—"Nightlife," by Kenickie, a wonderfully girlie British bit of power pop crossed with just the hint of snarling brattiness I wanted. Plus it was short, which was good because I didn't know how long I could pull off my bravado. But the element I'd missed in my practice sessions was the cheering crowd. Even if all I did was hold the glowing torch above me and look pretty, they'd be won over. Even Brenda, I soon realized, as my flame reflected her beaming smile, her usually been-there-done-that attitude gone in a swarm of pride for me. I soaked it in, loving every second as I played with the fringe, used the stick to emphasize the loud girl shouts, then got ready for the moment of truth.

I stretched it out as long as I could, crossing my legs, one against the other for support, then tilted my head back, grateful for the expertly coiled bun Courtney had fashioned my hair into, and opened wide. I held the stick above me, then twirled it down in one move as I'd practiced. I opened my eyes to see the flame heading toward me, then closed them and visualized me and Brenda fucking through a blaze of fire, ready to burn for the thrill of touching each other's bodies. The flame dove perfectly between my lips and I'd extinguished it so quickly I almost didn't notice my mouth touching the pole, then instantly opened my lips and pulled it out. There were a few more seconds of music that I let play on while I held the cooling stick in both hands above my head in victory, leaned forward and shook my tassels, then spun around to provide a view of my ass, and marched off. I sank into a chair immediately and stayed slumped there through the next two acts, relieved and grateful to have survived.

Finally, I was ready to head back out there. As the show wound down, I saw that a seat had somehow opened up next to Brenda. I slipped into it, and her hand immediately reached for mine, like we were some old couple. It wasn't merely a friendly hand-holding either. Her fingers immediately started massaging mine, soothing me, calming me. "You were beautiful, darling," she whispered in my ear, letting her lips hover there for just enough time to make my nipples bead against the heavy bra. She was telling me that tonight was the night, not simply because of a won bet or a technicality, but because she wanted it. Maybe she'd known exactly what she was doing all along with her incessant flirting, or maybe this time apart had made her think about me, and us. Whatever it was, I was grateful, and rested my head against her shoulder, breathing in her vanilla scent as she put her arm around me. We watched the rest of the performers. When it came time for the winners to be announced, Brenda clutched my hand tightly, almost smashing it when it was announced that I'd won second place. She gave me a huge kiss before ushering me onstage, and told me that I was robbed; knowing I was number one in her eyes was all I needed.

Then the time came to leave. I just put my long coat on over the bra and panty ensemble, too high off the night's energy to change. People had been coming up to me all night congratulating me and asking questions, and for the very first time, I was the star instead of Brenda. She didn't seem to mind though, but she did keep her hand clasped in mine, guarding off would-be suitors.

We strode out and walked the five blocks to my apartment. I'd stocked up on all kinds of sex toys, candles, and snacks, and had redone my bedroom, hanging gauzy pieces of fabric over the windows and lights, buying even finer, softer sheets—only the best for my girl. "Wait right here," I told her, pushing her down onto the living room couch, giving her a brief peck on the lips, then racing around and lighting the many votive candles dotting my room until it glowed with a dusky light. When I went to fetch her, she had her eyes closed and I worried that she might be asleep. When I approached, she stirred, staring at me with lust and awe—the same way I'd been looking at her since we'd met. The look on her face told me that whatever had happened since she'd issued her ultimatum, she was here for the same reason I was—she wanted me just as much as I wanted her. Our first real kiss found my lips crushed against her heavenly ones, her surprisingly strong hands gripping me tight.

"You're so beautiful," we echoed each other, our fingers tracing each other's faces. I still almost couldn't believe that *my* Brenda was actually in bed with me. The pressures leading up to this night seemed to melt away, even though part of me knew I was still riding the adrenaline high of baring my body—and my bravado—in front of so many people. Still, in some ways, being so intimate with Brenda made me even more vulnerable, which is why I decided to take control.

"Now, my darling, I've been so patient waiting for you to

see the light, I think I deserve a little prize for all my hard work today—don't you?" Before she could say yes or no, I'd fastened a blindfold over her eyes. Next I sucked on her earlobe, tugging the tender flesh between my teeth. I slipped a finger into her mouth, feeling her tongue instantly seek out its tip, sucking me deeper inside. Oh, yes, I had my sly little Brenda pegged all right—she was one of those tough-on-the-streets, submissive-slut-in-the-sheets kind of girls.

"Now you really look beautiful," I told her, as I lifted her arms above her head, trapping them between fur-lined hand-cuffs. She moaned as I placed them around her, not making a single movement to escape. She wanted this, and from the throbbing in my pussy as I bound her wrists together, I realized that I did too. I'd known it, but I hadn't really known what a rush I would get out of controlling my favorite little vixen. "Now I'm really going to heat things up," I said, the sound of the match striking the matchbook echoing loudly against our ears. Just seeing the flame reminded me of what I'd done earlier, but whereas that had been all spectacle and sass, blaze and glory, this was a calmer fire, a private one. I lit a purple candle, transferring the heated glow and blowing out the match.

I took the candle and lazily trailed it along her skin, tipping it so the flame hovered several inches above her stomach, enough so she could feel its warmth. "Ow," she giggled, a very un-Brenda-like sound yet one I longed to hear again. I let a drop of the wax collide with her belly, watching the purple pool against her pale skin. She whimpered, her body rippling as she angled away and then toward the flame, afraid to want more, even though she did.

"Hey, I did what you wanted today, you can take a little

wax, can't you?" I asked, smearing in the warm, gooey cream of it as she grinned at me. My other hand trailed down to her pussy, finding the trimmed red hairs there and tugging on them gently. I swept my fingers across her inner thighs, pushing my short nails along her delicate, pale skin. I wanted to be inside her so badly, but I knew I had to wait. I spread her legs, noting the moisture along her sweet lips, then took the candle and made lines going up and down her thighs. "I'm going to fuck you so hard, Brenda, you'll be feeling it for days. Just as soon as I pour the wax from this candle all over you," I said, my words making her shudder.

Watching the wax cover each new part of her, her body assimilating its heat quicker and quicker, made me proud. I watched as the liquid dribbled onto her; tested myself by aiming at certain spots, diving lower with the flame, then pulling upward as it arced all the way down. She thrust against her bonds, shifting slightly, but not enough to dislodge the blindfold. Her lips kept opening and then closing, yearning for something to taste, something to suck. When the candle was nearly done, I took pity on her, blowing it out and offering her the waxy, non-wicked end. My little slut took even that, though I only made her taste it for a moment, more a test of wills than anything else.

My fingers dove along her slit, parting her lips and entering her heated sex. "Oh, you're ready all right," I said as she drew me deeper inside. Whether or not she'd ever fucked or been fucked by another girl no longer mattered—she wanted me. I'd saved my favorite toy for last, and in mere moments, I had gotten naked and slid the cock into its harness. I mounted her, greedy to shove the fat dildo into her dripping hole. It was the biggest one they'd had at the store, but she took it like it was nothing, like it was my finger, or the slim candle, and I rocked against her. I'd been planning to untie her, but the look on her face as her arms strained against the cuffs, her eyes shielded, her mouth seeking, was too precious. I thrust the cock in and out of her, watching its black surface emerge sleek and shiny, her juices coating it from the start. I was so horny I imagined I could feel her squeezing the dick, giving herself to me again and again, just as I'd given myself to her today. It was all worth it as the cock pressed against my clit while filling her completely, and I made sure to take her right to the edge, then pause. I peeled some of the pretty purple wax off her, but left most of it, then concentrated on pumping her fast and hard. Her nipples beckoned to me, and I heeded their call, twisting one as I balanced my other hand against the bed. She shuddered as I pinched her nub between my fingers; this new, needy creature before me not quite the girl I'd pursued so valiantly all these weeks, but someone hotter for showing me this new side. Eating fire was nothing compared to sinking my cock—myself—into Brenda, the moment purely ours as we joined together. I let my hand wander down to her clit, stroking her nub until she buckled, spasming against my touch, her body jerking all around. I lifted the blindfold so she could watch as I thrust into her a few final times before I too came, then collapsed on top of her, our sweaty bodies pasted together by wax and desire.

"You didn't really mean it, did you—your ultimatum?" I asked, pinching her cheek lightly. "You wanted me all along, I can tell." The thought was just now sinking in.

"Maybe," was all I could get out of her, but her twinkling eyes gave her away. I didn't mind though—it's not every girl I'd eat fire for, and most girls wouldn't even think to ask.

ONE SOLID YELLOW ASTER

Zaedryn Meade

I knock on the door and wait. Five flights up
to the run-down Chinatown loft and they're
not even home. Great. I knock again. Finally,
a girl answers the door wearing nothing but a
thin white robe, somewhat sheer, dripping off
of one shoulder. It looks silky, soft. She may
have nothing underneath. It covers her knees
but is loosely tied, generously gaping at her
thighs. I don't stare. I try not to think about
how cliché this is. Her eyes light up at the sight
of me, my black-and-white delivery uniform,
the huge bouquet of spring wildflowers cradled in one arm. Ten stems of larkspur, seven
blue iris, and one solid yellow aster, accented
with "lush greenery and festive purple-tinted
foliage." One of the more popular deliveries
now that it's spring. Pretty, but not a lot of

imagination, which is unfortunate; this girl clearly deserves something unique.

She looks familiar, actually, but I can't place her face. Maybe I've slept with her before.

"Delivery," I say, looking down at the well-organized list on the clipboard in my other hand. "For Rachel…" I recognize her last name and suddenly struggle with it.

"That's me," she says, leaning slightly against the hallway just inside the door, an amused smile on her face. "What, you don't remember me, Zed?"

"No, I do, I'm sorry, I uh…you cut your hair," I try to justify.

She fingers the back of her neck. "For a play, a few months ago. It's growing out. Taking a lot of getting used to. Are those seriously for me?" she asks, eyes on the iris.

"Just sign here." I offer the clipboard, then hand over the vase.

We stand awkwardly for a moment, then she says, "Come in, have a glass of something."

"I can't, I…" but before I can answer she's already turned, walking down the hallway, readying the flowers for display. She leaves the door open and doesn't look back to see if I'm following; she knows I will.

"I didn't know you moved to Manhattan," I start. "Last I knew you were in Queens, with…what's her name?"

Rachel rolls her eyes. "Alexis. Don't remind me; that was a mess. Well, I'm here now. Who sent the flowers?" she asks, smoothly maneuvering the conversation in that way she always could.

I check the clipboard. No name. We tend not to allow that, actually; too many weirdos. She's examining the bouquet: no card. I wonder if it was Alexis. I wonder how long ago they broke up. "Don't know," I say. "No name. Your girlfriend, boyfriend, one-night stand from last night maybe?"

Rachel rolls her eyes visibly. "Not possible," she says airily, running the stems under water as she slices them and puts them back in the vase in some particular Rachel order. I lean against the counter. "I'm not seeing anyone anymore. They aren't from you, are they? Some far-fetched attempt to get back with me?"

"We were never together," I remind her. "But no, they aren't from me. I didn't even know you lived here."

"We should've been together," she purrs, leaving the flowers and moving close to me, closer, a little too close. She's going to kiss me or grab the waist of my jeans any second. "You know it. Are you sure it wasn't you? You always were so...bold with me."

Her hair smells like girl product, flowery and fruity. I notice it's a little damp. "Did I interrupt you?" I ask, touching the tie of her robe that would unknot with the gentlest tug.

"I was in the bath," Rachel says, turning back to the flowers, twisting a few stems, fingering the petals. She picks up the vase and moves to the cream-colored couch—the two rooms connected and open—setting them on the end table, and calls, "So, you still single?"

I swallow. "Actually, yes. Actually, I'm not even really... sleeping with anybody these days. It's been quite a while."

She looks at me questioningly, eyebrows raised. "Really. That's different, for you. Well, me too," she offers. She settles onto the couch, pulls her knees up underneath her, pats the cushion next to her. "I miss being with someone, but it's kind of nice to have time to myself."

"I think what I miss most is the kissing," I say, setting down, getting into it. "Really deep, or light, or whatever, just lots of kissing." And her mouth is so fucking pretty. It's hard not to think of kissing.

"Yeah, I miss the kissing...and I miss light touching...the kind that almost tickles."

"Yeah, I love that," I answer. "Especially after."

"Yes," she says, breathes in. "After."

Her lips curl and part and I can almost see her warm breath moving between them. I try not to stare. "I love it when you smile like that," I say quietly.

She doesn't really hear me, or maybe she does, but keeps going. "I tend to want to hold on to the person I'm with after. Lots of silence and breathing." Her eyes soften.

"I love that. That closeness can be so intense, and beautiful. When you feel like your bodies are so close and connected...it can be amazing."

"You know what else I miss?" Her voice gets anxious, faster. "The intense feeling of being wanted...the *before*. The moment when you suddenly feel so wanted...so sexy...just from the energy coming off of the other person."

"Yeah, I miss the wanting," I agree. "I always feel so transparent. I always think I'm hiding it, but I wear my emotions so obviously."

"Oh, me too. I become bold in certain instances, though. I start saying what I'm thinking out loud. I stop being embarrassed." Rachel's eyes shine playfully.

I'm still thinking about her kissing comment, and her mouth, her skin, her taste. Kissing everywhere. "Kissing is so similar to...going down on a girl, too, which I also just love, and miss."

"Jesus…" she says, almost under her breath. Her body flutters a little, which is exactly what I wanted. "I haven't had the pleasure of doing that in…over a year," she says. "I haven't done it that much, but I miss it, a lot actually. It seems I miss a lot of things."

"Yeah, there's a lot to miss." I pause, then continue, absently brushing my hand against her knee, exposed through a gap in her robe. She watches my fingers. "I love that moment when it turns from kissing to sex."

She leans her head back just slightly. "That moment when a hand slips under your shirt just slightly. Like it's asking for permission. And then when your body gives it, by pushing back just so."

"I miss the throw-down, the taking control. I love that feeling, when I have permission to do it." I'm feeling bold. She always could do this to me.

"And I love surrendering. In that sudden, amazing moment where I feel completely taken care of…so I no longer need control. Control is so vital for me in most of my life…so when I'm able to give it up…it's thrilling."

"I miss having someone trust me like that." I stop again. Something occurs to me, and I smile. She's caught. "Are you trying to seduce me?"

"What," she says, eyes sparkling, "am I not making it obvious enough?"

She moves toward me, as if to straddle me, but I move to push her down onto the couch at the same moment and instead, neither of us goes anywhere. I get caught up, ahead of myself, and shy all at once. But it's her, Rachel, my Rachel, the girl I used to dance with every weekend at Meow Mix, who I used to run into everywhere, who I used to fantasize about while getting off with someone else. Something about her hips, the perfect roundness of her breasts, her fucking perfect mouth. I've wanted her for so long. Shit. I laugh, mostly at myself, softly, to cover up the desire. "Why do I feel so…? I've had a crush on you since—when? Ninety-seven?"

"Ninety-eight. And it's mutual," she says, gazing at me with that seductive Rachel look. "Don't be shy."

I run my fingers along her cheek, then her jaw, to the back of her neck where her short hair is still a surprise. "A long time."

"Yes," she says. "A long time." Damn, she is *on*. I breathe and clear my throat again. Nervous. I look around her new place and admire her music posters, theatre posters, delicate decorations. The early afternoon sun creeps through her windows and the airy orange-yellow curtains paint pastel tones through the open rooms. Most of her shelves and walls are still bare, and small stacks of boxes are tucked in between the furniture.

"How long have you been at this place?" I ask.

She stiffens a little, but doesn't falter. "More than a month," she says. "It's starting to feel like home, but…I haven't even unpacked my vibrator yet. Isn't that awful? It's not lost," she corrects herself. "It's just hiding out. It's been…six months I think. I've lost my drive entirely."

I glance at her sideways. "You should unpack it."

"I should unpack it, huh? So it can sit in the nightstand." She sighs dramatically. "This conversation has depressed me. Lord, and you always said that I was the tease."

"I'm not trying to depress you, rather the opposite—to inspire."

"Well. Yes." She presses up against me, lowers her voice, lowers her eyes, lowers her hand to my crotch, attempting to be subtle and still obviously checking to see if I'm packing. "Do that. Inspire me. Please?"

"You really haven't had sex in six months?"

"Seven." she says, recalculating, certain this time. "Seven months."

I clear my throat, swallow. There is little more that I would rather do than spend the afternoon in bed with this beautiful girl. But I'm so loaded down with deliveries today, and I need to get ready for a date tonight—pick up some wine, tidy the apartment. How can I exit gracefully? "Rach...I have to go, I have more deliveries, a full schedule this afternoon."

"Yeah I know, I have work to do too. I'm supposed to be at the theatre in half an hour. But...I just want you to...tell me more."

I look at the clock on my cell phone and gauge my afternoon, counting the minutes in my head. I see her watching me. "Fifteen minutes," I offer. I can't just leave, not with her all smooth and bare and begging on the couch next to me like this. "We'll see how far I can get."

"Yes," she nods, and kisses me, gives herself over, her mouth like a ritual offering. Warm, soft. She's already making those little *oh*s and *mm*s from her throat.

I don't waste any time. I pull her robe from her shoulders and press my hands inside, touching her skin, her beautiful curves.

"Bedroom," I say, an order and a question. She moves her tongue over her lips where I've pulled away, her body thick and wanting, then stands and leads me. Her robe is falling off of her everywhere and she doesn't stop to adjust it.

Her bedroom is set up in an elaborate romantic scene of lit candles and slow music, with soft blankets on the bed. It's darker than the living room because the curtains are thick, but there's still some daylight trickling through. I wonder if I had been expected. If she'd known I was going to come. I slip the robe to the floor and lay her down naked, taking my time, slow, excruciatingly slow, lying next to her, kissing, hands everywhere.

She pulls on my black pants, my button-down white shirt that seems strangely formal next to her naked skin. She's trying to rush me, wants me up in her, wants me exploding in her, wants me everywhere all at once. I notice massage oil on the nightstand. No vibrator, but oil. I imagine her in here after her bath, skin supple and puckered from soaking too long, slathering oil along her freshly shaved legs, hands, elbows, breasts. Sitting alone with the oil on her skin.

I pick it up and rub my hands with it, put my hands on her belly, her legs, her hips.

"Why would you make me wait, after all this time, huh?" Her eyes flash, she's curious and frustrated and desperate all at once.

"Because I can," I say. "Because you're looking at me with all that want. I can feel it from here."

"So what, you're going to torture me?"

"Maybe not entirely. And you'd like that, anyway." I see right through her.

She breathes in, sighs. "You know me too well."

I keep going, lovely soft touches, lots of kissing. She tries to get to my buttons, the seam of my pants, and I have to grab her wrists every once in a while, set her arms above her head, hold them to her sides.

"I can be pretty good at doing what I'm told," Rachel whispers. "Just ask."

"I want to touch you," I say. "I want to see if you can just lie back quietly and feel me, without moving, without responding. Just lie back and feel me." I feel her relax, and run my hands over her skin, run my fingers along her legs and arms; her sides, a little ticklish; her back; her stomach. She tries to stay still, she does, but it's hard for her not to move. Her back has a tendency to arch at will. It's beautiful. I can hear her breathing deepen, grow heavier. Her skin is all honey and smooth, sweet and dimpled, freckled in places, contoured perfectly. I don't know how many times I've been up against her begging for this to happen, don't know how many times I've been at home alone wishing for this skin to be under my hands. I maneuver my body above hers, between her legs, softly; she opens quickly and her hips curl, knees bend. I hold myself up by my arms, not really touching her, watching her eyes, her skin as she flushes and struggles for control over her desire.

I kiss her, soft and deep, and let some of my weight fall on top of her. She has trouble keeping quiet. Whispers and sighs and moans.

I feather my fingers over her chest, trace her breasts, barely touch her nipples. "You're so beautiful," I whisper. It takes restraint not to press inside her, hard, not to fuck her *now*.

She whimpers a little. "This is hard," she says. "I'm really trying not to just...open my legs so you can feel me."

"I could get used to this view of you, naked under me like this," I say. She's open, so open. All blushing and wanting.

She circles her hips and tries to remember that I asked her to be still. "I have wanted you to fuck me for a very long time," she says slowly, choosing her words deliberately, making sure I hear every single one and all she's not saying in between.

I start with my fingers, just barely touching her thighs, the creases at her hips, her stomach; touching the hair between her legs but only so she can feel where my fingers are. I kiss her, soft, slow; moving against her, agonizingly tender. I move the other hand to her hair, so short now, and stroke the back of her neck.

She starts pressing up into me, whispering, "I want you."

I pause, smile into her neck, kissing. "Yeah? How much?"

She moans. "So much," she offers. "I haven't been...like this...in so long. You're softer than I imagined you'd be."

I harden temporarily. "I don't have to be soft," I say, almost defensively.

"I know you don't... I can't stop thinking about how you'll feel inside me... Please, I want to feel you, I can't wait... I don't know how much longer I can keep still." Her eyes are pleading, her lips parting. Her skin is amazing, all cream and sugar. I'm sure the folds of her are, too. It's so pale in places, stretched taut over muscle and curves, I sometimes expect to be able to see through it. My fingers are still between her legs, giving feathery touches, teasing. I slowly, slowly start letting my touch get firmer, cupping her cunt with my palm, feeling the heat of her in my hand.

"I'm asking you to," I say again. "Just a little longer. I know you want to please me."

She breathes and her body quiets. "Yes." She focuses on my fingers, the sensation, my weight on her hips, pushing her legs open.

"Good," I say. "That's good. You deserve a reward." I barely touch one finger between her lips, dip it in just a little, and wait for her to push against me, taking it inside. She does, immediately. Hard against me, pulling my index finger into her, the pulse of her around me, wet, slick and tight.

"This is beautiful," she whispers, closing her eyes.

"I want more than one finger inside you," I whisper. One of the few moments of explicit permission I'm going to pull from her.

She breathes out. "Yes please." I love feeling as the muscles change and clench from inside. I leave my fingers still, let her move on them, two fingers, three. Moving inside, curling against the muscles, but not moving in and out.

She whispers yes. Yes. Her hips thrust against me. I can feel her, swollen, squeeze around my fingers. I raise myself above her, hold myself up; she knows why and unzips me, pulls out my cock; apparently this morning I had packed it just for her, yellow and solid and thick. She puts her fingers around it, feeling the length and girth of it. This wasn't planned. She's so open already, so expertly sliding her fingers along the shaft and head of it, pulling, tugging my hips toward her. I try not to think of what it would feel like sliding into her. It makes me wet and hard and sends my hips bucking without even trying.

Her mouth is open, legs open, arms reaching, eyes glazing and thick. "Please," she says, fast, whispering, just a hint of desperation behind her tongue. "I need it inside me."

I touch just the tip of it to her cunt and feel her pull me inside. Then I am still again, I let my weight rest on top of her, just feeling her around me. I slowly pull out, then press back inside, deeper. She feels amazing under me like that. She's made for my cock, the exact contours of her were built for this moment, this motion, this cock inside of her, fitting perfectly.

"Take me, yes, I want you to take me," she whispers, gasping. "Yes...oh yes, exactly. Like that." She is so wet for me. Under me. She slides her fingers in my mouth and I suck. She touches her clit and I can feel her shudder while I'm inside and holding her.

"Let me come around you," she whispers into my neck, arms wrapped around my shoulders. I groan. God. I kiss her neck, her cheeks, her lips, her collarbone; press in and out of her, match her rhythm. I stay slow and soft and deep, over and over; look into her eyes, kiss her.

"God, you're so beautiful," I say.

"I'm so close…" she gasps, eyes tightly shut, fingers digging into my arms, then looking up at me, right into my gasping face, panting, thrusting against me. "Do you want me come now, like this?"

She's under me, my cock in her, my weight on her, taking me in all the way, I can feel how tight her muscles are, pulling me in deep. I shudder, my eyes rolling. Fuck. Do I want her to come like this? Is there anything else I have ever wanted more? She could probably say anything and it would send me over the edge right now, but damn that was a good choice of words. The fucking nerve of her sometimes.

"Yes, god yes, I want you to come, just like this." Her legs are squeezing around me, her slick pussy lips around my cock, and she's kissing me until she can't and her mouth opens in a quiet scream, pushing against her muscles, against her body, against the edges. I feel her stomach curl and pulse. Her muscles tense, she gasps for air, the smallest smile on her lips. I keep my mouth on hers, hold her close to me, the weight of me on her, between her hips, still thrusting in her, steady and hard, until she shudders against me and makes me stop.

I hold her after, curl around her; feel her skin where her scars are, where she's bruised, where she's ticklish. But I have to go. I'm going to be behind already, will have to rush the rest of the afternoon. I pick up the thin white robe and slip it over her skin, then button my shirt, buckle my belt, tuck my shirt back in.

She walks me toward the door, hands me my clipboard with the florist orders on it, her signature bouncy in the middle of the top sheet. "So," I say, "who really sent the flowers?"

She shrugs, dismisses the question. "I wouldn't know."

"Come on, admit it. You sent them yourself. You knew I'd show up to deliver them."

"Are you kidding?" she asks. "As though I have time to hunt down every hot dyke I've crushed on." But she wouldn't have had to hunt me down. I've worked at this same place for years.

Rachel kisses me once more, and closes the door behind me. I believe her, almost.

A TASTE OF SIN

Fiona Zedde

Dez sat on her bike outside the bar smoking a cigarette and waiting for her best friend to show. The night's entertainment seemed promising. Women walked past, darting their eyes over her even as they clutched the hands of the men by their sides. Dez's tank top stretched taut over her chest, cleaving to the tight body, the small high breasts and flat stomach. Worn blue jeans, a thick leather belt and Timberlands completed a package that Dez knew was fuck-worthy. She didn't have to see the want in these women's eyes to know that. But it didn't hurt.

"When you're done posing, you want to come into the bar with me?" It was Rémi, who'd just ridden up on her bike, the laughter rich in her voice even under the dark helmet. She wore all black today. And spurs on her motor-cycle boots.

Inside, they turned their helmets over to the bartender and parked themselves at the bar with two shots of tequila, a pitcher of beer, an ashtray, and a pack of cigarettes between them. The crowd was hot tonight—affluent, beautiful, a nice mix of races and cultures. A conversation in Spanish tickled Dez's ear from halfway across the room and from somewhere else a hint of Jamaican Patois rubbed up against Haitian-accented French. Rémi knocked back her tequila.

"Nice." Her glance traveled around the bar, taking in the view.

It didn't take long for the festivities to begin. A silver-bangled arm nudged Rémi's, then the accompanying body did the same.

"Excuse me," the stranger said. "I didn't see you sitting there."

Liar. The brown-skinned *mami* licked her gaze up and down Rémi's body, taking her time at the highlights—breasts, hips, ass. She wasn't bad either, with her curvaceous form poured into a Donna Karan dress of the same luscious tone as her skin. But she had on too much makeup.

"Please, excuse *me*," Rémi said, moving neatly back and out of her way. Reaching to ash her cigarette in the heavy silver disc in front of her friend, she turned to Dez. "I wonder what's keeping Ricky. You can't trust boyfriends for shit, huh?"

The pretty stranger almost swallowed her tongue in surprise. She ordered a drink she probably didn't even want and fled.

"That wasn't nice."

"What do you want me to do, give her a pity fuck just for trying?" Rémi snorted and took a sip of her beer, balancing her cigarette between her fuck-fingers and the glass. "I didn't see you offering your pretty little self in my place."

"It was you she wanted, not me."

"These days I'm not settling for just anything."

"When have you ever had to settle?"

"You'd be surprised." Smoke spiraled up from Rémi's cigarette and she squinted against its bite. "Nowadays any pussy that comes to me has to be good pussy, or at least interesting pussy. It can't just be any old shit."

"I still don't know when the hell you've ever had to take just whatever."

"Two years is a long time, isn't it?" Rémi put down her drink and looked at Dez. "There's actually someone—"

"Baby, you must be a model," a voice interrupted. "That body of yours is just *too* fine."

Dez looked past Rémi to the guy with the midnight skin, beautiful teeth, and asshole leer. His eyes eagerly drank Rémi in, while next to him, his friend smiled quickly at Dez.

"You play ball?" the second one asked.

Rémi turned to look at the two men. That was an original question. What else would two six-foot-tall black women do for a living or for fun?

"We don't play with balls." Her amused eyes flickered over them, then turned away in dismissal.

The friend eyed Dez and tried a leer of his own. "How about you? Can I buy you a drink?"

Whenever they were out together and straight boys saw Rémi first they always asked if the women were models, trying to lure them into some vanity trap because of Rémi's pretty skin, quiet self-confidence, and devil's mouth. But when they saw Dez first the lead-in was usually about basketball or some other height-requiring sport. Never mind that the two women were the same height.

"No thanks, I already got what I'm drinking," Dez said.

"What about you, baby?"

"Same thing," Rémi said, holding up her beer.

Admittedly, most men often saw what they wanted to where women were concerned, but wasn't it obvious that she and Rémi were dykes? Or was this about the challenge and a potential foursome? The men looked expectantly at them.

"We're not interested," Rémi said firmly.

"You sure?" the first one asked, looking her up and down.

"Very."

The two women found something much more interesting to look at when a dark-skinned honey slid up to the bar, insinuating her body between Rémi's and the interloping men.

"Hey, handsome," she murmured, leaning in even closer to Rémi. "I would *love* to eat your pussy."

The silence in the immediate area was deafening. Dez and Rémi sized her up—striking features, including pillowy lips touched by a hint of lip gloss. Close-cut hair and long silver earrings dangling to her shoulders. Short skirt showing off lean legs and a juicy ass. Very nice.

The two women exchanged looks. Very, very nice.

"Want to make it a threesome?" Rémi looked her over again. "My friend here really loves your ass."

The woman glanced from one to the other. This was probably the best two-for-one deal she'd ever been offered. "Sure. My place is just up the street."

"Damn! It's like that?" The cocky boy who'd hit on Rémi first was the first to speak. A domino effect of speculative murmurs sped around the bar.

Dez and Rémi quickly settled up with the bartender, grabbed their helmets, and followed the woman out the door. They rode the short five blocks behind the woman's black Infiniti truck. All they knew was that her name was Jeanne and she lived in a townhouse near the beach. No roommate, boyfriend or girlfriend at home.

The two women parked their bikes in her driveway, refusing the use of the space behind her in the garage. They weren't going to stay that long. Once they were all in the house, Jeanne's cool composure melted.

"You are so fucking hot." She grabbed Rémi, touching her through her clothes and kneading the solid muscles with wonder.

The tall woman let Jeanne caress her, chuckling while the slim hands burrowed beneath the leather and cotton. She grinned at Dez over the woman's head. Rémi lived for moments like this, when a woman appreciated how much time she spent making her body look perfect.

Jeanne reached back and tangled her fingers in Dez's shirt, pulling her up hard and rubbing the sleek, denim-covered thighs as she angled her head up to sample Rémi's mouth. She leaned back into Dez and purred.

The woman felt hot against Dez's breasts. Dez nuzzled the back of Jeanne's neck and reached around to cup the heavy breasts in her hands. *Oh. What's this?* She fumbled to unbutton Jeanne's blouse, but the woman eluded her, pulling back from Rémi and Dez to watch their faces as she tugged off her blouse and tiny skirt. She wore no panties.

Oh, yeah? Jeanne wore nipple clamps, silver beauties pinched tight to her fat nipples with a chain dangling low on her belly and attached to the matching clamp on her clit.

Rémi's eyes became megawatt bright.

Jeanne stood posing in the middle of the spacious living room, the light bouncing off the Y-shaped chain attached to the clamps. "Would you two like a drink?"

"We don't want anything to drink," Rémi said. "We want to fuck. Isn't that what you brought us here for?" She took off her jacket, then pulled a pair of latex gloves from her back pocket, put them on, and coated them with lube. "Come here."

Jeanne came obediently, but still teased with her head held high and her mouth curved in a secret smile that said she was doing Rémi a favor by walking across the room to her. The chain wriggled against her skin as she moved.

"Nice jewelry." Rémi gripped the chain where it caressed Jeanne's belly, and tugged.

The woman gasped in pain, even as her ass rolled and turned up asking for more.

"I'm going to change your script a little," Rémi said, meeting Dez's eyes over the woman's head. She wanted that ass. Dez nodded and backed up to sit in a nearby armchair, a pretty floral thing that smelled faintly of perfume, and wait. Rémi was running this show.

She kissed Jeanne, sucked her plum purple mouth, and turned the woman's ass for Dez to admire. When Rémi bent Jeanne just a little, Dez licked her lips at the glistening pink slit and the darker pucker of her asshole that Rémi fingered and teased, her gloves wet with lube.

Rémi worked the woman, caressing and kissing her, tugging on the Y-chain until Jeanne gasped and the tips of her breasts became swollen and distended. Her thighs gleamed wet with cunt juice. Rémi turned her again, showed the woman's tits to

Dez as she squeezed them from the back, then ran her gloved hands down Jeanne's belly and toward the swollen clit while Jeanne's eyelashes beat uncontrollably and her mouth fell open to gulp more air.

Dez eased back in the chair and undid the buttons of her jeans. She slid the pants down and over her ass as she watched, her pussy getting juicer, tightening, anticipating the mouth that would surely lick it wet then dry after all this buildup. Her tits throbbed with a sweet pain under the little tank top.

Rémi spread Jeanne's legs and pushed her slightly forward toward Dez, as if Jeanne was asking her for a light or something equally incendiary. Jeanne's face changed when Rémi started to fuck her. She seemed to stretch, elongating herself to accommodate Rémi's fingers and her desire, her face becoming taut and hard, needful. Low, long sounds left her mouth. Jeanne leaned forward, bracing herself on Dez's chair. Rémi slowed the pace of her fucking.

"Make my friend come," said Rémi. "At least twice. She's very particular. No hands, and don't put your tongue in her pussy." She flicked Jeanne's clit and the woman jumped, almost falling to her knees in front of Dez. "No matter what, don't stop. Understand?" When Jeanne nodded, her body quivering and damp with sweat, Rémi reached into her pocket for a pack of dental dams and took one out. "Use this."

Jeanne reached blindly for Dez's naked pussy, opening her mouth wide for it despite the awkward angle of the jeans rucked up at Dez's knees. Even through the barrier of the plastic, her tongue was heaven to Dez. Her heated mouth, the flat of Jeanne's tongue against Dez's shaved pussy and the hot suction on Dez's clit were all heaven as Jeanne anchored her hands on her hips, her head bobbing with each yawn and snap of her mouth. Dez loved the hungry noises the other woman made in her throat. They made her pussy feel wanted, made it open up and salivate, eager to be devoured. She pressed Jeanne's head deeper into her pussy. The thick hair tickled her palms as she guided the skilled mouth to exactly where it needed to be.

Jeanne knew what she was doing. Even with Rémi working her pussy hard from the back, fucking her with a lovely liquid sound, she focused on the task at hand. She damn near swallowed Dez's clit. The come snuck up on her, lifting up her hips and carrying her away on a swift tide of sensation that left her breathless and shaking, but still wanting more.

Beyond the rising peach curve and cleft of the woman's ass, Rémi fucked her with gloved fingers, plunging in deep with her face a hard mask of concentration and her lips skinned back against her teeth in a feral grin. Her breath whistled with each exhalation. As Dez shuddered in the throes of her first come, Rémi pulled her fingers from the sticky sheath of Jeanne's pussy and slapped her hard. The woman jumped, bumping her mouth hard against Dez's clit.

"Shit!" The woman's muffled cry of surprise sent a jolt of electric heat slamming between Dez's thighs. She moaned and widened her thighs as far as the jeans would let her.

Rémi slapped her again and again, the sounds thick and hot in the room, mingling with the slurp of Jeanne's mouth on Dez's pussy, her groans, and the steady heavy breath whistling through Rémi's teeth. She slapped her asscheeks, her thighs and the tender flesh between them. Jeanne gasped and jerked, eating Dez's pussy in earnest as the pain spread through her body. Dez knew exactly how she felt, could feel the heat in her own thighs, the sweet clench of her pussy at that twin-edged pain. A fiery wave rolled through her. She threw her head back and held on. This one was going to be good.

Rémi started to fuck their little playmate again. Jeanne's tongue flew over Dez's clit, licking the tender bundle of nerves harder and faster. Through the haze of pleasure Dez looked up at Rémi. Her friend nodded. They pulled off Jeanne's clamps at the same time. The woman screamed and her knees buckled, but Rémi held her up. Jeanne kept at Dez's clit, licking and sucking until Dez's wave crested and she bucked against Jeanne's mouth, holding her head steady while Dez's pussy fisted, flooding come against the plastic barrier of the dental dam and on the pretty floral chair.

"Fuck yes!" Dez groaned.

Jeanne's head hung low as she panted between Dez's thighs. "Damn."

They weren't done yet. At a signal from Rémi, Dez stood up despite her wobbly knees and moved aside so that her friend could take her place in the chair.

"Now, if memory serves, you mentioned something at the beginning of this evening about my pussy and your mouth." Rémi tugged down her zipper, showing off her thick, curling bush. "Come. I'm ready."

BINGO, BABY

Radclyffe

"Honey, let's go in drag tonight."

I looked up from the newspaper and tried to suppress a grin. Shelby is a femme. Not ultra-ultrafemme—no superlong nails or heavy-duty makeup, but she doesn't leave the house without eyeliner, either. Plus, she's small. Okay, *petite*. Her head comes to my chest. But she's perfectly built—every part of her—from her pert, high breasts to her nicely rounded, squeezable ass. But no one, nohow, would take her for a guy. Not even with a twelve-inch dick. "Sure, baby, but we only brought one dick."

It's tough packing toys when you travel, and the security people at the airport in Provincetown check *everything*. But then I guess they've *seen* everything, too, and there's no way I was going on vacation without my equipment. Still, I couldn't bring a complete complement either, so we both wouldn't be able to dress in full gear.

Shel's lush pink lips parted, her tongue peeked out as she ran it lightly over the velvet surface, and my mind turned to oatmeal. "We only *need* one. For me."

I got hold of myself and dragged my thoughts away from what she could do with that tongue. "Huh? What am *I* going to wear, then?"

"This," she replied sweetly as she held up a tiny swatch of leather.

I paled. "That's a skirt."

"Uh-huh."

"It's yours."

"Uh-huh."

"I can't wear *that*." I started to sweat. I started to look for the exit. I was in boxers and nothing else. I couldn't run.

"You might be taller, but your hips aren't that much bigger than mine. It will just be a little short."

"A *little?*" God help me, I actually squeaked. Just the thought of the skirt was making my clit shrink. "That won't even cover my crotch!"

"This will."

She held up a black satin thong, and my clit fell clean off.

"Oh no—no fucking way."

"Please, honey?"

Not fair. Not fair, not fair, not fair.

"Then we'll *both* be in drag," Shel pointed out, twirling the thong around her index finger. "It *is* drag bingo, after all."

Ordinarily, the sight of Shelby within twenty feet of a thong makes me want to start at her toes and lick my way to the top of her head, but today all I could think about was how much that tiny triangle *didn't* cover. Especially on me.

"We don't have any drag clothes that will fit you. My jackets are all too big." I tried a different tack. Shel was very particular about her clothes.

"Don't worry about me. I'll manage something." She leaned over the sofa, cupped my crotch, and resurrected my clit as she squeezed. "Didn't fall off, now, did it?"

"Ha ha," I muttered as she stuck her warm tongue in my mouth. It was a few minutes before I thought about much of anything except how clever her fingers were. When she stopped doing that wonderful up and down, round and round thing she was doing with her thumb, I groaned in protest. "Hey—what—?"

"Later, honey." She gave me another little tug and kissed the tip of my nose. My clit gave a little jump right back. "I have to get dressed. And so do you."

That effectively killed my healthy, happy hard-on once and for all.

I dawdled. I balked. I downright stonewalled. Okay, okay—I mostly sulked. I showered but then I refused to get dressed. Shelby ignored me as I sat on the foot of the bed staring at the floor, naked, immobile—a pathetic rendition of the *Thinker* facing a firing squad.

"What do you think?" Shel asked softly.

I turned my head and found myself eye to eye with a pair of black silk boxers that tented out suggestively over the gently bobbing dick inside. Now I have to tell you, I think wearing a dick is about the sexiest feeling I've ever had—except, of course, fucking Shelby with one. But I've never particularly been interested in being on the receiving end. Fortunately,

Shelby has never complained. So I'd never seen her strapped before. I couldn't take my eyes off her smooth, tanned belly encircled by the broad waistband of the boxers and the jutting prominence below. She is such a girl in every way, and I wouldn't have believed how hot she'd look with all that girl power dancing inches from my face.

"Jesus," I breathed in awe.

She made a little sound like a contented purr. And then she reached down and wrapped her dainty fist around the silk-sheathed cock and gave it a little shake. My mouth dropped open and my clit stood at attention.

"Does it always make you horny right away when you put it on?" she asked a little dreamily.

"Usually, yeah," I muttered, watching her hand action speed up a little bit. "Baby?"

"Hmm?"

"If you want to jerk off with that, come a little closer and I'll help."

"Oh no." She laughed knowingly, giving the dick one final tug before letting go. "You just want to distract me so we'll miss bingo."

"That was the furthest thing from my mind," I protested. It was true, too. In that moment, all I could think about was holding on to her ass and putting her dick in my mouth. *In my mouth? Jesus Christ. What's happening to me?*

"Come on, honey. Stand up. Let me dress you."

My brain was still a bit addled, and without thinking, I complied. The next thing I knew, I was wearing a sleeve-less mesh top that was so tight my nipples nearly protruded through the tiny holes, the black satin thong that barely kept my clit covered, and the leather skirt that hit right at the bottom of my buttcheeks. I don't know why she bothered to put me into clothes at all. I took one look in the mirror and almost fainted.

"I can't go out like this."

"Sure you can. I promise your butch credentials will not be revoked."

I turned, ready to take a stand, and got a good look at her as she buckled a thin black belt around her waist. She'd gone for the simple GQ look, and it worked perfectly on her. She wore an open-collared black silk shirt tucked into tailored black trousers with dress shoes and the belt. She'd slicked back her short blonde hair and wore no makeup. She resembled an androgynous Calvin Klein model, one of the ones that I always feel a little bit guilty about staring at. I glanced down. She looked like a handsome young man with a very substantial hard-on. *Oh baby.*

"You gonna walk around town like that?" I felt myself getting wet. This was so confusing.

"Why not?" She gave her hips a tiny bump. "You do."

"Well, yeah, but that's different."

She stepped closer, cupped my jaw, and stood on her tiptoes to kiss me. When she leaned against me, I felt the firm press of her dick against my thigh. Now I was wet *and* hard. I put my hands on her waist and moved to turn her toward the bed. To my astonishment, she pushed me gently away.

"Uh-uh. No touching."

"Oh, come on, baby. Let's just stay home."

"Nope." She slid a slim leather wallet into her back pocket and buttoned it. Then she held out her hand and gave me that smile that I've never been able to resist. "Come on, honey. Time to go to drag bingo."

We stood in line along with half the population of Provincetown to get through the white picket fence and onto the grass-covered front lawn of the Unitarian Universalist Church, where dozens of metal folding tables had been set up for one of the highlights of Carnival week. Drag bingo. The space was crowded with tourists and townspeople, drag queens, and here and there, a drag king. It was a party atmosphere, and everyone was taking pictures of everyone else. We wended our way toward a free table, carrying our fat color markers and our stack of bingo cards.

I would have felt self-conscious in my less-than-flattering outfit, except no one was paying any attention to me. The drag queens were so flamboyant, so outrageously wonderful, that all eyes were on them. Except for those of the dykes, who were unabashedly eyeing my girlfriend. I had a wholly unfamiliar urge to start scratching eyes out. *Scratching eyes out? Who the hell am I?*

"Can't you strap that thing down?" I said in an irritated whisper after the third time I spied some sexy femme staring at Shelby's crotch.

"It's as down as it's going to get," she said with a grin. "You ought to know."

"Well, *I* never get cruised the way you are when I'm packing it."

She gave me a fiery look. "Oh yes, you do. You just don't know how to stake out your territory. It's a girl thing."

"Then sit down," I hissed, indicating one of the few free seats left, "and hide that before I have to hurt someone."

"I was wondering," she whispered, leaning close as I took the seat next to her, "if it always makes you want to come in your pants really bad, too."

I groaned. I would have banged my head on the table, but they were starting to call out the first of the bingo numbers, and everyone around me was in a frenzy to mark his or her cards. You didn't interfere with some of these people at bingo, not and keep your body parts.

It's not easy to sit very long in a skirt, I discovered. I tried crossing my legs, but my feet went numb. If I didn't cross my legs, I forgot to keep my knees together, and although I welcomed the breeze, I was afraid that I'd be advertising to all and sundry exactly the state I was in. Which, considering the fact that every few minutes, Shelby would run her fingers up the inside of my thigh underneath the table, was one of terminal arousal bordering on coming in my seat. When she casually picked up my left hand, moved it under the table and into her lap, and pressed it against the bulge in her trousers, I almost did.

"You're driving me crazy," I growled into her ear. "I'm going to the bathroom to stick my head under the cold-water faucet."

She laughed as I walked away.

I passed by the long lines for the Porta-Johns outside the church and walked around to the side entrance. Having been to more than one show in the church auditorium, I knew there was another small bathroom just inside. Fortunately, not many other people thought of it, and the line was short. Two of the three stalls were occupied, and as I stepped into the third—the farthest from the door—I felt a hand against my back and another person crowded in behind me.

"Shh," Shelby whispered before I could say anything.

I couldn't even turn around, we were pressed so close together, with her behind me and my knees nearly up against the toilet. When she gave my shoulders a gentle shove, I reflexively reached out with both hands and braced myself against the wall in front of me. It's a good thing I did, because a second later she slipped her hand under the back of my skirt and between my legs, and my knees nearly gave out. For the first time, I appreciated the ingenious nature of a thong. With a practiced flick of her thumb, she swept the material aside and slid her fingertips between my labia.

I heard her groan as I drenched her hand, and I had to bite my lip to hold back a cry of my own. I think I've mentioned how good she is with her hands, and I was already pushing my hips back and forth in an attempt to rub my clitoris against her fingers. I'd been so turned on for so long, I knew I'd come in seconds. To my surprise, she pulled away before I could get there. Then I heard it, and my heart stopped.

The unmistakable sound of a zipper slowly sliding open.

When I moved to turn around, she cupped the back of my neck in her hand to stop me with a whisper. "No."

Off balance, still braced against the wall, I had no room to do anything but wait. I felt as if my whole body were waiting, waiting to be touched, waiting to be filled, waiting to be taken. It was wholly unfamiliar and completely natural. With the first brush of the smooth, cool length of her dick between my legs, my clit jerked and I tightened inside and all I wanted was for her to make me come. I pushed back again, this time against the fat, firm head, and felt it slip inside. I moaned. I couldn't help it.

"Feels good, doesn't it, honey?" she murmured in my ear, her breath hot and ragged.

I knew what she was feeling, the pressure against her clit from the base of the cock, the sweet power of being inside her woman, the need to give and take at the same time. I could only whimper and nod my head. I wanted more, but I was afraid. Afraid to be other than I have always thought myself to be; afraid to be not less, but more. She knew, and she helped me.

She moved her hand from my neck around to the front of my body and underneath the edge of the tiny skirt. She held my clitoris gently between her fingers and began to slide it back and forth the way she knows always makes me come. As soon as she started, I pushed back onto her dick and she slid deeper inside. As I stretched in body and mind to take her, the pressure surged into my clit, and I knew I was going to come.

She stroked me, I rocked against her, she pushed deeper. Once, twice, and then I felt it—the slow, rolling contractions in the core of me that in another minute would burst shooting from my clit.

"I'm coming," I cried softly. I felt her weight against my back, her body trembling as she worked herself inside me. I heard the quick, high-pitched sound she makes when she's nearing orgasm. Just as I crashed over the edge and lost all sense of anything but her, I heard her triumphant voice in my ear.

"Bingo, baby. Bingo."

KIKI

Jolie du Pré

"Close your eyes."

The tall grass tickles my face as she lowers my head to the pond. One hand rubs my hair, while the other showers it with the water.

"All right, baby. You're done." We stand. She lifts up her T-shirt and pats my eyes with it.

Now my blonde locks are black. My parents never let me do it when I was at home, but that's not why I bailed. That's not the half of it.

I grab a strand, letting it slide between my fingers. Its dark color triggers an ache in my pussy, which gets even stronger when I look over at Kiki's face.

She's smiling in that way that says she wants to fuck me, the new me with my slick black locks.

"You look hot!"

"I want a mirror."

"Yeah, when we're at the store we'll get one."

What she really means is we'll steal one.

Kiki's bald, but she still has tiny little hairs on her head that feel good under my fingers, fuzzy like a caterpillar's. I move closer to her, kiss her lips, roll my tongue over her stud. She's got another piercing on her nose, five on her eyebrow, and a bunch on her ears. She hooked me up with one through my belly button.

The clouds are forming above us. It looks like rain. We head back to our place under the bridge, just before it starts to pour. Don is there. He sits on a tattered blanket, playing his guitar and singing to the sky. His voice is gravelly and sometimes he'll hit a note and nothing will come out. The skin on his face is tough like leather and he's missing three of his front teeth. Kiki says he's about fifty and that he's been drinking since he was ten. The kindest man I know. Last week, when I was crying, he sang me a song and I pretended that I enjoyed the sound of it, because I love him. He's my family.

Not my real family, who told me I was going to hell for being a dyke. Who beat me. Who sent me off to a Christian boarding school. I'm twenty now. Haven't been home in about two years. I don't miss them, never have.

Kiki walks over to the spot on the grass where she hid the box, and then she digs it up. Crack, the only thing she loves as much as me.

She lights some. Her face looks like she's close to coming after she blows it out. The smoke burns my eyes and smells like burnt alcohol. I turn my head.

I don't want it. But if I look at her, at it, I might change.

Later, we sit in a restaurant and look at the menus, acting like we're going to order. Then when some customers are finished, we take the money they leave on the tables. About ten dollars today, enough for lunch. We didn't eat yesterday.

When we're done with our meals, we take a walk. It's Saturday. Lots of people are out and about, shopping at all the expensive stores. Kiki decides she wants to scare some "rich brats" again. She makes faces, which I tell her she doesn't need to do since she looks pretty scary anyway, at least to them.

She runs up to some kid. He's dressed perfectly in matching designer duds. Standing there, eyes bugging out of his head, frozen like a statue, he starts to cry. That's when his mother notices and runs over to grab him. She clutches her purse as they hurry out of sight. I try not to laugh.

Kiki grabs my hand and we find an alley. She's brought one of the rocks with her and her pipe. She takes a hit and then she's ready to fuck. We go to the train station, head into one of the bathrooms, and lock the door.

Pressing me against the wall, she puts her mouth on mine. Her lips are chapped and her breath is stale, but her kiss is firm. She takes my shirt and pulls it up. Then she leans down and puts one of my tits in her mouth. Since I'm small, she can suck it all in. While she's doing that, her fingers play with my other nipple. I feel a tingle in my pussy and she knows it. She knows what gets me hot. She puts her mouth on mine again. I push my tongue inside and find the stud. I like the way it feels. I like to play with it.

We pull down our pants and panties and let them fall to our feet. Then we push our bodies against each other, rubbing our pussies together, starting a fire. I slide three fingers into Kiki's cunt and nibble her ear.

"Fuck that pussy," she says.

And that's what I do; hard and fast my fingers go in and out of her hole, juice all over. I lick her neck and reach under her shirt to feel her breasts. I want to make her come. I push even harder into her. Soon she's hunched over, holding on to me for support, until I hear her moan and feel her pussy close around my fingers. I pull them out and put them in my mouth. She's glassy-eyed and smiling as I taste her.

Now we're back under the bridge. Kiki doesn't rest much. The crack has turned her into a zombie. But for once, she's sleeping. I lean my back against the concrete wall and hold her head on my lap. Don is next to us, stretched out with his mouth open, snoring. Even though the city lights are bright, I can still see some stars.

I make a wish for us, and then I close my eyes and go to sleep.

LAST TEN BUCKS

A. Lizbeth Babcock

I call you, late and unexpectedly, and ask if I can come to your home. You say I can, which was my hope (of course). I come in a taxi, the better way, despite what the Toronto Transit Commission would have me believe. I wear only nylons and a short, sleeveless dress under my winter coat. My legs are clad in thigh-high boots. Your favorite. I am completely focused on you. Focused on what is about to happen. I struggle to ignore the incessant chatter of an annoying cabdriver, offering only a monotone *mm-hmm* where absolutely necessary. I am polite. I always have been.

Finally, I arrive. You have left the porch light on for me. It is blazing on your darkened street, like a firecracker in the sky. I give the driver my last ten bucks, but I would have paid anything to see you tonight. I would have found a way to come.

My attire does not surprise you but you are pleased, like when you anticipate that something will taste really good, and then it does. You tell me to go downstairs. I do. I wait, and soon you come too. You are wearing leather. You are fully dressed, fully butch. The sight and smell of your gear arouses me before we even touch. You are harnessed, already. I tell you what I need, even though I think you know. You pull the front of my dress down, exposing my tits. You don't touch them, only look at them, and approve of them.

You pull out several different toys from your special chest, where you keep your sacred treasures and the means through which you attain your most sadistic desires. I have never seen the full contents. They are sacrosanct, secured by lock and key, like dangerous weapons or precious jewels. You control them, and tonight, me.

You make your selection, telling me why you have chosen this one over and above all of the others. You want to mark me, make me scream and squirm. I listen to your words like an eager student who has an aching crush on her teacher…the kind of crush you share with your girlfriends on the telephone while giggling, screeching, and making promises not to tell.

You want me on my knees in front of you, and although I am cooperative, you push me down aggressively. You place the heel of your hand on my mouth and slide it across my face, making a messy streak out of my blood red lipstick. I offer up my arms to you, holding them together, my wrists exposed. Methodically, you tie my hands in front of me, always my preference with a newer playmate.

We talked about that on our first date when we met for

a late-night drink at a local pub. It was your intensity that struck me then—that held me there well beyond my self-imposed curfew. You looked deep inside of me that night, and everything around us was superfluous and inane. It was packed, as usual. But all of the other people were nothing more than moving colors, blends of light and dark around us, incoherent fusions of sound. I described to you my darkest fantasies and told you of my experience thus far.

You watched my eyes and lips with intention as I spoke. Your sense of your own power was what made me wet, and I secretly pushed my crotch against the edge of my chair like an animal in heat. I imagined you fisting me right there—the table our stage, the patrons our audience. I was present but lost all at once.

When I excused myself to use the washroom, you followed me in. You told me to lift my skirt for you, and you felt what you had done to me firsthand. You slid your fingers under the edge of my panties and fondled me. I stared into your eyes, completely defenseless. I leaned back against a long counter of sinks and let you have your way with me. I wanted to come all over your fingers in that moment. I wanted you to play with my clit mercilessly until my moans became so loud that you would have to cover my mouth and force my silence. You didn't do that though. You didn't let me come. You gave me just enough to make me want more. Just enough to make me need more from you. It was humiliating in a way, being forced to show you my wetness only to have you smile and walk away. I left that night with a sense of your ability to control me, to control a situation. And you did this with a seductive ease.

I hold my hands in place as you manage the heavy twine. I love giving myself to you like this. Fully. You pay close attention to each knot you weave, like ritual, like religion. Upon completion, you guide my tethered hands back down toward the floor. You gently place your right hand under my chin and tilt my head so that I am looking up at you—way up—looking straight into you, into your steel blue eyes. Your stare is so intense in this moment that my inclination is to look away, like when you see something you're not supposed to. I resist that urge. With a voice equally as intense and unwavering you say, "I am going to make you my bitch tonight, got it? I'm going to take your cunt."

Your statement is quickly followed by a harsh slap across my face. I do not wince. I do not look away. My eyes remain connected with yours. My faith in you keeps me still. I want this. I am flooded with disorganized thoughts and scattered images of how your objective will be achieved. You order me to walk to the other side of the room and bend over a table in the corner. It is an old wooden table—strong, stable, and firm—like you. You have been working on its repair for some time; skillfully crafting and successfully manipulating it to become what you want it to be—your very own.

"Now," you direct sternly as you shove me forward. I do as you say and it feels a bit like walking the plank—like a final destiny. I feel your eyes on me as I move across the room, my arms immobile and my head down. I bend over the table with a teasing hesitation, stretching my arms out over my head and grasping the far edge of the surface with my fingertips. "Like this?" I ask as I lean into the mastered project.

There is no response to my question. You are coming toward me, telling me that I'm going to get it, and making me tell you that I want it. I do. You lift my dress up, progressively, exposing my ass. You take a few steps back. Then it comes, the hard *whack* of the mindfully chosen flogger. It is harsh against me—the hit so severe that I cry out in a voice I do not recognize as my own. My heart is racing. You spank me again and again, harder and harder. There are only brief moments of relief.

My nylons provide no shield from the pain, and no compromise of the pleasure. I ask you to wait, but you offer little time for recovery. I can tell that you like me like this—yours. You are tough. Cold. Totally on top. This is my favorite way for you to be, so far. I begin screaming with each wallop, and I can feel my asscheeks heating up, on fire. You do not ask if I am okay. You know that I am. We have an agreement, something we started developing during that first encounter. It's a nice feeling, like a safety net ready to catch you during a particularly dangerous stunt.

Prior to that first night, we had been mere images to each other; our faces scattered among a thousand other lonely dykes seeking connections in cyberspace; our words complicated by template descriptions of who we are and what we want. Did we have the same favorite movie? Did we long to travel to like destinations? Who cared? This was real life. Full force. Our instant chemistry had led us here to this moment, and this moment was all that mattered.

I start chanting just one word, "Please." More like begging for mercy, or praying for forgiveness. You tell me that I will address you as Sir tonight, and I incorporate that into my hymn. When I writhe out of place, you pull me back, making me take more. "Don't fucking resist me, whore. I'll tell you when I'm finished with you, understand?"

"Yes, Sir."

"Yeah, I'm gonna decide when we're fucking done here, got it?"

"Yes, Sir."

"And you're gonna be a good little slut for me tonight, aren't you?"

"Yes, Sir."

"Tell me!"

"I'm going to be a good little slut for you, Sir."

"You're gonna do as you're told, right slut?"

"Yes, Sir. I'm going to do as I'm told, Sir."

"Louder!"

"Yes, Sir. I'm going to do as I'm told!"

"Dirty fucking whore," you mutter under your breath as the discipline subsides.

You tell me that I better behave. And you mean it. You are designedly detached. Strict, demanding, and fierce. I am dizzy with delight. Numb, yet feeling. Hurt, yet wanton.

After a brutal spanking, you pull me up by my hair and force me back down to my knees in front of you. You are cocky, and not just because you have one. You order me to suck you off, and I obediently take you into my mouth. Your fingers are tangled in the roots of my long hair, commanding my movement. You like me like this—your little victim. Our mutual rhythm is hypnotic and spiritual. You make me take you in so far that my eyes water. I can feel the tears escaping from the far corners and disappearing into my hair. You tell me that I am good—a good girl. I am. I love that you say this when you are being so rough with me. The tenderness in your tone makes me feel completely safe and protected. Your hand slowly encourages me to take in even more. I gaze up at you as I struggle to suck your cock just the way you like it. I am completely focused, committed, devout. I want to please you, Sir. Honor you, Sir. You act like you don't care, but I know that you do—inside.

You say you are going to fuck me now. Hard. And I am not surprised. You shove me back up into my original position, my ass in the air, my legs spread—forced open by the kick of your boots. The redness from my beating blushes through my thin veneer of protection. My nylons are a minor barrier. While acting as an obstacle on the one hand, they also serve as gift wrap on the other. And this is how you see them. Something good is inside, and you want to open your package, claim your prize. You are like a kid on Christmas morning, but more controlled. You reach for a sharp knife, and begin to slice the thin material. You are careful, strategic, as you gain access to my wet pussy. Fuck, you are my dream come true.

You slice the fine fabric just enough to push yourself inside. I breathe heavily in anticipation as you prepare to enter me. My head is spinning, as you plunge your whole cock deep inside of me. I shift with some discomfort in response. "Don't you dare move, bitch. This is what you want, so fucking take it." I teeter on that perilous edge of pleasure and pain. Screams escape from my lips, like water running through my fingers. I can feel every detail of your solid cock inside of me, every nuance of its shape. It is wicked. It is miraculous. Again and again, you tell me that I am yours now.

You make me beg you to fuck me every few minutes, and I plead with you to keep going. "Please, Sir—don't stop. Don't let me go." You pull out every time I work up to a climax, and make me wait. You watch me struggle to catch my breath and you push my face hard against the table. "Not yet, you fucking slut." You reenter me with such fullness and force that my moans vacillate between ecstasy and anguish. I revel in my sense of helplessness.

"Who does your cunt belong to, bitch?" You demand an answer as I lament and whimper. It is you. You are fucking me harder than I've ever been fucked—it is as if my life depended on it. The friction from my face rubbing against the wood burns as I submit to the motion of this invasion. "Are you going to come, bitch?" You ask knowing that you are in complete control. "What do you need to do, bitch? You need to ask for permission, don't you? Come on, bitch, ask me if I'll let you come now." I am speechless. You shout, "Do it!" in between each violent thrust, treating me like a whore you have paid for.

"Ple-ease, Sir. Please, please will you let me?" My moans are irrepressible. My words are broken. You control every aspect of my letting go, and I feel completely owned. I am indeed your dirty whore, and yes, a fucking slut. But most importantly, I am your bitch tonight, Sir. In this flicker of time, this is my offering to you.

And that was exactly the way it was supposed to be. Just like that. The right amount of everything, and not too much of anything. You fucked me like that until you came. I could feel your cock dripping with wetness when you made your final exit. You told me that next time you were taking my ass. You said it as a cold hard fact.

I left when you were finished with me that night. I borrowed a token from you and hopped the streetcar home. The purpose that evening was not to linger. It was not our date night, just an intermittent hello. Tonight we will meet at a quiet upscale restaurant on Church Street. We will have a candlelight dinner in a private booth. The glow of the flames will light our faces. The theme: romance.

THE WORLD TURNED UPSIDE DOWN

Jean Roberta

Let the record state that I, Francis Henry Vincent Edmund Paine, seventh Lord Barrenfield, have sworn before God to tell my damning tale to all who wish to hear it.

Lady Alison Sweet was my fiancée, and she wore the diamond ring that I inherited from my grandmother. Our wedding date was set and our union was heartily approved by her parents and mine. Her property was attractive to me, of course. I have never denied the importance of practical considerations in the taking of a wife. That I loved the lady for herself, however, was clear to all who knew us both.

Before I make my confession to you gentlemen, I appeal to you: consider the spell that my lady cast on all who knew her. Some of you felt it yourselves. Could you feel her radiance between your hands, soon to be yours forever, and not do as I did?

Even now, the image of Alison lives in my heart. She was like a spirited mare who needs the right master to shape and mold her talents, which even she could not properly name or understand.

Here is her portrait in miniature. Note her shining chestnut hair, her robust pink complexion, and her laughing dark eyes, which hint at the secret she was carrying. You can just see the creamy swelling of her bosom above her favorite green gown. At the time, I believed that she wore it to remind herself of the woods where we met whenever we could, away from profane eyes.

My story begins when we had gone a-Maying in our own fashion. What year, you ask? It was 1805, a time not long past.

I have been told that a thorough confession will unburden my soul, and even convey such benefits to my audience. If this is your desire, know this: my lady and I were married in all but name. She had given herself to me when she consented to be my wife, and her passion was greater than I had expected. How she seemed to love me!

On the day when the dart of suspicion first pierced my heart, she ran to me in our usual trysting-place under the oldest oak tree in the woods that belong to her family. She greeted me with a kiss, nestling into my arms, but I fancied that her bonnet resembled the bronze helmet of a female warrior. I untied the ribbons and lifted it off her dear head, freeing her to loosen her hair so that it fell down her back in natural waves.

If you are to understand my actions, you must understand

that Alison was never a modest maiden. I believed that it was her immoderate love for me, and nothing worse, which prompted her on occasion to shed her garments and dance for me in her naked glory like a wanton houri in a sultan's harem. After I freed her from the prison of her corset, she threw all her undergarments atop the muslin gown that already lay on the grass like an impromptu tablecloth. The scene was set for a love-feast worthy of the ancient gods.

The sight of her high, girlish breasts; her slender waist and the round, firm globes of her buttocks almost sent me into a frenzy. My soldier stood at attention, demanding to be released from my breeches.

She taunted me like a dryad, hiding behind trees while calling to me to come find her. She gained the advantage while I removed my boots, my breeches, my shirt, my waistcoat and the myriad other items which distinguish a gentleman from the honest savage whose state he envies at such moments.

As a man in the prime of life, I was well prepared to overtake a fleeing, unshod woman, especially one who wanted to be caught! She shone like a capricious beacon in the shade as she ran laughing from tree to tree, luring me on.

I seized her from behind, grasping her warm breasts, which seemed designed for such a purpose. She squealed with pleasure as I rolled her tender, swollen buds between my fingers and told her that she was my captive and must yield to my every whim.

Do not blush like schoolgirls, gentlemen. You have asked for a complete account of all that has led me to the feet of blindfolded Justice, and to you as her seeing representatives. I intend to answer your demand.

"Oh sir, have mercy!" she begged sweetly, tormenting my

manhood by rubbing her backside against it. "Will you ravish me?"

"As thoroughly as you wish, my nymph," I answered. "It is your fate to be possessed by the one you have tempted."

I placed her small white hands on a tree trunk at the height of her shoulders while I held her haunches steady. I sought out her womanhood with my fingers, and found it slippery with welcoming fluid, and hot as a volcano.

I eased my lance into her until it was in to the hilt. Dear God! Did ever a woman afford such pleasure to her lover as Alison? Her cries were like a beautiful song in my ears, and never did she protest her ill-usage, even as I plowed her like a madman.

After our mating had reached its climax and our blood was cooling, I resolved to show her the tenderness she deserved. I turned her to face me and held her against my chest as though to shield her from the harsh judgment of society. I murmured the endearments that women so long to hear. I promised to be her loving husband as long as she remained my loyal wife. Deceived as I was, I was happier then than I have been from that moment forward.

Hand in hand, we returned to the spot where our clothing awaited us. A folded square of paper lay on the grass where it had evidently fallen out of its hiding place near my Alison's skin. I bent to pick up the incongruous paper, and saw that it was a letter.

"Leave it!" warned Alison before she could compose herself to speak more sensibly. "It is nothing, Frank dear."

"We have no secrets from each other, my darling," I reminded her. "And I am interested in all your correspondence, from your shopping lists to the invitations you receive from your lady-friends."

Alison looked as though she might faint. She busied herself with her stockings, deliberately turning away from me.

I unfolded the letter and read these words, as I remember them:

> *Dear Mistress Alison,*
> *How odd it seems to address you in this way after what has passed between us. Please understand that I intend no presumption, but in any contest between nature and the silly laws of Man, nature will win. It is best if you do as I have said. I will count the minutes until two o'clock in the afternoon on Tuesday next, in the place you know. Do not be tardy unless you wish to be punished!*
> *Your devoted, etc.,*
> *Mary*

I felt as though I had been thrown from my horse. "Alison," I spoke her name more harshly than usual. "Is this a letter from your maid, Mary Bentley?"

Alison's confusion spoke more clearly than words. "Is it?" I repeated.

"Yes," she admitted softly.

"This is outrageous," I told her. "You must dismiss her, or your father must do it. No servant with an ounce of common sense would write such words to the one she serves. The woman is clearly out of her wits, or more depraved than you can fathom, dearest. She is as poisonous as a viper, and you must not keep her under your roof for another day!"

I was somewhat pleased to see that my Alison looked truly ashamed. She blushed so prettily that I was tempted to tumble her again, but my parents had asked me to bring her to tea, and we had little time to waste.

I tore the letter into tiny pieces, and offered them to the breeze. As I helped Alison into her gown, the previous location of that insolent parody of a friendly message troubled me a great deal. "Darling," I asked her, "why in heaven's name did you carry that letter on your person?"

She turned to face me and looked boldly into my eyes. "Would you have believed it, Frank," she asked, "had you not read it yourself?"

"Perhaps not," I mused, startled by her sangfroid.

"Then you see," she explained, "why evidence may be valuable."

The oddness of this remark, expressing as it did a certain feminine caprice, caused me briefly to lose my composure. I realized momentarily that my Alison needed the protection and guidance of a husband in her dealings with servants. As Lady Barrenfield, she would certainly need to know how to run a household with grace and authority.

Pardon me, gentlemen. Recounting my dashed hopes is exceedingly painful for me.

When we arrived at my parents' home, Barrenfield Hall, I am sure that we both presented an appearance of youthful gaiety, perhaps shadowed slightly by the many concerns involved in planning a wedding. While listening distractedly to tea-table chatter, I could not help thinking about Mary, the lady's-maid who presumed to have such a perversely intimate relationship with my Alison.

Mary Bentley had been employed by the Sweet family for five years, I believed. Her whereabouts before that were open to speculation. When I made inquiries during the following days, I was told that she had worked in a tavern where she was, in effect, a woman of ill repute. There she had enjoyed the patronage of gentlemen of quality who were willing to supply her with the necessary letters of reference to gain her entrance into a respectable household. Far from being a trained lady's-maid, she was apparently an experienced procuress.

No, gentlemen, I have no proof of the veracity of this information. Your insinuation that I might have known the woman in question in her previous circumstances is highly unwelcome. Furthermore, I defy you to deny that personal reputations have currency in a court of law.

From direct observation, I knew that Mary had a certain disagreeable forthrightness of manner that made her expressions of deference to her betters seem subtly mocking. Her features had a masculine boldness of line that is admired by some painters, but not by true connoisseurs of feminine beauty. She expressed herself with greater eloquence than one would expect from a woman of her station. When I remarked on it to Alison, she innocently explained to me that Mary claimed to be the bastard child of a sea-captain who had provided her with an unusual education. The captain's mistress, whom he had probably met in the sort of establishment where sailors seek diversion, had undoubtedly intended to further her own ambitions through a daughter who could not hope to be satisfied with her lot in life.

To return to my narrative, however: I decided to investigate the mysterious appointment referred to in the fateful letter. After reminding Alison that her maid must be dismissed and that she must be prepared to dress her own hair until a suitable replacement could be found, I told her that I had an appointment with my solicitor on the following Tuesday afternoon.

I assured her that I needed to make financial arrangements which would ensure her security as my wife.

Half an hour before the appointed time, I waited behind a hedge on the grounds of the Sweet family home for a sight of my beloved. She appeared, looking apprehensive, and walked briskly in the direction of the woods. Before she could disappear from my view, I followed stealthily.

As silently as an Indian scout, I followed her into the woods and at length to the banks of a stream where, in a happier time, Alison and I had dined in the open air after a leisurely rowing expedition. Now the figure of a man in hunting clothes approached my Alison, striding vigorously from the opposite direction. I reached for one of the pistols that I carry with me on occasions when I may be required to protect those in danger.

To my horror, Alison flung herself upon the stranger before I could ascertain his identity. The familiar angularity of his face and the sensuous ease of his gait led me to recognize him as Mary Bentley!

"Come, my girl," commanded the male-female monster abruptly. "We must not be seen." The two figures retreated into a secluded opening in the woods. I had to adjust my own position behind a bush in order to keep them in my sight.

"You would fool anyone, dearest," laughed my faithless Alison between the aggressive kisses of the one who held her. It was unbelievable! I felt rooted to the spot with revulsion, but also with a sickened curiosity. I needed to learn the extent of Alison's betrayal of me, and of her corruption.

"My angel," demanded Mary, "will you accept me as your husband in America?"

My senses seemed as heightened at that moment as those

of a man on his deathbed. I perceived everything in vivid and even excruciating detail: the mournful rustling of leaves, the splashing of fresh water over stones, and the cawing of crows, which sounded to my stricken ears like an ironic comment on Mary's ridiculous proposal.

"My husband!" laughed Alison with horrid glee. She no longer appeared to be even a distant cousin of the young lady with whom I had fallen in love. "My husband, my mistress, my lover—if the old words will not fit, I will make up new ones, my love. In America or anywhere else. Oh, Bentley, how I wish I had known my own heart sooner! Are you sure you can forgive me?"

In answer, Mary kissed her passionately on the mouth, then left a trail of kisses down her soft neck and the creamy skin that led to her décolletage. "Silly goose," chided the female seducer. "There is nothing to forgive. Papa's ship sails next month, and we will be aboard. No man can claim you as his property when you are beyond the laws of this kingdom. The salt air will melt away your promise to Frank, and his ring will fetch a pretty price in New York. The Devil shall be forced to give up your soul."

Mary stroked Alison's hair, adding further assurances that the breaking of a sacred vow would be of no consequence, that it was even the duty of every woman who loved freedom!

The confused Alison clung to the clever-tongued Mary, who pressed her to her bosom and lowered her to the ground. Both women unfastened each other's garments in an energetic dance of mutual unveiling. Mary's male disguise was removed, piece by piece, and the body of a strong, voluptuous woman emerged into the light of an unblinking sun. Her arms held Alison with a strength that seemed better suited to the work of a laundress, while her melon-like teats seemed to bask in the warm air like those of a shameless animal. Her robust, sun-browned form served as a foil for Alison's rose-and-white delicacy.

I ought to have shamed them both by bursting from my hiding place to interrupt their sordid game. Inexplicably, I could not do it. I remained languorously still, as the pain in my heart warred with the discomfort in my breeches.

I did not even protest when Alison lowered her mouth to Mary's unfettered dugs and sucked like a calf. "Ah!" sighed the coarse object of her attention. "Little nursling."

There followed such fondling, tweaking and kissing that the two women fell into competition as to who would first penetrate the other's inner sanctum. "Impudent girl," chided Mary, holding one of Alison's arms behind her back in a way that forced her lovely breasts into prominence. "Do you need a taste of the birch?"

Writhing in her companion's arms, Alison confessed her perverse desire. "From you, Bentley," she replied in a whisper that fell on my ears like sweet-tasting poison. "I am so naughty and so frightened that I need correction from your stern hand. Yours alone."

Like a miserable sailor who has been forced onto the deck to watch his younger brother be flogged, I felt compelled to watch as Mary dragged Alison by the hair to the foot of a tree where several slim branches lay waiting for her hand. She selected a supple branch adorned with budded offshoots.

Seating herself on a large rock as though it were her throne of office, she pulled Alison to her, and the obedient girl complied by arranging herself on the lap of her she-master with many seductive movements of her hips and bottom. Mary passed one of her work-coarsened hands slowly over the soft, pale skin on which she intended to leave her own cruel imprint, and smiled in triumphant pleasure. "Tell me, dearest," she coaxed, "for what you deserve to be punished."

"For dissembling so well," answered the helpless captive, hiding her blushes behind her veil of hair. "For hiding my plans from Frank, who thinks we have no secrets from each other! For responding to him with such passion that he cannot guess how much I fear the life of a wife and mother for which I have been trained. Oh, Mary! I am afraid of a long sea voyage with a rough new country at the end of it, but I cannot stay here! I would go mad as Frank's wife, even if I am destined to starve to death in America! I am no purer than a common whore who has been caught stealing a gentleman's purse, and my word is not to be trusted. My own soul is like a bog full of vile creatures half-hidden even from me."

"What a dreadful confession, my love!" exclaimed Mary, as judge and executioner. "Your soul must certainly be examined and scrubbed as clean as it can be made." As she spoke these words, Mary spread Alison's legs apart with a hand that appeared to be holding a kind of stuffed leather pouch, the sort of thing the French call a *godemiche,* which their women use to console themselves in the absence of their husbands. In despair (as though I were already an insubstantial ghost), I watched as Mary pushed this device into Alison's obliging cunt. The young lady whom I could no longer call my own sighed loudly.

"There," chuckled Mary. "You have a choice bit to fill you while I give your outside something to contemplate. Are you ready, my dear?"

"Yes, Mary," answered the willing Alison. "Only, if I may

ask a favor." The doomed culprit hesitated, as though suddenly overwhelmed by indecision.

"Ask now, Alison, or be silent until I am through with you," warned Mary.

"Will you begin with gentle strokes? The first few are always such a shock," complained the pretty captive.

"If I do," returned Mary, "I will strengthen my strokes until your lovely bottom is sore enough to spur you to good behavior until our next meeting."

With that, the depraved Mary firmly grasped her branch of chastisement and commenced to apply it to the buttocks that surely deserved as much pain as they could bear. Alison responded with quiet moans, which soon grew to muffled yelps and then to strangled screams, as the sting of the birch echoed in her flesh and stirred the obscene object inside her. Dear God! How well the oath-breaker deserved to be flayed alive, and how sorry I was that I had been too tenderhearted to do it myself! Yet how little she deserved any attention that could satisfy her, even at the price of bruising her skin.

While watching this near-inconceivable display, so suggestive of the vilest performances of the most abandoned harlots, I could scarcely remain silent myself. As Alison shivered violently in her own ecstasy of sin and repentance, I could not remain unaffected. My outraged love reached its own crisis, and I was thus enabled to remain patient for a while longer.

How subtly corruption lays hold of the most unsuspecting soul! While trying to recover my composure, I could well imagine the terrible relief in surrender that must have affected those hapless ladies and gentlemen of France who found themselves bound by drunken ruffians beneath the swift, shining blade of the guillotine. When all hope—or *l'esperance*, as they must have called it in their prayers—had fled, what calm anticipation must have flowed through them in their last moments. If this is God's compensation for injustice, I hope it will not fail me when I face my own end.

I continued watching the two naked females as the tear-stained Alison knelt between Mary's knees to kiss the bearded lips between them. With no sign of distaste or hesitation, Alison used her rosy lips and tongue to give pleasure until Mary shuddered and panted like a hunting dog in full chase. The graceless pleasure-seeker caressed her willing servant's hair and face, and told her that it was enough.

"My beautiful girl," murmured the self-styled she-husband. "I love you so much. Have courage, dear. You are stronger than you know, and I will be with you always."

Alison rested her head on Mary's knees. "Darling," she asked, "do you think that women in America have all the rights of citizens?"

"I am sure they have," responded Mary. "The Americans are allies of France, and their government was founded on the same principles: *liberté, égalité, fraternité*. They can hardly deny us any of the Rights of Man."

"Oh Mary," sighed the juvenile and misguided young lady. "I would give up everything I own to be as free as a man! I want to earn my keep, but what trade could I follow in America?"

Mary gently raised her companion up until the two were standing together, wrapped in each other's arms. They swayed gently in a rhythmic, silent dance as Mary sought to comfort Alison without words. I was given a clear view of Alison's red bottom, which aroused me despite the distastefulness of my position. We three seemed wrapped in a strange and potent spell.

Mary broke the silence at length. "You are a clever pupil, my darling," she assured her, "and could learn any trade you please." She continued: "You are a good shot with your bow and arrows, and a fair rider. You could be a huntress in the wilderness, as free as the goddess Diana. And I can always keep us by the skills of my hands, if not by my wits. Now we must dress ourselves again to face the world, my good wife."

Alison seemed to be assailed by doubt. She touched her own belly, tears shining in her eyes. "What if I were with child, Mary? What could I do?"

"You would bear it in our new home, dearest, and we would raise our son or daughter with love to spare. No child of yours will ever be called a bastard while I am alive, Alison. You must trust me."

After much kissing and exchanging of sounds too low to be heard clearly, the two deluded women helped each other into their clothes. And then Alison spoke my name in a tone which assaulted my ears like a blow. "What if Frank discovers us, my love?" she demanded. "He distrusts me already."

Mary laughed like a fishwife who is accustomed to shouting in the streets. "Even if he were watching us now," she boasted with arrogant deliberation, "would he denounce me as his rival and challenge me to a duel? Would he inform the police that his fiancée has been stolen by her own maid? Would he take you to be examined by a physician who would confirm that you have been ruined? Would he carry you off before the wedding day? Not he. His own pride will protect us until we make our escape."

At once, my own cowardice rose up in my throat like bile. Had the two females intended to lure me into the foul pit of their degeneracy in order to watch me suffer? Had the whole world turned upside down so that those who had once been lowest now held all power? Intolerable!

"Damn you!" I roared, springing to my feet. Before I could control my emotions, I seized one of my pistols and aimed it at Mary, the cause of my Alison's downfall.

"Frank!" screamed my former sweetheart, eyes wide with fear. "No!" She threw herself upon her lover to shield her. I realized that I had fired when Alison sank to the ground, blood pouring from a wound in her neck.

From that moment, I was like a man possessed. The fiendish Mary, dressed as a man, moved toward my poor fallen Alison, and I felt as though I would lose my wits at the sight. How many more young lives would the unnatural being destroy if she were allowed to live?

"Stand back!" I commanded, causing her to stand motionless, staring fearfully at my weapon. Even when faced by the man she had wronged, she breathed no word of remorse, and expressed no feminine desire for forgiveness.

I discharged a bullet directly at her heart, hoping to dispatch her at once. Her vile screams were so maddening that I scarce remember what I did next. Even when half-mad, I knew that I could not leave her to suffer. I fired at her head, the seat of her depraved schemes, and at last she lay in deep and utter silence.

How strange I felt, standing alone in the rustling woods with no sound of a human voice in my ears! Despite her treachery, my heart swelled with grief at the sight of my Alison, once so full of life and now permanently lost to me in death. How still were the two bodies! I felt no triumph, but a grim sense of having followed the prompting of Nature at her most relentless.

As a gentleman, I could not leave the dead unburied. On leaden feet, I returned to my home to fetch my most trusted and stalwart servants to help lay my late fiancée and her seducer in the earth to which we must all return in our time.

And so I stand before you, gentlemen, charged with the murders of two helpless women because I played the part of a man. Would any of you have acted differently under such provocation? And have I no claim on the mercy of the court, although none was shown to me?

I submit myself to your will. And if I must keep an appointment with the hangman, this sordid tale will at last end with no consequences to a living human heart. I have been told that hanged men spill their seed at the last, and thus my future heirs may die before their conception on the weathered wood of the gallows.

Perhaps the world has turned upside down after all. If that be the case, may my testimony reach the wondering ears of another audience, like a ballad of doomed love that cannot die as long as it is still sung.

HEAVENLY BODIES

Andrea Miller

Aries

"Forget social niceties," Aries said. "Let's screw in the bathroom."

Refreshingly direct, I thought, but there was no way I'd follow her to *that* grimy stall. And the problem wasn't the graffiti on the door or the overflowing trash can. No, the problem was that since Aries moved to town, she'd humped scores of women hovering over the toilet here at the bar and I refused to be next. Nope, I liked her too much for her to leave me in a washroom high and dry, or even high and wet. As perverse as it sounds, I wanted a relationship with Aries. You see, I'd a sixth sense about her—that under the tough butch exterior she was a lost lamb.

"You horny bitch," I said, smiling. "We're

gonna fuck in a bed." Then I grabbed a fistful of her short hair and dragged her outside. In the parking lot was Aries' car—red and low to the ground. We got in and she started the ignition.

"I'm not sure," she said, putting the car in DRIVE, "that I can wait for a bed." Aries slipped her hand up my skirt, proving her point, and the proverbial sparks flew. I still wanted box-spring dignity, but I began to reason that a car was good enough. I spread my legs to give easier access. Very easy—I wasn't wearing panties.

With one hand on the wheel, Aries simultaneously made sharp turns through empty streets and soft strokes against my fur—so soft and teasing that I realized she was making me wait for making *her* wait. I rolled into her hand, wanting more, harder. Yet she continued with her light touch and occasional no-touch as she changed gears.

Finally Aries turned onto the highway and sped up, her foot pressing into the gas pedal, her finger plunging into my hole. I moaned and rammed back at her. Aries went faster, dodging cars; streetlights and inky night blurring past us. My heart raced and I tried telling her to stop driving. But a part of me—the slick, throbbing part—didn't even want her to slow down and the words jammed.

Aries pinched my clit, then rolled it with her fingers. She was being rough now, but the rub was bringing me to the edge. I lifted my hips off the seat and, jerking hard, came wet against her hand.

Aries pulled over onto the side of the road, gravel crunching under her wheels. Is it free will or destiny, I wondered, that doesn't have a bed for us? My slit pulsing, the stars twinkling, I couldn't tell.

Taurus

"I had a craving for brownies," Taurus explained as she dipped her finger in the pot. "Taste this, sweetie."

My mouth watering, I leaned in to lick the long delicate shaft of her finger and to swallow every trace of the just-melted chocolate. Leaned in to suck as if I intended to tongue her very bone. Taurus pulled out and took the chocolate off the heat. "The next step," she said, "is to beat the butter."

She put two yellow sticks in a green bowl and started the hum of the mixer. But the taste of her finger had left me hungry for more than brownies, and now I nuzzled her neck where the neat line of coffee-colored hairs met bare skin.

The butter growing light and fluffy, Taurus sprinkled in the sugar as I pressed against her—feeling the hard bone of my cunt sink into her generous ass. She added the chocolate and I fondled her breasts, her nipples stiffening under my touch. She cracked the eggs, mixed in the flour, folded in chunks of white chocolate. And all the while my hands strayed lower—across her round belly that was a sweet contrast to her limbs knotted with muscle—and down to her clit that was plump and prominent.

Taurus spooned the mixture into a buttered pan, put the pan in the oven and set the timer; we had twenty minutes. I nudged Taurus to the counter, getting her to lean over it with her legs spread and her back to me. I pulled down her boxers, baring her butt. Then, I slipped a finger into her pussy. She squirmed into it, moaning, and with my other hand I reached for the butter open on the counter. I took a generous swipe and greased her crack with it, making it so slick my finger easily slipped in. I felt the rub of my own fingers through the thin wall separating her two holes and my cunt throbbed. The kitchen was thick with the deep, heady smells of slit, sweat and chocolate.

Taurus turned to look at me with her liquid-brown, almost bovine eyes. "Now," she said. "I need to come now." Still pummelling her ass, I ripped my fingers from her gooey cunt and pressed them to her clit—her clit so hard it felt like it had a stubborn bone lodged inside. Taurus bucked between my hands. Her flanks straining. Her neck muscles bulging.

"Baby," she grinned, with a final shudder as the timer rang ready. "You can ride me anytime."

Gemini

The Gemini sisters kissed and it looked perverse—like someone pressed against a mirror, lips on the glass. Impossible to tell apart, they both had long limbs, pale skin and hair streaked blonde. I'd just met them earlier that night at the theatre. A double feature had been playing: two sexy French movies with convoluted plots. Neither twin had needed the subtitles. Both were good with tongues.

One Gemini circled my waist with her arms, pulling me in. And the other coaxed my mouth open, slipping her tongue between my lips. "Forget social conventions," whispered the twin whose hand was roaming from my waist to my breast. "We're all consenting adults," she continued. "And you like it, don't you?"

My nipples growing hard and my slit growing wet, it was obvious I liked it. But I didn't *want* to. *This is wrong*, I thought, feeling a twin roll my nipples between her fingertips. *We shouldn't do this*, I thought, sucking the other one's throat. *This isn't normal*, I thought, creaming all the more. Yes, some taboos are like that. Terribly, deeply titillating.

Stroking my ass, my breasts, my cunt, the Geminis unzipped my zippers and unbuttoned my buttons. It felt like they had a million hands all blowing over me and like my hands would never be enough to know their double curves. One Gemini latched her mouth onto my nipple and chewed slightly; the other lodged her thigh between mine. And the three of us humped hard, smearing juice across each other's skin.

Suddenly one Gemini had a fat dildo—double headed with snaking silicone veins. She and her sister lay down opposite each other, legs butterflied open, and brought the cock to their holes. Then, gyrating, they swallowed. The twin bed underneath us moaned with each thrust and the yellow duvet got wetter. How many other women, I wondered, have the Geminis brought to this apartment of theirs and fucked on this tiny bed? Then the Geminis pulled me on top of them and I wondered nothing.

My tits hung in one Gemini's face; my cunt hovered over the other's mouth. And with me spread wide like that—perfectly exposed to their darting eyes—all their quick movements suddenly stopped and they simply studied me. The shape of my lips, hood, clit. The size and slope of my nipples. I waited for what seemed like a very long time, desperate to have their two tongues wash over me.

"Beautiful," sighed one Gemini, her breath blowing cool over my slit.

"Lovely," agreed the other, taking a taste.

Cancer

The porch light was on and soft music leaked out through the window. Slipping my key in the lock, I pushed the door open and heaved my suitcase over the threshold. Inside were the smells of roasting and stewing, candles and Cancer. Hearing my footsteps, she raced to me and crooned, "I had a feeling you'd arrive around now and I'm so glad you did." Then she looked at me with her large wet eyes and kissed me slowly, deeply, her hand cool on the back of my neck.

We'd been together for years, but we still didn't like to be apart, even for just a few days. And during this business trip—a seemingly endless week—I'd missed her with particular sharpness. Missed her pale, translucent skin and her face round like the moon. All I wanted now was to melt into her warm breasts. "Come," Cancer said, leading me to the bathroom.

The tub was a gorgeous old-fashioned claw-foot and Cancer had just filled it with deliciously hot water and a sprinkling of white rose petals from the garden. Anticipating a long soak, I started to take off my blouse, but Cancer caught my fingers mid-button. "Let me do it," she said. "You need pampering."

Her hands moved over me—slipping off my skirt, rolling off my stockings—until I was naked except for the thick steam clinging to everything in the room. Cancer, however, was still in her bathrobe. I tugged the satin belt and the robe opened like curtains—revealing full breasts and pale pink nipples. "Oh, I'm not getting in," Cancer said. "I've already bathed and I want you to have the whole tub to yourself. I'll stay with you, though."

Lowering myself in, I tried pulling Cancer in too. But she insisted on staying out and positioned herself behind me on the rim of the tub. She began to massage my shoulders and it felt like the hot water and her touch were seeping into my bones, soothing me. I could feel the brush of her satin sleeves and the rose petals clinging to my thighs.

I turned to face Cancer. Her parted legs were propped up on either side of the tub and she was leaning against the wall behind her—exposing the cleft moon between her thighs. I followed the blue webbing of her veins with my mouth, kissing the tenderness of her inner thighs and their jasmine musk. "You smell," I sighed, finally arriving, "like home."

Leo

I imagine she smelled of nutmeg and cloves and that her skin felt warm, like peaches in the sun. But the truth is, I never got that close. Leo lived next door—in the house with the deck decorated with pots of marigolds. And during the summer that's where she stretched out lazily in her lounging chair, watching me watch her from my second-story window.

I remember her working slick coconut oil into her calves and thighs as carefully as if she were polishing precious metal. And then, her long legs glistening in delicious contrast to her scanty orange bikini, her hands crept upward. Smeared oil along the length of her arms and over the curve of her hips—so slowly I squirmed impatiently. Was she toying with me? Would she hold back this time? I pinched my nipples to feel the soothing bite of nails.

The bikini top clasp rested between her two suns and just when I thought I'd burst, she undid it—showing me both her perfect generosity and her brutality, her nipples sharp like claws. I'd never spoken to her, but I adored her and ached to have her rake over me, over my cunt. I jammed a hand down my pants and rocked on my finger.

Leo flicked her long blonde hair and took a sip of her cocktail, an umbrella on the rim spearing a pineapple wedge. Spearing a cherry. Then she looked up at my window and, with even more excruciating slowness, she undid the bikini bottom ties resting over her hips. I saw the amber triangle between her luscious thighs and I began to sweat, to pant.

Her toes curling and extending, Leo lightly stroked her secret mane. Then she slipped a finger into her mouth and licked it with flashes of her pink tongue until it was perfectly wet. Yes, everything was wet; cream had gathered between my legs, too. Leo slid the juicy finger to her cleft and made precise circles. Her lips were parted and her eyes were half closed into pleasure slits—such the perfect lust look I wondered if she'd practiced in the mirror. But then her expression and even all her movements turned suddenly raw. And separately—together— we quivered against our hands, moaned like animals with deep throaty sounds floating through the open window.

Virgo

"According to the book," Virgo said, taking a sip of tea. "There isn't one correct way of performing cunnilingus. Correct is simply what the recipient prefers. Have *you* noted much variation in *your* partners' predilections?"

Giving head was one of my favorite topics and I strained to keep my voice as clinical as Virgo's. If I ever hoped to get down her pants, I couldn't blow it with dirty cunt talk. She wasn't that kind—not yet anyway. I suspected, however, that if I could just spread her legs, her repression would crumble to an uninhibited, hungry hole. "There's a great deal of deviation," I finally answered. "Much depends on the vulva's shape."

"Do you mean the size of the labia?" Virgo asked. "I read that women with large inner labia sometimes like having them sucked, yet women with small or absent inner labia are unable to experience this."

"The size of the labia is important but so is the size of the clitoris," I replied, marvelling again at the perversity of Virgo's sexuality. Although she'd never been with a woman, she had thorough book knowledge of lesbianism. She worked at the public library and apparently spent every free moment combing just a few special shelves.

"When a woman has a clitoris that juts out," I continued, "her partner can suck on it as if it is a small penis, but when a woman has a hidden or small clitoris, her partner is only able to lap at it." I tried to imagine the form of Virgo's clit and I felt mine pulse. We'd been having these chats every Saturday for months and they still always got me wet.

"Is there anything that all women enjoy?" Virgo asked, just as the waitress arrived with our scones and cream. "Don't you think, for example, that virtually all women prefer when the clitoris is not sought out immediately?" Virgo took a tiny bite and looked at me with clear eyes.

"True, it's best to begin by...slowly licking the area where vulva...and inner thigh meet...." I crossed and recrossed my legs but the rest of the thought stayed jammed in my throat. *Slipping the tongue between inner and outer labia. Gently retracting the hood. Sucking the clitoris.* Virgo smiled elusively.

"Would you excuse me for a moment?" I said. Then in the bathroom I made it fast and dirty and solo. Leaning against the wall with my hand rammed down my pants, I imagined Virgo using—just for once—the nonscientific terms.

Libra

We'd been dating for just a few weeks, but we were already packing for our first romantic weekend getaway. "Which toy should I bring?" Libra asked, her voice clear sugar coming through the line. "What've you got?" I answered, stuffing a swimsuit into my suitcase.

"Well, I have seven…. The first one's a finger vibe that fits perfectly—nice and snug—over the tip of my pointer. You'd love it," Libra assured me. "It feels delicious on the clit, so precise." I imagined her making tiny humming circles over my nub and assured her that I was sold—that she should definitely pack the finger vibe up.

"Wait," Libra said. "Make an informed decision; hear about *all* the toys before choosing." I cradled the phone against my shoulder, getting ready for Libra to talk my ear off. "I also have a dildo with a hollow base," she continued. "It's bright purple and intensely ribbed. The problem is, it's massive so it's only really good if you want to be ripped open."

"I could handle that," I said, setting Libra giggling. "Do you have a bullet vibe to stick inside the base?"

"Of course," she answered. "And when turned on, it purrs like a pussy and even makes some women ejaculate. It's fantastic, but on the other hand so is my elegant glass wand. Glass, you know, is rock hard and frictionless. You can fuck and be fucked with it all night long." I pictured Libra ramming such elegance up my cunt and then cleaning off the juice with the bow of her mouth. I tried to interrupt and insist that she bring the glass wand, but Libra barrelled on.

"I also have a double dildo," she said, bringing my packing to a distracted finish, suitcase left gaping. "Can you imagine us being filled at the same time?" Imagining just that, my cunt creamed and I couldn't take any more. "You know," I said, my voice cracking. "We don't need a toy. Your fingers would be just fine."

There was a slight pause on the other end of the line. "All

right," Libra finally answered. "But what hole would you like them in first?"

Scorpio

Scorpio's cock was too long, too thick, too red. Too much to hide in the folds of a skirt without magic. But no, I didn't notice the bulge when she led me through the beaded curtain to her chamber flickering with candles. Nor when she took my hand and traced each line with a bold crimson nail.

"This curve in your heart-line," she said, pinning me with her penetrating gaze, "indicates a tendency toward lust. Is that true?" Scorpio smirked like she knew the answer and placed her hand on my thigh. "Is your pussy often wet?" she continued. "Is it wet now?"

I blushed and mumbled incomprehensibly, but Scorpio's creeping hand *was* making me moist. "You're not communicating," she said. "Your throat chakra must be blocked. I'll have to open it."

Scorpio stood and released her skirt, revealing the glory of her cock. "Now," she said. "Strip."

I stared with my mouth gaping. Her beauty that stark, that sharp. Yes, Scorpio was so lean it seemed she didn't have enough skin and that her bones might tear through. Yet somehow she had juicy breasts the size of plums. I slipped off my clothes, hands shaking.

"Kneel," Scorpio ordered. Then when I got into place she walked around me three times. Her footsteps falling hard and her circles strangely binding me without rope until my arms were pinned behind my back and she stood facing me. Her cock filling my vision. "I know you want your mouth fucked," Scorpio said. "So beg for it."

I whimpered, cowed by her ability to know what I craved, and she cracked a slap on my face, making my ears ring. "Please," I bellowed. "Please."

Scorpio stroked her cock and then jammed the head in my mouth. It was so big it strained the circle of my lips and I feared I couldn't take any more, that if she rammed deeper I'd choke. "You can," she said. "You've no choice."

Scorpio rolled her hips and the shaft rubbed against the back of my throat. My eyes watered, my mouth watered, but she fucked harder. Bucked her hips until my throat numbed and then cracked open. She yanked my hair, thrusting one final time, and I swear I felt jizm spray hot and spread through me.

Scorpio pulled out. "Come back again and I'll open your swadisthana chakra, located here," she said, running a crimson nail over my cunt.

Sagittarius

"You're Moon Double Cock," Sagittarius declared, yanking off my T-shirt. "And this is your coronation ceremony."

Never having heard of a Mayan ruler so named, I raised a dubious eyebrow. But Sagittarius plowed on. "Below," she continued, "are one hundred thousand people here for the event and they're transfixed—watching me ritualistically disrobe you."

I looked over the edge of the ancient pyramid and saw nothing and no one—just the outline of lush rainforest stretching on forever. "How can they see us?" I asked. "The sun set an hour ago."

"No, the sun's at its zenith—just as this city, Tikal, is at *its* zenith." Sagittarius regarded me with fiery eyes and swept the entire park with a wide gesture. Then she knelt, kissed my feet, and stroked my legs, and I, helplessly, softened into her fantasy.

"And who," I asked, "are you supposed to be?"

"Oh, I'm the priestess leading the final stage of the ceremony."

"Final stage?"

"Yes, the bloodletting to ensure the prosperity of your reign."

"Hmm, I know some people like that, but hon, you hate blood."

Sagittarius grinned and cupped my pussy. "This is the good kind," she said. "The pop your cherry variety."

Of all the things Sagittarius had ever asked me to imagine, being a virgin struck me as the most ridiculous and I snickered until she jammed my mirth with her finger—shoved fast into my hole. "The spectators and the young queen gasp," Sagittarius said, smiling at my surprise and slipping in a second finger, then a third. "The priestess feels blood trickle down her wrist," Sagittarius continued. "And another wetness even more sacred."

Planting my feet into the cold stone, I braced myself to ride each thrust and I looked down over the pyramid's edge. My clit swollen into a fat bead, I could now see Sagittarius' vision—the one hundred thousand people watching and sliding inspired fingers into their robes, into those of their neighbors.

Sagittarius pressed her head to my cunt and flicked her tongue like a snake. "Come for the good of the people," she said between licks. "Listen to them fucking. They want your divine ass and they're screwing each other dreaming of it."

"Yes," I panted. "The spectators are a web of mouths and crotches—everyone both sucking and getting sucked. They're heaving, writhing, shaking and—now—they're coming together with the seismic force of an earthquake."

I jerked against Sagittarius' mouth, my moan ricocheting out into that surprisingly twenty-first-century night.

"Queen Moon Double Cock," she said, as soon as I'd caught my breath. "I think park rangers are coming...."

Capricorn

Still slicked with sweat and slightly panting, I was relieved to have finally reached the top. All the way up the mountain I'd had my eyes fixed on nothing but Capricorn's tight ass and now I had plans that didn't include the picnic she was unpacking. I heaved off my knapsack and rummaged through it.

"Can you believe the view?" Capricorn asked. "Isn't it incredible?" Without looking around, I nodded yes and spread the blanket.

"Come here, hon," I wheedled, slipping the sandwiches from her hands. "You didn't want to stop mid-mountain, but we're here now...." I pulled her down and kissed her like kissing was everything. And I caressed her from back to buttocks to thighs, her muscles rippling under my touch. We'd been together for two years now, but Capricorn still always needed it soft and slow to get wet.

Our eyes locked and I fell into the rich, brown earth of hers. "I want you buried in me," I whispered, setting her hands on a trail to my cunt. "And I want to be buried in you," I continued, undoing her belt.

Capricorn stroked the fur between my legs and then squeezed and massaged the lips. She had strong, capable fingers and everything she did with them was perfectly precise, perfectly designed to send tremors through my slit. I mirrored her movements—stroking with the same softness and then slipping between her folds. We lingered over each other's clits, drawing small moist circles, and finally we thrust simultaneously into each other's holes. Moaning moans that sounded like sighs.

Yes, I'd been waiting so long for her to ram my cunt that now my bones were almost melting with relief and I could finally open my eyes to see. To see the clouds soft against the mountains in the distance. To see the trail far below us twisting and curving—sometimes steep and rough, sometimes lush with velvety green. Yes, Capricorn was right. We were at a gorgeous dizzying height and we were getting close to the edge. Her thumb pressed into my clit and mine pressed into hers, we were just a few strokes from coming.

I bucked harder and drove my fingers deeper. Feeling like we'd been reduced, or perhaps elevated, to just the connection between us. Yes, that we were nothing but two pussies clamped wet onto knuckles, jerking faster and faster until we would slump into each other. Into the earth. Yes, we were as high at that moment as we'd ever be again.

Aquarius
With me and Aquarius sharing the tiny bench, our thighs touched. We were in room 11—a closetlike space dominated by a screen and the bluish light it threw off. There were sixty-nine channels on offer and I was letting Aquarius choose. This was, after all, her opportunity to learn.

I'd met Aquarius at a peace rally a year before. She'd been hard to miss as she'd been practically deep-throating a microphone, belting out chants. Also, with her silky hair and chiselled features, she'd appealed to me in a patchouli kind of way. We took up drinking fair trade coffee together every week, yet despite my longing to make it personal, our talk was always political. Then Aquarius mentioned Andrea Dworkin and I saw my opportunity.

"You can't understand pornography," I'd declared, leading her to Slut Cinema. "Until you've seen a variety."

Now Aquarius was picking a channel and the screen was filling with two stewardesses. One was topless, though she had a jaunty scarf tied around her neck. And the other was taking a miniature bottle of wine from the drink cart. Stewardess number one cracked open the wine and splashed it over number two's tits. Licked it off and then splashed on some more.

"This is a parody of lesbian sexuality," Aquarius huffed. But I said nothing. She was right—I'd never seen an actual dyke with so much makeup. Let alone such long nails. I was hoping, however, that Aquarius would soon forget about the blue eye shadow. I *knew* I would.

Stewardess number two poured the remaining wine into her costar's mouth, letting it drip from her face like cum. Then number one yanked up her skirt and wriggled out of her lace panties. The camera zoomed in, filling the screen with crotch—fleshy hairless lips, a ring through the clit. Feeling my own cunt throb, I looked at Aquarius. Her green eyes had gone big and round and she was crossing and recrossing her legs. I snaked my hand between them and, through the thin fabric of her skirt, cupped her hot pussy. Surprised, she stiffened, but then stewardess number one spread herself open and Aquarius relaxed, thrusting into my touch.

Stewardess number two looked appraisingly at her costar's juicy slit and jammed the empty bottle into her hole. Then as she slipped the bottle in and out, Aquarius slid her hand between my thighs, moving the panties to one side. Yes— finally—Aquarius, who could always be counted on to think outside the box, had her mind (and fingers) deep inside of it.

Pisces
In the surf we did kicks, flicks and side steps—mamboing together in bare feet. We didn't have music, but twilight gave us a naked rhythm.

Pisces was my partner, a woman with such grace she seemed to never walk but rather glide. A woman with tiny feet and gorgeous heavy-lidded eyes full of strange light. Pisces was a dancer by profession and passion, so she led. And I loved her, trusted her enough to let her take me into peculiar and beautiful steps.

Our mambo melted into tango—tango with its tragedy of old Argentinean nights and its sensuality of Pisces' thigh too fleetingly between mine. Then she dipped me, hard and smooth, and I felt our breasts crush together. We surfaced and slipped into another dance. This time whirling like der- vishes with our right hands lifted to heaven and our left hands pointed to earth. Our skirts billowing with each turn. "The fundamental condition of existence," I remembered Pisces telling me once over wine, "is to revolve." Now, reeling faster and faster, I understood. Neutrons, electrons, protons, wheeling through each sky. Venus, Neptune, Mars, wheeling through each cell. Pisces and I growing dizzy, flushed.

Pisces took me in her arms and we slipped into a waltz. The waves falling in three-quarter time, we step-step-closed with them, slow enough to feel not just the softness of the sand under our feet, but also its sharpness, its grit. With the strong accent on the first beat, I kissed her hard. Our tongues twisted together like two pink seals and her teeth chewed my lips.

The waltz dissolved, but the dance came back—rough—raunchy—all crotch. Yes, with our hips gyrating we were looping like music and the rub was making a slick fire. Pisces, without missing a beat, brought us to the ground.

Muscle slippery like a fish, she slid against me, letting me feel the hot press of her cunt. I dipped a finger in and wriggled through her juices. Then I pulled out, giving it to Pisces' mouth. She parted her lips and flicked her tongue over the wet finger—gorged on it as if it were a small, delicious cock. I dipped back in and sucked the fringes of her pussy lips. Her shaved slit looked like an unusual and delicate sea creature—best served raw on the half shell. It smelled like mermaid perfume and it felt like nothing else. Pisces grabbed my hair and yanked me to her clit, grinding her crotch into my face.

"This is heaven," I murmured when I finally surfaced. "This is heaven."

SUBTEXTS

Peggy Munson

1

Daddy puts on his Duran Duran album
and I run through the woods. It's the same
recurring nightmare but I am awake. The
red velvet hood brushes my cheek, soft as
blood splattered on rabbit fur. The last lights
of day cut through the trees like a series of
incisors. Daddy is a feral version of Simon
Le Bon wailing, "I'm on the hunt down
after you." The echoing music makes the
branches quiver. Everything is salivation and
footfalls and panting breath. My cape flutters
in the jet stream off my back. I don't know
why Granny has chosen to live in this spot,
but she's Germanic and odd in her need for
privacy and shade. I catch my breath at her
doorstep, glancing around with paranoia. I

fondle the laces on my corset. Granny likes me hemmed in.

Granny isn't really kin. We call her Granny because she's been in the scene longer than anyone. In the front room, her whips hang on nails and her teacups rest on hooks. Everything looks normal, except that her boi's dog crate is open. He's usually there, curled up and resting between chores. Maybe she sent him to buy lube at the general store. I pry open her door. I see Granny's frilly bonnet heaving on the bed. "I brought baguettes," I say cheerfully. "And your favorite whiskey, Granny G." But something is not right. I have a feeling of déjà vu as I lean over her protruding nose and utter the lines: *My what big teeth you have. My what big teeth.* Granny has always been proud of her Ashkenazi nose, but the flaring nostrils are not hers. "Better to eat you with," snarls the thing in Granny's nightie.

The figure lurches out of bed and pins me to the maple floor, singing "Hungry Like the Wolf" between drooling snarls. "Eeek!" I scream. Daddy has duped me. He bites at my velvet cape, tearing off pieces like flesh, red filaments flying everywhere. "Grrrr, you tease," he snarls, fumbling for my wrists. I struggle to get away as his nostril-steam and claws leave white contrails on my chilly sky-blue skin. I grab his throat and squeeze it until he is pawing the air for breath. I pull myself away, with half of my cape ripped off, and my corset and panties still on. "You whore," Daddy snarls. I hope he molests me on the half-mulched autumn leaves.

I take off running.

I should have known he'd be in Granny's bed. Daddy sometimes bottoms to Granny. She probably made him eat her out, something he's very good at with his long, wolfish tongue and nicking teeth that terrify a clit just enough to make it stand up. Maybe she got the munchies after he made her come, and went with her boi into town. I shouldn't have stopped in the woods to drink my bottle of Orangina. Daddy pants down the trail as the trees slap me on the ass with their branches, and try to pry their way inside of me. Daddy and the supernatural trees are in cahoots. Daddy calls out to a sugar maple and then its gnarly blackened arms seize me and pull me to its bark. It stuffs a hunk of gingham in my mouth—the handkerchief that fell from my basket of food. It flips me around so that I'm facing a woodpecker hole. "I've got her," says the tree.

"Stop it, you wooden jerk!" I yell as I spit out the handkerchief. The trees cackle. They look so wholesome and Rabbinical with their long beards of moss, but they are dirty, voyeuristic bastards. I rip at the bark with my fingernails. But it's too late: Daddy strolls down the trail, swinging his tail. His fur pokes around his leather chaps. He spanks a paddle against his left hand. "Toro, toro," says Daddy, and takes the last of my red cape in his mouth and tears it off. He yanks my panties to my ankles, then spreads my legs out until my panties rip. "You're too tempting to the animals," says Daddy. "Tsk-tsk." He whaps my ass with the paddle and his long, scratchy tongue runs down my ass crack. He starts rimming my asshole and his nose burrows in my crack. He slides his long nose between my legs, sniffing my wet pussy. "Ahhhhhhh," he sighs. "You smell like a rained-on clove cigarette. No—like a puddle full of dimes." He has to mull over this for a while, his nose nearly fucking me as it prods around my hole, and his tongue lapping at my pussy juice. I start to whimper from the abrasion of his tongue on my clit and my pussy lips. My clit feels swollen. I thrash against the branches that are holding me. I stare with one eye into the darkness of the woodpecker hole. "No," says Daddy finally, after he's teased me for a while. "You smell like a girl who fucked herself in the woods." Now he's angry. "A girl who is not supposed to FUCK herself without PERMISSION." He slams the paddle very hard on my ass, so I flinch and retract. He is right. After I finished my Orangina, I stuck the bottle in my ass. I noticed the bottle was shaped like a butt plug, with a big bulbous end that wouldn't slip in and a narrow shaft. I thought how Granny might flog me for being late, and I rubbed my clit and fucked myself with the bottle on my picnic blanket until I came.

"I'm sorry, Daddy," I'm begging now. "I didn't mean to—"

"Bitch," he yells. A birch tree turns around when he says *bitch* as if he's called its name. It thrusts a bunch of branches toward Daddy for him to make a switch. He starts to beat my ass, the branches stinging up and down my legs. I moan and plead for him to stop but wow, it feels incredible. "Oh, Daddy," I moan gleefully. I'm swimming in endorphins when he pins me fast against the bark. He mounts me from behind and pumps his cock into my ass. He fucks me for a while like that, his hot breath scalding me. "Oh fuck me fuck me fuck me," I scream, stupid as a little girl with nothing but a ruthless id. Before I come, he pulls his cock out and slips another condom on. He tells the trees to look at me. "Look at my little whore," he says. "Look at my puddle full of dimes."

"She's hot," the trees exclaim in unison. They point between my legs where I am dripping wet, where I am opened up for all to see. "Look at her lipstick cave." They're leaning in, blocking the moon and stars so that I only see the shining eyes of animals.

"Her lipstick cave," says Daddy. "Yes, that is exactly what it is." He takes his finger and he spreads my pussy lips. He sniffs me with his nose again, and pries the hole with nose and teeth so I am gasping, moaning for his cock. He pulls a tube of lipstick from my satchel, then applies it all around my pussy so it makes a little mouth. "I want to hear you scream," he says. "And plead and beg for help. No one can hear you here. Meanwhile, I want a blow job from your cunt." He rams his cock inside of me.

I squeeze his cock with all the muscle I have left. He rocks and heaves and thrusts.

The trees begin to clear away as he is fucking me, so that I'm floating in a meadow, lashed to just one tree. He's burning up my lipstick cave. He's ripping all my animals to bits of bones. I am the dissolution of a hundred fairy tales. I am a girl made up of screaming, hungry red. "What big—" I gasp. "What big you have."

"Just come, you little bitch," he orders me, and wraps his arm around my throat. "Come like you've got some teeth."

2

When I see Lo I have the most awful impulses. I have the most gnawing, stabbing, torsion-of-stomach pains. I have dirty, vile, horseshit-covered-cobblestone ideas. I am a French novel used as toilet paper. I want to do things that would make you sick. In bathroom stalls, in alleys lined with fire escapes and brick: I want to fuck this girl until she cries out Uncle, skewered on my dick.

She is older than her namesake, but not by many years. She twirls hair around one finger, oblivious, only as old as the gap between us, working her

Barely
Legal tender
Currency.

I am a wretched, pummeled heap of human bones watching
from across the street. I am *that* dirty old man in an archetypal
trench coat, pulling my meat beneath the tweed. The sky is a
single ironed crayon, translucently cornflower blue. Lo buys
one baguette, and butters it from top to bottom before settling
in to eat, her plucky lips noshing the edges, teasing all she
ingests. Her coffee melts into tanned skin. Her fingers give a
hand job to the baguette. Every gesture she makes is so erotic.
I stroke my stiff cock and gasp. The whole world hangs where
it is—a hundred wordless games of hangman—until she gets
up to leave the café. Her skirt forms a coy paper fan.

I grow flushed looking at her. I am the rosiest rube.

Then wagging tongues follow her like rattling cans.

She has read the *CliffsNotes* and knows this story. How one
day she will peel me off of her like old tin that has crashed
around her body, how needy and car-wrecked I will be. At
night, she kisses my hip bones, bending them like luthier's
wood. She sees the harmonics of her laugh and my stiff dick.
I know I'm a sick old man. Ah, but I drive down the winding road of her body. Ah, down the blind, sexy curves (with
cut brakes of cut nerves). I skulk behind her tall-backed chair
as she does her homework, then press her hands to the stiff
wooden arms. "Gotcha, whore," I bark. I run my fingers
over the front of her T-shirt until she is writhing, making the
chair dance around. I slide her skirt away and shove aside her
panties and make my way inside her carefully, carefully. Her
pussy is dripping. I tell her: *Take it hard, make it fit.* Later,

she holds her narrow fingers over my eyes and implores me, "Don't peek." Then she works her poisonous mouth on my dick. Later, I watch her pomegranate body unpeeling, all of its encapsulating red. She laughs, my little Lo, and lo I am done in.

It would be perfect to hold her still. Pin her to her innocence. But who am I kidding? She is more knowing than I. I do pin her into door frames, against walls while she tries to squirm away. I fuck her and kiss her and make her come. I pin her to her own capitulation.

It wasn't until forty that I really embodied my dick. Before that, I was amorphous and bookish and repressed. I had wan lesbian sex with nonrepresentational implements. Then something rustled in my briefs, just as corn shoots up audibly at night, and from that day on I sought the feelings I found with twenty-year-old Lo. I was once afraid of my desires, but I am no longer afraid. I have met the gutting knives of her gazes, and savored the bloodless high as my entrails spilled from me. Lo's young lust has liberated me.

"Come on, come on," she says impatiently, tugging my hand. She takes me to the edge of the city, where the caverns begin. I punish her for casting a glance to the rocker boy stoking the bonfire outside as we enter the cave. I shove aside her skirt and fuck her against graffiti and she becomes a limp vowel, her sweet juices spilling on me. "You're mine," I tell her. "You fucking tease." I push her down to her knees by her head. She makes lipstick graffiti on my cock. She is thin kindling and I am an illusion: flat as newsprint. When I fuck her, I am a flat-hatter skimming her rose bushes, flying away so fast she does not know what left her so turned on and trimmed. I am certain she sees me as a transparent chump, but she doesn't let on. She acts like this is not the most threadbare perversion in the literary canon: a dirty old guy and a nymph. Later, she moves one hand up my pant leg, teasing out my blood, pushing it to a mottled point. She has no idea how she turns me on. All she has to do is rub a straw between her lips, cross her knees. Unbeknownst to her, even her fabric comes on to me.

When we kiss, when I unbutton her blouse, when I lift out her breasts—and, best of all, when I make her lips part: it is too much. Life spills out of her, and I scoop it into my pockets, as the old do. My skin biodegrades like cellophane each time she exhales a little breath.

Then I fuck her: oh *god*. I fuck her with my mind, my hands, what lays wait in my pants. I fuck her in my dreams, in my car, under weeping willow trees. I fuck her in hotel rooms where I use pseudonyms like Mr. Wood, and she pretends to be my daughter in a strappy dress. I tell her to ride my cock harder while the curtains snap closed in disgust. I tell her to spread wide, then wider, for my cock. Every part of her swallows me, every membrane breaks. I am the black widow's dinner and I'm willing, I'm there. I give my spindly self over to her.

It is the way she touches me. We used to watch water bugs gliding across the creek: like reflections trying to escape a mirror. She touches me so lightly and delicately until I am just honed glass, no longer a likeness. I have never felt so touched as when she touches me.

And how she kisses me. The gasp of suspension bridges, hummingbirds with sugar water, things that feed only on sugar and air.

In my dreams, her head is in my lap, and we are simple. In my nightmares, my car is spinning out of control, and she has stolen the steering wheel. I wake up gasping, my rubber dick the only steel rod holding my flaccid bones in place. "Lolita," I'm screaming, but she is no longer there.

Lo pretends to be morose, wears little goth skirts and dark eyeliner and dyes her hair black. She listens to my old Smiths albums and puts safety pins through her skin. Sometimes, she nearly rips my cock out of my pants, starving for its girth. Sometimes, she has fits about how she can't take living with an old *perv*. She goes to clubs and comes home at 3:00 a.m. I am tortured to think of the boys and girls who bite her lower lip, but relieved when she walks through the door sullen and drunk and wanting me. Even when she tries to appear somber, the day skips around her whims. She lifts up light wherever she walks. She has piercings all over, reflective metal on skin. I stare at her necklace and want to unlace her, fuck her angry and raw. I run my fingers under the clasp, tease her vulnerable veins. I play with magic and metalurgy. She gasps. She gives in. Then I am sliding my fingers into her, cupping her liquid in my palm.

She is not dragging invisible chains like I am.

Oh, my little Lo, if only I could always have her burrowing around my sheets or giggling, flopping her legs over my lap. If only I could keep her collared and tied. If only I didn't have to resort to Japanese rope bondage, and chain, and clothespins I use to decorate her skin. If only she didn't like to be bound and tied and crosshatched by whips. If only she didn't like to be bruised and spanked and cajoled and stripped. If only she didn't like to be on all fours, like a colt. Or splayed out while I fuck her up the ass. If only she didn't kiss like a cottonmouth, and like cotton. If only I could crawl into her skin, and be that young again. If only it weren't so terribly taboo and wrong. If only the dark roar within me didn't feel like a religion, this twisted psalm. If only it didn't make me pray to the child who would lead me, lead me home.

3

The tittering old nurses adore Finny. He indulges their gummy speeches about the good old days at boarding school. They tell him how handsome he is, what a *catch*, then giggle about his gender camouflage when they give him sponge baths. I call him Granny's boi because they like him so much. They read him books from the library and giggle over the dirty parts. I don't care how Nabakov got his rocks off: I like bois. I adore Finny's salmon-hued cheeks.

"They gave me a suppository last night," he says provocatively when I walk in. "I'm a clean mean pooping machine."

"Very kinky," I reply and nervously pace near the window. I can see the tree from here.

I made him topple from the branch to get a piece, a separate piece of him, for me. What good was a God in the sky? The eloquence of his body tumbling was a ripped treble clef, and I could not bear any more singsong choirs with the war raging overseas. War made us horny and confused. We did not know what to do with the bulls in our balls. So I jiggled the branch, and Phineas fell to the ground, and broke his bones. I shook the branch to understand my own desires. Haven't there always been casualties from that impulse?

From the infirmary window, all I can see are maples. Wood waiting for confused bois who want to maim something so they don't have to go off and kill. Our lives here are a denuded fairy tale. I grab my belt to jiggle my package. "I hate this fucking wheelchair, G.," he says. "Nobody understands me but you." I'm too shy to look at his trousers, to see the bird folded in the nest, bring the worm. In the wheelchair, he is my prisoner of war. "I know, Finny," I reply. "You deserve a hero's welcome." I slowly unzip my fly. My shirttails, like a stage curtain, part. My dick is the star attraction: no longer his understudy. "I've got to tell you something," I say. I am jittery, but I turn around and face him. "But first, I want you to put my cock in your mouth. It's your one-gun salute. Your dicker tape parade."

He grins. He takes my rubbery dick in his warm hands. I can't bear his serene confidence, how he shines without fuel. I want to make him gag on my poverty, my putrid soul. "Tell me anything," he says, rubbing his hands on my shaft. "I'm your man." Even many of the nurses don't mistake him for a girl: he's not obvious like me.

I'm the geek. I need philosopher's proofs. A Kantian escape from the cunt. I'm not a sculpture brought to life, a body that makes everyone believe that he or she can thrive and live eternally. I am not he. "I'll tell you this much," I say. "You're a born cocksucker. You've got gunpowder in your gullet."

I grab a clump of his perfect hair in my fist, so forcefully he gasps. His lips are scarred with a color too red to persist. In times of war, life has to downgrade, or it will ache. My cock is too big for his wet red lips, but he wraps his whole mouth around me, starts moving it down while he grips my pockets. "Mmmm." Finny moves like hummingbird wings. He'll give to me no matter how bankrupt I am. He sucks me perfectly. The best blow job ever. He never gags, not even when I rough him up, and force my cock to the back of his throat. I moan and glance over my shoulder at the door handle and then, suddenly, I start to sob. I'm just a little boi. Finny grabs my ass and holds me. He licks slowly up my cock. He sucks my grief right out of me.

"I did this to you, Finny," I cry, barely scraping out a whisper. "I shook the branch and made you fall." His eyes grow big and blue: the madness of porphyritic bedpans. He will not let me pull away. His hands form a swing for my ass.

"Stop saying that! Don't be an animal," he shouts angrily, then slaps my cheek hard. The sting moves all the way through my groin and I moan. It's so hot when he gets angry. "That isn't funny." He slaps me a few more times, harder with each hit so the tears are shocked out of me. He turns me and sits me down on his lap and reaches around and jerks me off. "I'll shake your fucking branch," he whispers. "Close your eyes, boi. Fall."

The knot of guilt sinks through my torso and splits into big, aching acorns in my balls. I fall back and whimper as he makes me come by jerking his hand on my strapped cock and pressing its base into my little boi-dick underneath. He kisses my ears. "Don't mess with me like that," he chides sweetly. "You'd never hurt a fly." I turn around and press my lips to his and flick my tongue in his mouth. He grabs a crutch and swings it toward my head. He knocks me lightly on the skull so I fall over, dizzy, laughing. Then I start crawling toward his chair and I pull out his cock. "God, Finny," I say hungrily. "I want to fuck your cleaned-out ass so bad." I wrap my lips around his cock. He starts groaning and raking his fingers through my hair as I tease the head of his dick.

Before Finny, I was little more than a wooden foot soldier, a chess pawn. He was the one who rippled the nervous tic that shook my legs that shook the branch. I've wanted to be inside of him forever. Finny has never let me fuck him up the ass. I've thought about it every single night while staring at the moonlight squinting through the trees. "I'm helpless, Gene," he finally says. "You pretty much could prison rape me any time in here."

I reach an arm behind his back and lift him out of his chair. He is perfect. Even the scribbles on his cast are calligraphic, well-penned. He is breathtakingly pure.

I lay him down gently on the hospital bed and put his broken leg in traction and his other leg to the side. I shove some pillows beneath his lower back to lift him. I grab a tube of lube from the hospital tray, and work a little around his hole with my finger, teasing the opening as the tender skin pulses. I kneel at the end of the bed and start to rock my cock into his ass. His hole clenches around my cock, then lets go—like the pond swallowing a jumping boi. It feels amazing, and I hold down his arms and pump deeper. Finny's face goes starkly peaceful. I hold his hand as if I'm a hospice aide. "Let go," I say. I cock back my swollen cock and aim and fire. Just as he's moaning "Oh, god," I look out the window and see the headmaster's daughter pulling strands of gum from her mouth. She must be the angel of death.

Much later, a woodpecker plays its own version of "Taps" and I feel senselessly alive. The funeral party has gone off to eat a smorgasbord of food. The woodpecker leaves a hole in the tree that looks like Finny's sphincter. Pushed by my roughneck hormones, I shove my pecker in the hole and thrust. My cock is just a piece of rubber tree, but all life blooms inside its awful rage. I violate the tree. I shake its trunk in rage. I bone upon it and I try to make myself as hard as Finny would have been, as brave. The bark abrades my boi-tits and arouses me. I wrap my arms around the tree and hug it, fuck as deep as I can get. The leaves are dying slow, civilian deaths. My trousers drop atop my knees. I take my other hand and pull my tie, to choke myself a bit. The air teases the little hairs around my ass. My dick is growing from the swell of choral voices changing as they steel up for the war. I'm coming as he's passing out of here and melting into sky.

I smoke a cigarette, then climb the very branch I shook. Up high, I look around and all I see is sex, the green that is so vast it is almost unbearable. The anti-war.

The temporal beauty of this arbor I abhor.

4

I've wanted to get to the marrow of earth, its watery depths.

I've been on a hunt for as long as I can say, for thundering butches with whitecaps in their veins. I've ridden seas of cocks and fists, gone deep-sea fishing with sailor-mouthed sods. I've fucked the sperm whales with realistic cocks that squirt fake cum, the codpieced pieces of work who think courtship is a Renaissance religion, the clammed-up stones who speak in a Morse code of thrusts. They have wailed inside pussy trying to reach my belly, cast fishhook glances with their eyes, bit my lips bloody. They have held me by the scalp and circled my wounds, as hammerhead sharks would do—butting me with their cocks.

But I just want Melville.

I sink into the bar stool at the Pittsfield Whale and gaze at her. Her hair is bristly and uneven, as if she cuts it in the dark. I watch as she works one hand with a dishrag, moving it like a fin around a damp glass. She doesn't raise her face to look at me when she plunks down my drink. She curls over one bent arm at the other end of the polished oak bar fabricated from an old ship's deck. She talks to a pride of butches with Massachusetts accents, their salty voices a creak of metal shoring up against the relentless cold. "Wicked starm, eh?" one says. "Yep, pissin' down snow," the other answers. They glug frosty ales. I have only lived in these parts a few months, and I seek out the Whale most weeks.

I know her two fetishes: sappy karaoke and fishnet stockings. Whenever I wear fishnets, her eyes snag upon me for a moment, checking out my legs. Tonight, she sings "Rio" by Duran Duran. Her hands form twisted shipyard knots on the microphone and, knowing snow is piling up outside the door, she wails, "Her name is Rio and she dances on the sand." By the time she finishes, all cars in the parking lot are buried. The trucks make their way to the road, but my pathetic Volkswagen is unrecognizable, a Galápagos turtle that has taken a bad turn. I stand in the door of the Whale shifting my feet. I feel the wind howling through the holes in my fishnets. Melville lumbers up behind me.

"It would be unseemly for me not to offer a ride," she says, her jocular potato-print face spreading into a shy grin. Her Ford pickup could chug through any weather. I am wearing next to nothing, still Southern in my need to expose a tasteful bit of skin. "Yeah?" I ask. I have a ridiculously poofy down coat that I bought before I realized I was allergic to it. It turns my skin bright red wherever it touches, and makes my nose run. "Where you headed?" she asks.

"Cummington," I reply. "I'm renting a space near the old artist colony. You know it?"

"Don't think," says Melville.

"It's an hour," I add. Snowflakes stick to my eyelashes as I flutter them.

"Hardly a drive," she replies, guiding me into the cab. I push over the tools on the seat. There is a coil of rope on the floor and I poke my heels into its gaps. The fishnets rub my pussy. Melville wants to thrash against their flimsy barrier: I can tell.

She drives carefully. Melville is just the kind of butch I like: shy in the streets, confident in the sheets. Snow hits the truck in a dizzying hurl. The roads are so rural we just pass thickets of tall pines. Then, the snow begins to grow more treacherous, blocking visibility except for a few feet away. I notice the edge of the horizon wobble. Suddenly, Melville loses control. Without warning, the truck goes black: the headlights shut off, the motor stops dead, and the whole vehicle coasts over a bank, bouncing on its shocks. Melville pumps the brake but the truck doesn't stop. She tries to turn over the engine but it makes a wheezy grind. It is as if the battery has been thrown into water. We coast amphibiously into the dark. "Oh god," yells Melville.

We glide through the marshmallow fluff landscape. I am sure we are going to hit something—a tree, a pole—but the car stops abruptly in a sea of snow, just floating there. We both jerk forward against our seat belts and then the cab rocks back and forth. It seems like we are rocking in water, not on solid ground. The snow looks like froth on top of surf. I see a few protruding rocks that look like dorsal fins. Melville's face casts an odd light: round as a lighthouse lantern.

"Are you okay?" she asks with alarm, putting her hand on my knee. I scan her face, then see it in the dark: her giant dick, protruding from her fly.

"I'm fine," I say, and point. "But your bone is sticking out."

Melville's eyes shoot to her crotch. "So it is," she laughs. "See what your hot self could have done to my fibula? At least I have a splint for this." She takes one hand and wraps it around the base of the cock, jerking it gently as she stares intensely at my face, then at my fishnets. The truck is rocking back and forth like a schooner, the Berkshires rising in swells. I whimper when I see Melville handle her cock. I almost start to salivate, like a man on a hunt.

"So, baby, do you have a blowhole?" she asks, and my face wrinkles in confusion. Then she traces a finger on my lips. "Oh," I answer. "*Blow*hole. I guess I do."

She guides my head down over her soft leg. I pull my hair back with one hand, then wrap my lips around her dick and suck. Melville grips my tangled kudzu of hair so I can work with free hands and knead her thighs. Her hips rock gently into my throat, making me gag a little so I'm struggling back. "That's right," she sighs. "Take my cock in your blowhole, baby." She starts jerking and heaving into me like she's going to come. I pull up for a moment and beg, "I need you to fuck me."

Melville says, "Let's brave the storm and crawl into the back. I've got lots of wool blankets under the truck cap." She pulls me to her side of the cab and the rope follows with me, tangled in my legs, so that I trip when we tumble out the driver's-side door. Then we sink down so far into the snow it seems liquefied. Melville grabs the door handle of the truck, and swings the rope to hook the corner of the rear bumper. Then she drags us through the snow, holding me tight with one arm, until we can crawl into the capped space in the back. We shake off snow and then Melville drapes me in blankets, then warms me up with her body. She takes off her down vest and rolls up her sleeves so I can see her naval tattoos: an anchor, a school of fish, and a pinup girl on her forearm flesh. She slides a hand up my leg. "What are you trying to catch with these fishnets?" she says.

"You know what," I answer. "Your Moby Dick."

"You ain't seen nothing," says Melville. She fumbles under the covers for a minute, then puts a flashlight in my hand and guides the light down her own body. She's strapping the biggest dick I have ever seen. A whalebone of a boner. "Spread your netting," she orders me gruffly. She twists the rope around my wrists and ties a slipknot. "We'll moor you til you can't take any more." She pries one finger through a hole in my fishnets. "Oh baby," she moans. "You're a stormy little thing." She rams her cock against the fishnets, trying to force her way in. Her cock is so huge she has to throw me on my back and get on top of me and grunt and push to get it through. I pull her by her belt loops. Once she breaks through a square of string she has to conquer my hole. The cock is huge and Melville has to really work to get it in. Her big seaworthy hands push my thighs up in the air. I bang sideways against the cold metal of the truck, rocking us further into the drift. All my life, I have been a landlocked mariner and a tongue-tied storyteller. I have been shipwrecked and parched of words. I have been pirated and buffeted and overturned. I've had a need so big and shameful that I couldn't even speak of it. Melville holds my mouth closed with her hand so I can barely whimper through. "It's okay, baby, take it all," she says. "You've got an oceanic need." She epic-fucks me all night long with her behemoth cock. It is a pleasure I would drown to get.

SWEET HUNGER

Skian McGuire

It's hot in the sugar house, with the fire that never goes out and the sap boiling off in clouds of steam. Too hot for clothes. There's nobody to see me, and the old warped windows are fogged up anyway. When the time comes, the fog will clear, and there will be a face looking in. That's the way it always is. The magic, as near as I can tell, is supposed to be done naked as you're born and naked as your soul is when you die. Sugar is what comes in between, and pain.

It used to be a collective, dykes in the woods and dykes in the milking barn and dykes coming out the proverbial wazoo. Good part of the world to find them, next to all those women's colleges and the leftovers hanging around. I was never a college girl; I've been here on this farm since there were still Indians for neighbors. But for a time it was lesbians, and you could say that's what She likes best. After all, She's the one that makes the maples' love come down in buckets, in the spring, when the whole world is getting pregnant.

For a time it was wimmin's land, that's the way they wrote it then though it sounds the same regardless, for a little minute in the history of the world. They came looking for the simple life, or safe haven from the men who raped them, or to be pure in the holy spirit of womonhood. Some came looking for Her, and it was these last—few and far between—that made the sugar with me.

They were good women. The ones who came for their own reasons left for their own reasons, too, and I can hardly remember them now, but Hers are burned in my mind just like splashes of boiling sap have left white scars on my hands and arms through the years. There was Bethie, who went back to school to be a doctor; and Sue, who left to marry a man; and Chris we lost to breast cancer. And Patty, who died in that terrible car crash; she was the last of the ones who chose by daylight, and what went wrong with it was not her fault. I suppose you could call them lovers, for what we did in the spring. Now I take such help as comes, when the glass clears. I don't remember their names.

I know what they see through the streaky pane. A tall woman, powerfully built, broad of shoulder and hip but narrow in the waist, breasts high and full, lush ass, round thighs. I am their dream of womanliness. Tied-back hair sprung loose in wisps that plaster themselves to my sweating face, and its color is always the color their mothers' was, when they were tiny children. Their eyes drop to the triangle of hair between my legs, and something about my sex casts a spell on them, that and the smell of the maple, to be caught in the sticky sweetness of the air.

They have wakened in the night and gone for a walk to ease their restlessness. That is the way it always is now, and they are always women, because, as I said, that's the way She likes it. It would be women, I think, even if it weren't for the clientele I make purpose to court here at my B&B, which is what the farm has come to. It's advertised in all the lesbian magazines. A down-home Yankee vacation. Perfect for your same-sex honeymoon—I even put in a hot tub. I cook them a breakfast and I leave them alone, which seems to be the way they like it. The sugar house and the maple trees figure in all the advertising photos, though I never mention these things by text. Let word of mouth bring them here, when it's time. When the sugar comes.

I keep the boiler going all night as long as the sap is running; a couple of local boys help during the day so I can get some sleep, not that I need much. It's at night I have to be here, chucking in cord wood, adding sap, skimming froth, waiting. The steam swirls up, sweet enough still to make every surface sticky. Sometime—never the first night, but always before the last gallon is finished—there will be a cool draft, and a pale shape in the foggy window will become a face behind the flickering orange reflection of my fire. I will watch her expression change from curiosity to surprise, and her eyes will pass down my body as her expression changes again. I know what desire looks like. I open the rattling old latch of the sugar house and let her in.

She takes my hand as she steps through the door, and my hand is as soft and young as hers. I don't need to say anything.

I pull her toward me, her eyes glittering with the fire inside her, her lips slightly parted. She is breathing fast. I am the one who has to push her big heavy coat off her shoulders, undo each button of her flannel shirt. The clothes are cold from the winter night. They fall in a heap on the rough floor. She is as compliant as a child, lifting her arms obediently for me to pull her thermal shirt over her head. I pull her to me, then, pressing my sweaty breasts against her cool ones, and she gasps as our flesh meets. I lower my mouth to open lips for a kiss.

She is hungry for it, letting my tongue invade her and answering it with her own. Her breathing quickens still more as we kiss hard and long, until she moans deep in her throat and her hips move against mine and her cold hands slip around me to pull me even tighter to her.

I break off the kiss to push her away and find the elastic waistband of her sweatpants. Even as I slip my fingers under it, against her flesh now warming to my touch, she is toeing off her unlaced pac boots. Her hands come to my hips to steady herself, as she hides her face against my shoulder. Is she ashamed of her desire? Her infidelity to the lover left sleeping in their room? I have never known why, since this is a woman's offering to the secret Goddess of her heart, and nothing shameful. I try to keep from smiling, because it is always the same: however shy, she is not wearing panties, and never more than the loosest, most easily disposed-of clothing. Whatever dream sent her here, it sent her here ready. When I part her legs with my hand, she is slick and swollen with wanting. My two fingers slip right in and she clutches me tighter, her legs suddenly made of rubber. I lower her to the floor, to the heap of clothing and the blanket I laid there ahead of time. After the long winter, like the quickening Earth Herself, I am ready, too.

I lay her down gently, kissing and licking and nuzzling as I go. She licks me too, idly at first but then as purposeful as a dog, for the salt of my body and the sweet of the maple steam. I let her lick until I have slipped down, out of reach.

Her nipples are tight and pink as oak buds. She shivers when I tongue them each in turn, gasps when I suck one hard, cries out when I take it in my teeth. I force myself to be gentle, and suck for a long time, like a baby, while my fingers explore the landscape of her body, the firm ridge of ribs, the swell of belly, the crest of hip. My body presses her legs apart, and she spreads them even further. My mouth follows the trail my hands have blazed—gentle, gentle, my teeth grazing lightly across the surface, taking only a tiny carefully restrained nip. I must not draw blood. I know that now. Poor Patty.

She is bucking her hips now, trying to draw me down, moaning. Now she is as slippery with sweat as I am. I bury my face in her pussy and her moist thighs clamp spasmodically on my shoulders before surrendering. She is so wet her juice is like a liquor I can dip out of her on the curled end of my tongue. She shivers when I do. I take my fill.

When I take her with my hand at last, her cunt is like a ripe raspberry ready to drop from the cane, soft and juicy and bursting. Sometimes she has already come in my mouth; sometimes she comes as soon as I plunge into her; sometimes she comes again and again as I drive my fingers in and out. The one that has come to offer herself tonight spreads her legs for me to ease my whole hand inside her while I hold her in my lap, one arm cradling her, the other squeezed in the dark hot cave of her cunt. I churn my closed fist while her pleasure rises and ebbs and rises again. I breathe in her musk, lush and fertile and clean as the breeze through the June marsh grass.

It's the summer that has risen in her, like Persephone returning from the underworld, like the sweetness that the trees held
back until the sun had come round again. When she is limp
and spent, I pull my hand from her, careful not to wipe the
juice away on our discarded clothes, and rise.

The time has come to open the tap that lets the sap down
from its collection tank into the boiler. It is icy cold compared
to the heat inside her. I taste the crystal-clear sweetness of the
maple on my palm, suck the savory richness of her from my
fingers, the two flavors mingling on my tongue. Now spring
can come. The magic is done, the world is remade, from the
molecules of sap that will boil for hours before becoming
syrup, to the metal of the boiler and the rough planks of the
sugar house walls, to the hard winter earth beneath us, to the
she-bears giving suck in their sleep, to the budding trees to the
house where other guests lie sleeping and my own bed waits.

The syrup itself carries magic into the world, too, not just
the act of making it. Sex and sweat and the rising sap itself
are power enough, no need of blood to turn eros into something else. It's no business of Dionysus, with his bloodthirsty
wild-eyed girls strewing chaos, like the chaos that tore this
women's house apart when once I was not careful. Now I
leave that for the vintners and brewers and the moonshiners
who boil something stronger than sweet amber syrup. What
magic gets bottled into gallons and quarts and pints and why
is beyond my knowing, except to know it's there. Is it for
love? For healing? For fruitfulness? That's Her mystery. All I
know is the magic of making it. There must be other places
where sweet desire is tapped and made into something the
human world can use, shut off as most of it is in concrete and
steel and rhythms based on prime time and season premieres

instead of sunrise and the circle of the year. This is my part.

I rouse my guest into just enough wakefulness to restore her to her clothes, push her boots back on her feet, bundle her into her coat. She leans on me heavily as I guide her back to the old farmhouse, up the creaking steps to the room where her lover lies sleeping. Has one of them ever woken in the night, nothing but an empty place cooling in the bed beside her? Did she lie there, waiting, becoming afraid? Did she shiver by the window, wondering if she ought to pull on her jeans and boots and go out looking? If she did, she thought better of it and climbed back under the heavy quilt to fall into dreamless sleep, her memory of the night haunted only by the faint scent of wood smoke and sugary steam and the bite of the cold night air. I know how it goes: they will wake together at daybreak, ravenous for each other, and if their lovemaking is a little rougher than it usually is, well, whatever slight sweet bruise, whatever red imprint of a grasping hand, whatever soreness of a woman well-fucked might linger into the light of day, there will be reason for. And neither of them will remember anything else.

The moonlight from the hall window is bright enough to see the liver spots on my gnarled old hand, bright enough to catch a glimpse of my white hair in the mirror by the stairs. I move stiff and slow with weariness, but I must return to keep the fire on til morning. No bed for me, yet; no release for my own want, which the years have never quenched. I am crone now, but maiden still. There is power in that, beyond what comes from the sugar and the rising sap and the hunger of women's desire for each other.

I bottle the syrup and sell it like any other, never knowing where it goes in the world or what it's for, except to knit the green earth's lust for life back into the human heart where it's grown so stale of late. That's not my part. Here in the woods, women come and bring me their hunger for sweetness. I take it and give more back, and mix the two with what the winter trees draw up from the waking earth and send it out to make its magic in the world.

ABOUT THE AUTHORS

Zoë Alexandra is a twenty-one-year-old student at Southern Connecticut State University. She has studied creative writing at New York University and has been published in the summer 2005 edition of *Deconstruction Quarterly*. She is involved with Food Not Bombs New Haven and she likes to cook vegetarian delights, ride her bicycle and hang out with her Shiba Inu, Sasha. She is currently working on a collection of erotic poetry.

D. Alexandria (d-alexandria.com), "Boughet-to Princess," a Jamaican descendant, hails from Boston. Her work has been published in *Best Lesbian Erotica 2005* and *2006, Ultimate Lesbian Erotica 2006* and, under the pseudonym Glitter, in *Queer Ramblings Magazine* and

GBF Magazine. She is a regular contributor to Kuma2.net. She is currently penning her first novel and a collection of black lesbian erotica.

TARA ALTON (taraalton.com) lives in the Midwest where she works as a travel consultant. When she is not working or writing erotica, she collects tattoos and worships Bettie Page. She has contributed stories to online magazines such as *Clean Sheets*, *Scarlet Letters*, and *Mind Caviar* and her work has been included in the anthologies *Best Lesbian Erotica 2006*, *The Mammoth Book of Best New Erotica*, and *Best Women's Erotica*.

A. LIZBETH BABCOCK lives in Toronto where she has done extensive work in the queer community, including counseling LGBTQ youth, conducting anti-homophobia workshops, facilitating groups for children of queer parents, and developing programming for lesbians with substance use concerns and for people living with HIV/AIDS. She likes beaches, puppets, and street sausages. This is her first published work.

ANNETTE BEAUMONT is a self-described risk taker. Racing skeleton sleds down iced tracks at speeds exceeding 80 mph paled in comparison to coming out in her late thirties in fear of losing her children. She still enjoys a life of multiple identities. A CEO by day, she finds balance in extreme sports and adventure travel. She bravely admits to attempting her first novel, but her greatest thrill comes from her two children who openly take pride in their lesbian mother.

SUKI BISHOP lives in Northampton, Massachusetts. She has most recently been published in *Painted Bride Quarterly* and *Blithe House Quarterly*. Her story, "Where the Story Lies," has been nominated for the 2006 Rauxa Prize for erotic fiction.

RACHEL KRAMER BUSSEL (rachelkramerbussel.com) is senior editor at *Penthouse Variations*, writes the "Lusty Lady" column for *The Village Voice* and hosts In the Flesh Erotic Reading Series. Her books include *Up All Night, First-Timers, Glamour Girls, Naughty Spanking Stories from A to Z, Ultimate Undies, Sexiest Soles, Secret Slaves*, and *Caught Looking: Erotic Tales of Voyeurs and Exhibitionists*. Her writing has been published in over sixty anthologies, including *Best American Erotica* (2004 and 2006) and *Best Lesbian Erotica* (2001, 2004, and 2005), and in *AVN, Bust, Gothamist, Mediabistro, New York Post, On Our Backs, Velvetpark* and others.

JOLIE DU PRÉ (glbtpromo.com) is a writer of lesbian erotica. Her work has appeared on the Internet, in e-books and in *Hot & Bothered 4, Best Bondage Erotica 2, Luscious,* and other print anthologies. She is also the founder of GLBT Promo, a promotional group for GLBT erotica and erotic romance.

SACCHI GREEN writes in western Massachusetts and the mountains of New Hampshire. Her work has appeared in *Best of Best Lesbian Erotica 2, Best of Best Women's Erotica, Penthouse, Naughty Spanking Stories from A to Z,* and a thigh-high stack of other anthologies with inspirational covers. She coedited *Rode Hard, Put Away Wet: Lesbian Cowboy Erotica* with Rakelle Valencia, and their second and third anthologies, *Hard Road, Easy Riding: Lesbian Biker Erotica* and *Lipstick on Her Collar*, are due for release in fall of 2006.

LYNNE JAMNECK (lynne-jamneck.blogspot.com) is a naughty girl who doesn't look it. She's also a complete geek, a "Battlestar Galactica" fan and a biter of hypocrites. Her dirty little secret is that she's a fool of a romantic at heart. Her short fiction has appeared in numerous markets including *Best Lesbian Erotica* (2003, 2006), *Sex in The System: Stories of Erotic Futures, Technological Stimulation, and the Sensual Life of Machines* and *Hot Lesbian Erotica*.

SKIAN MCGUIRE is a working-class Quaker who lives in the wilds of western Massachusetts. Skian's fiction has appeared in many anthologies, webzines, and print periodicals. He is the founder and editor of *The Shadow Sacrament*, an online journal of sex and spirituality; the current issue and a call for submissions may be found at shadowsacrament.com He is currently in the process of transition from F to M.

ZAEDRYN MEADE is a queer self-defined sugarbutch whose erotica has been published in *Penitalia: Collegiate Erotica*, *Best Lesbian Erotica 2006*, and *Secret Slaves: Erotic Stories of Bondage*. Originally born in Alaska, she now lives in New York City.

ANDREA MILLER's writing has been published in various anthologies including *Best Women's Erotica 2005, Lessons in Love: Erotic Interludes 3, Tales of Travelrotica for Lesbians: Erotic Travel Adventures* and three previous editions of the

Best Lesbian Erotica series. Yes, with her sun in Sagittarius and her moon in Scorpio, she was born to write smut.

PEGGY MUNSON (peggymunson.com) is the author of *Origami Striptease* and the editor of *Stricken: Voices from the Hidden Epidemic of Chronic Fatigue Syndrome*. She has published in *Best American Erotica* (2006 and 2007), *Best Lesbian Erotica* (1998–2005), *Best American Poetry 2003*, *Tough Girls*, *On Our Backs*, *Blithe House Quarterly*, *Lodestar Quarterly*, *Literature and Medicine*, *San Francisco Bay Guardian*, and many other publications.

JOY PARKS writes articles, interviews and book reviews for the *San Francisco Chronicle*, *The Advocate* and many other GLBT and mainstream publications. Her book column "Sacred Ground" appears regularly in a number of websites and in print. She began writing fiction as a fortieth birthday present to herself and her short stories appear in *Back to Basics*, *Hot & Bothered 4* and *Call of the Dark*. She lives in Ottawa, Canada.

RADCLYFFE is the author of over twenty lesbian novels and anthologies including the 2005 Lambda Literary Award winners *Erotic Interludes 2*, edited with Stacia Seaman, and *Distant Shores, Silent Thunder*. She has selections in multiple anthologies including *Call of the Dark*, *The Perfect Valentine*, *Best Lesbian Erotica 2006*, *First-Timers*, *Ultimate Undies*, *Naughty Spanking Stories 2*, and *Sex and Candy*. She is president of Bold Strokes Books, a lesbian publishing company.

CYNTHIA RAYNE's first erotic book was written when she was thirteen. The most risqué thing that happened in the book was a chaste kiss, but it was the talk of her middle school! Since then, she has had quite a few of her short stories and novellas e-published. She lives in Ohio where she is currently working on a novel.

JEAN ROBERTA teaches English in a Canadian prairie university. Her erotic stories have appeared in numerous places, including *Best Lesbian Erotica* (2000, 2001, 2004, 2005 and 2006). She sings with Prairie Pride Chorus, which has recently released its first CD, *Watershed Stories*, two suites of songs about GLBT life recorded by the Canadian Broadcasting Corporation.

KYLE WALKER has had a notorious and checkered career, including appearances onstage in Ed Valentine's *Women Behind the Bush* with En Avant Playwrights, as a karaoke-singing biker in a promo for PBS, and as a contributor to *Best Lesbian Erotica* (2003-2006), *Best of the Best Lesbian Erotica 2*, *A Woman's Touch* and *Friction 7*. Kyle is forever working on an erotic novel, *What People Want*.

ANNA WATSON is an old-school femme living in the Boston area. She is in a long-distance relationship with her butch Beau, which gives her lots of time for daydreaming about naughty things. Her work has appeared in *The Tokyo Journal*, *Common Lives, Lesbian Lives*, *Mothering*, *Unsupervised Existence*, and the anthology *Shaking the Tree* among others. When she's not writing smut, she can be found on butch-femme.com chitchatting and having a gay old time.

FIONA ZEDDE (fionazedde.com) is a transplanted Jamaican lesbian currently living and working in Atlanta, Georgia. She spends half her days as a starving artist in the city's fabulous feminist bookstore, Charis Books and More, and the other half chained to her computer working on her novels and on an endless collection of dark and dirty stories that she hopes to get published some day. If you see her, please don't make jokes about her getting a life. She might bite. Those starving artist types tend to do that.

ABOUT THE EDITORS

Born in Dublin in 1969, EMMA DONOGHUE
(emmadonoghue.com) is a novelist, play-
wright and literary historian. She is best known
for her contemporary and historical novels, which include *Stirfry*, *Hood* (winner
of the American Library Association's Gay
and Lesbian Book Award), *Life Mask*, and
the best-selling *Slammerkin*, which won the
Ferro-Grumley Award for Lesbian Fiction.
Her books of short stories are *Kissing the
Witch*, *The Woman Who Gave Birth to Rab-
bits*, and *Touchy Subjects*. She has also edited
the anthologies *Poems Between Women* and
The Mammoth Book of Lesbian Short Stories
and published two works of lesbian literary
history, *Passions Between Women* and *We
Are Michael Field*. She lives in Canada with
her lover and their son.

Tristan Taormino (puckerup.com) is too busy for her own good. She is the author of three books: *True Lust: Adventures in Sex, Porn and Perversion, Down and Dirty Sex Secrets,* and *The Ultimate Guide to Anal Sex for Women,* a new, revised edition of which was published in 2006. She is currently at work on a book about polyamory. She has won two Lambda Literary Awards for the *Best Lesbian Erotica* anthology series. She runs Smart Ass Productions, a porn production company, and recently signed on as an exclusive director for Vivid Entertainment; her first video for Vivid, *Chemistry, Volume 1,* was released in September 2006. She is the sex columnist for *The Village Voice* and *Taboo,* and the former editor of *On Our Backs.* She has been featured in over two-hundred publications and has appeared on dozens of radio and television shows including HBO's "Real Sex," "The Howard Stern Show," "Ricki Lake," and The Discovery Channel. She teaches workshops at colleges and universities, and sex and leather conferences. In addition, she coproduces the semiannual national sex event Dark Odyssey. Along with her partner and their three dogs, Tristan splits her time between New York City and Upstate New York.